Alderslay.

Val Portelli

Published by Quirky Unicorn Books

About the author:

You can find other books and free short stories by Val Portelli here:

Amazon author page:
https://author.to/ValPortelli

Goodreads:
https://www.goodreads.com/wwwgoodreadscomVal_Portelli

Facebook:
www.facebook.com/ValsTales

Blog:
https://voinks.wordpress.com

Twitter:
https://twitter.com/ValPortelli

Website:
www.quirkyunicornbooks.wordpress.com

YouTube: 'Val's Tales.'
www.youtube.com/channel/UCsmbM57q4SzHbOcx3CPbr1Q

Dedications:

With grateful thanks to Angela Ripley, who first became involved in editing this manuscript more years ago than either of us care to remember.

Also to Paula Harmon, without whose support it would probably never have seen the light of day.

Table of Contents

Murder of Changes

Chapter 1. Finding a home.

I fell in love with the ramshackle old house the first time I saw it. Would I have been so enthusiastic if I had known it held secrets worthy of an Agatha Christie novel? In my eagerness to tell my fiancé about it, I dialled his number, then hung up quickly when it went to voicemail and I realised he was probably asleep. Almost immediately a message came through.

'Gina, is everything OK? What's wrong?'

I responded, embarrassed my excitement had caused him concern.

'Paul, sorry, did I wake you? Forgot about the time difference but I might have found our forever home. Tell you all about it when you phone tomorrow. OK. Love you.'

We, or rather I, had been house hunting for ages but could find nothing that really had that *Wow* factor. For the time being, I was renting a one-bedroomed flat in a south London suburb. It was convenient for work but tiny, even for me on my own. When Paul, all six foot three, and fourteen and a half stone of blond hunk came to stay, I realised how cramped it was. At least having shared such a tiny space I knew when we finally did move in permanently together, space restraints wouldn't cause us to bicker.

Despite that I was looking for a home with plenty of room, big enough to have friends or family stay for weekends, and remote enough to have parties without annoying the neighbours. We also wanted somewhere we could make our own, and if this involved slumming whilst we did the restorations, so be it. When Paul's contract abroad ended, he would return to working in London so good transport links without spending half of our lives sitting on trains was a priority.

I spent hours on the internet investigating possible areas and calculating journey times and connections. Quite by chance, a friend who worked for a local council let slip there were plans to develop Biggin Hill airport into a commercial tourist enterprise over the following few years. The extensive scheme included a train link to provide a fast service into the centre of London so I widened my hunt in that direction. At that time the area was totally rural and difficult to reach except by car, but eventually it would make the perfect location, offering easy access to central London, the M25 and both Bromley and Croydon town centres.

Although we both loved the peace of the countryside, we needed to consider the practicalities, especially with Paul being away frequently on business. I started spending every free weekend driving around the area and hounding local estate agents. It was autumn and the countryside looked beautiful, with the leaves showing off their full glory in every imaginable shade of brown, green and rustic red. After a few weeks of being shown round possible homes I began to despair. The properties offered by the estate agents tended to be new development boxes, on modern housing estates in what they hoped would be a desirable area once the transport links were established.

It was dusk as I left yet another viewing with a *'Don't call me, I'll call you'* parting comment to the agents. Perhaps I wasn't concentrating, or just feeling miserable but for some reason I missed the turn off to my usual route and ended up on a country lane with no room to reverse. The high hedges blocked any view to the sides, and with darkness descending the twists and turns in the road made it impossible to see very far ahead. The Satnav had fallen silent and I had no idea where I was.

Despite the possibility of another vehicle haring round the bend and crashing into me, I decided to give it another five minutes before executing a twenty-three-point turn to head back the way I had come. The road narrowed and seemed to be taking me further away from the main road, but attempting to manoeuvre I noticed a small side lane where it would be easier and safer to turn. In the distance was a crumbling ruin, fronted by wrought-iron gates hanging off their hinges. Although it was nearly dark, I couldn't resist the temptation to drive up the lane, thinking perhaps someone lived there who could give me directions.

It was totally out of character for me to take silly risks, but as I climbed out of the car for a closer look, I realised there were no lights and the place was deserted. Why had I left the comparative safety of the car, and not merely used the space to turn and drive away? That's when I saw a decayed 'FOR SALE' sign almost hidden amongst the surrounding trees.

By the side of the ornate, heavy oak door an old-fashioned bell pull was set into the stonework. I couldn't resist pulling it, but wondered how to explain if someone answered. Standing in the silence with only a shaft of moonlight as illumination, I remembered the listener in the old poem *"Is there anybody there?" said*

3

the traveller, knocking on the moonlit door." The response I had was the same. None.

As the darkness deepened, my sensible head took over. What on earth was I doing standing alone at night, ringing doorbells on deserted properties? House hunting must be affecting my brain. I needed to get back in the car and find the route home. Nevertheless, I couldn't resist peering through the cobweb-stained windows. Although it was difficult to see clearly, the interior showed a high-ceilinged entrance hall leading into a main foyer, with a staircase reaching to the upper storeys.

Above the ornate frescoes was a balcony overlooking the ground floor, and my imagination took over as I pictured a Tudor banquet, with costumed guests imbibing mead, and throwing chicken legs onto the floor for the scavenging dogs to gobble up. My rumbling stomach reminded me I was hungry, and the quick reality check convinced me to leave the house and head for home. Using the extensive forecourt, I turned the car round and found my way back to my usual route.

Chapter 2. Will he, won't he?

It was a typical Monday and I suffered the normal commuting horrors, accompanied by torrential rain and a biting wind, forecasting the beginning of winter. I managed to concentrate on work through the week, although every spare moment my subconscious returned to the deserted house in the country.

When Paul answered my phone call for our usual catch up, for some reason I skirted over my adventures at the house. I mentioned it briefly in passing, but concentrated on giving him an update on all the unsuitable properties I had viewed.

With his usual intuition he read my mind and returned to the subject of the ancient ruin. Playing Devil's advocate, I explained how much work it needed, how it was in the middle of nowhere and totally unsuitable.

Laughing, his only response was, 'So what's the asking price then?'

God, do I love this man who knows me so well?

The next weekend saw me in the turn-off lane to the ruined house. This time it was bright sunlight and somewhat reluctantly the selling agents had given me a key to look over the property on my own. True to form, the key was not a small Yale but a large, rusty brass monstrosity. Nevertheless, excitement filled me as I fitted it into the lock. The door creaked open and I entered the house for the first time. It was even better than my glance through the windows had led me to believe. Despite the dust, dirt and years of neglect I could see what a beautiful home it had once been.

As I carefully climbed the broken, rotting wooden staircase the view from the upper floors was spectacular. The house looked out over fields and rolling hills with a glimpse of an ancient church spire in the distance, surrounded by the thatched roofs and stone walls of the village cottages. Even as my mind registered the amount of work to be done, I was already planning priorities and how each room might be decorated.

I decided the largest, south-facing bedroom would be ours. Tapping the dividing wall to the old-fashioned bathroom next door, I discovered it was only plaster board and could easily be converted to make our bedroom ensuite. Similarly, the box room on the other side could become my large walk-in wardrobe.

Exploring further, I discovered six more rooms of various sizes, which could become guest rooms and bathrooms. Carefully returning down the rickety stairs, I imagined them transformed into a sweeping marble staircase leading to the main reception area.

The kitchen was a disaster. That would probably be the biggest expense and take the most work. It was a huge room, leading on one side to a dilapidated conservatory and on the other straight into what appeared to have once been a garden patio area. The other rooms on the ground floor were a mishmash of designs. It seemed someone had tried to modernise the property without giving any thought to its ancient heritage. There was another smaller kitchen which had been updated in sixties style, and looked totally out of place and impractical. My thought was that it would make a good office area or TV room.

Before I became totally carried away, I wandered into the extensive grounds. To one side of the conservatory, I noticed an overgrown area which on closer investigation held the remnants of an herb garden. Further into the undergrowth I was intrigued by an area bordered by a high hedge on all sides. Pushing open a small wooden door set in the foliage I was astounded to come across a paved area, complete with swimming pool and wooden changing huts.

It was all too perfect.

Despite my enthusiasm I had to do some costings and think about budget restraints. All my practical thoughts about transport links had gone out the window, and I had to consider whether Paul would be happy living in a wreck in the middle of nowhere. I had no idea what the asking price was, let alone the cost of making it habitable. Too much time had passed day dreaming, so I reluctantly locked up and headed back to the estate agents before they closed for the evening. A signpost pointed in the opposite direction from the one I had come so I followed it, surprised to find myself in the village high street within a few minutes of leaving the house. It was much closer to civilisation than I had originally thought, although still difficult to find, unless you knew the area.

Whether the estate agent had given up on the hope of a sale, or was eager to go home, he seemed surprised when I expressed an interest in buying the property. Realising I was serious, he turned into full sales mode, even supplying me with a list of local tradesmen able to carry out the necessary renovation works. Considering the size of the property, the asking price was very reasonable, but I was sure I could negotiate a substantial reduction. After telling him I'd be in touch, I headed home, already determined to make it mine. That evening I phoned Paul long distance, informing him I had found our dream home. He was not due leave for nearly two weeks, and I could hardly contain my excitement and trepidation, imagining his reaction when he actually saw it.

The following week at work dragged, although I spent every quiet moment on the phone, setting up appointments with the local tradesmen to give me estimates. As I was only free at weekends, I spent my evenings giving them an outline of my ideas, and arranging for them to gain access through the estate agent to prepare their quotes. It was not ideal as I would have preferred to explain and see their reaction face to face, but it was the best I could do. Luckily, as they were all from the village or nearby, there was no problem with obtaining the key from the agent who they all knew personally. As the quotes arrived, together with the workmen's suggestions and observations on possible problems, I spent every evening compiling lists and costs for managing the project.

It would all be wasted if Paul didn't like it. Although I was looking forward to seeing him, as Friday approached I found myself becoming more and more nervous. As it was, his flight was delayed so he didn't arrive at my London flat until well after eleven.

'You look exhausted,' I exclaimed but had to curb my impatience until he had eaten and caught up with sleep. 'We'll talk in the morning.' I didn't want anything to put him off my dream for our future together.

'You're up early for a Saturday morning,' Paul said as I went to get out of bed.

'I'm eager for you to see the house,' I replied.

'And I've had a good night's sleep so I'm eager for other things,' he smiled as he dragged me back to bed.

It was almost twelve by the time we set out, and when we arrived at the agents there was a sign on the door saying CLOSED FOR LUNCH. Not a good omen. As usual Paul was his positive self.

'We might as well spend the time exploring the village, starting with lunch at the local pub,' he suggested as he steered me in that direction.

It was an excellent meal, the sun was shining and Paul was soon deep in conversation with the locals. In the short time it took him to order the drinks he was already on first name terms with the barmaid and a few of the regulars. He had also found out about the reputation of the tradesmen who had given me quotes, and learnt some of the house's history. I had begun to think of it as my project, but realised his interest was a good sign. We made a great team, and his personal approach perfectly complemented my paperwork attitude. Over lunch he updated me on what he had found out.

'Most of the tradesmen have excellent reputations except for one. He's let down several people in the village and tried to invent things that don't need to be done to earn more money. His work isn't up to standard, so he relies on strangers to boost his earnings.'

'Thank goodness you found out in time,' I remarked and immediately crossed him off my list, although luckily I had a back-up builder who was highly regarded. Paul had also learnt a wealth of history about the origins of the house.

'It was built around 1850 as the mansion for the local land owner,' he told me, reading from his notes. 'The village grew from all his employees, and he provided the cottages for their housing. The original lord of the manor, John Allston was a good and fair man, and the area prospered under his rule. His son James was not so dedicated to the welfare of his tenants who he treated like serfs, and unrest grew. This escalated when the grandson Henry inherited the estate. He was a gambler and despot who cared only for his own pleasures.'

I listened with interest as he continued, after taking a sup of beer. 'The cottages crumbled into disrepair as the workers moved away to find other employment. There were rumours of wild parties at the Manor, and several young girls disappeared under mysterious circumstances. This state of affairs continued for some years until eventually there was a revolt amongst the remaining villagers. It was not clear exactly what happened and there were conflicting stories. The only thing everyone seemed to agree on was that there was a mysterious fire, and the lord was never seen again.'

'Oh, wow,' I exclaimed, so intrigued by the story that it was with a start I realised well over an hour had passed.

'Are you sure you're still interested in buying it?' Paul asked.

'You're not wriggling out of it that easily,' I told him, dragging him up from his comfortable chair. Several people called goodbye as we made our way to the car and headed back to the estate agents. This time the door was open and the agent himself accompanied us to view the house.

On the way he gave us a spiel about the more recent developments in the history of the house.

'After the fire it lay derelict for many years until it was commandeered and used as a war-time base for code breakers. In the early fifties it was bought by a property developer who turned it into a hotel. He installed the swimming pool, and the second kitchen for use by the resident housekeeper. Being way off the usual tourist trails the owner went bankrupt, and once again the house was left to the vagaries of nature.'

He stopped as he turned into the lane, then continued, 'Some years later it was taken over by a hippy commune and finally purchased by a reclusive American millionaire. When he died with no close relatives a long drawn out wrangle over his estate ensued. The house fell into a state of disrepair until it was finally settled, and again it was put on the market. It's now owned by the trustees who are eager to dispose of the property, hence the low asking price.'

As we passed through the dilapidated iron gates of the house, I turned to look at Paul's face to see his first reaction but his expression was unreadable. He took my hand and listened attentively as the agent showed us round. I realised I had been thinking with my heart instead of my head as Paul asked all the pertinent questions. My dream was over before it had begun as I started to appreciate how big the restoration project was.

'Thank you for your time,' Paul said to the agent as we returned to my car for the drive home. 'We'll be in touch.'

Too upset to speak, I drove in silence for most of the way and Paul let me be.

'Shall we eat out?' he suggested when we arrived home. 'It'll save you the bother of cooking.'

In my morose state I nodded, so he booked our local favourite restaurant before going up for a shower. When he finished, I took a long pampering bath to cheer myself up. With time to think I decided I was being unfair on him, spoiling his precious free time by acting miserably. With a smile plastered on my face, I went back into the living room to find him closely studying the various quotes for the repairs to the house.

'It seemed a good idea at the time,' I said giving him a hug. 'What time did you book the restaurant for?'

'Eight o'clock and it's still a good idea,' he replied, taking me aback.

'Are you serious?' I asked, wondering if I had misunderstood.

'You love it and so do I,' he replied, drawing me to sit on his lap. 'It won't be easy, especially with me away so much, but it's feasible. Hey, don't cry. It'll make your mascara run, and I don't want to eat dinner with a panda.'

That's when I knew that whatever the problems and the arguments that were bound to ensue, we'd buy the house and live happily ever after.

Chapter 3. Sealing the deal.

'Of course we're having champagne. We have a lot to talk about, but first, let's order some food. The Dover sole looks good. You can tell me all about the builders once we've eaten.'

We talked about it endlessly over dinner before returning home a little tipsy, and falling into bed to celebrate by making love. Sunday morning we lazed around before having a late brunch. By mutual agreement, after deciding on the price we'd offer the agents we let the subject of the house drop, and concentrated on talking about other things. Mid-afternoon the sun came out, so a long, leisurely stroll was in order before returning home for an early supper.

'I hate to leave you, darling, but you know I have to catch the late flight ready for work tomorrow. How about coming back upstairs to say goodbye properly before I go?'

After seeing him off I had an early night, ready to face my own working week. Despite not wanting to appear too eager, by 9.02 a.m. on Monday morning I was on the phone to the agents, offering a price well below the one Paul and I had agreed on for the house. I didn't do much work that morning as I waited for their return call. Not surprisingly they turned down the offer.

'That's a shame. We can't go much higher but I'll consult my fiancé to see if we can scrape together a little bit more. We do like it but there's so much renovation work to be done. That's going to be expensive and the location is rather remote. Even if it was in good repair the history of the house could be a deterrent to any prospective purchasers. Sorry, can I phone you back?' I asked, hoping my subterfuge wasn't too obvious. 'I've another agent on the other line. He phoned me before with the details of a house which has just come on the market. It sounds perfect for us.'

I managed to hang on until lunchtime before returning his call, when I enthused about the "other property" and increased our offer by only £1,000. The afternoon dragged, and I was packing up to go home when he phoned again. Our offer had been accepted! I had to cover my face to stop him hearing my whoop of delight, but I'm sure he could hear the smile in my voice as I promised to call him the next day to sort out the details. Even though I knew Paul was working, I couldn't resist phoning him the moment I arrived home to share the good news.

'Hey, babe. That's brilliant. I didn't realise you were such a good negotiator. That's a lot less than we were prepared to go. Well done, you.'

Not surprisingly I didn't sleep well that night, although my dreams were not the happy ones you might expect. Instead, I woke feeling disturbed by a half-forgotten nightmare involving fires, witchcraft and rooms which were all a dark shade of red. It didn't put me off my dream home, and I soon regained my enthusiasm.

That week partly flew by and partly dragged. I had a million things to sort out, and had to work late to catch up with the ordinary tasks I had been neglecting. As the agent, architects, surveyors, solicitors and workmen were only available during the working day, it was logical to concentrate on them from nine to five, and catch up with my usual job after hours, often staying until gone eight at night. Even when I finally arrived home I was still grafting; ploughing through spreadsheets, plans, suppliers and design ideas. My "To-do" list got longer and longer, and I hardly slept. I spoke to Paul regularly giving him updates, which was important as he wasn't due any more time off for a couple of weeks.

We had the problem of him not being around to sign the purchase contract prior to exchange. Rather than waste time backwards and forwards with the mail, he suggested the house was purchased in my sole name. He'd arrange to wire his share of the necessary funds direct to my bank account prior to completion, and was amused when I laughingly suggested I could take the money and run.

'No way. You love the house too much, although if you change the locks I might have to break the door down to get in and ravish you.'

Although I wasn't happy the house wouldn't be in our joint names, I understood the practicality of his idea. After all, we could always sort things out later when the house was ours, and the renovations complete. Meanwhile I liaised with solicitors, signed and exchanged contracts, and by the end of October the house was ours, or rather mine.

The labourers had already been primed and started work straight away. The electricity and plumbing were the first priorities, with the builder working in tandem with his sub-contractors to demolish and renovate as they progressed. Luckily the roof was waterproof, although it would need to be overhauled in due course. I wanted the basics of heat, light and water available so the work could carry on during the winter months. I had plans drawn up for the main kitchen, but meanwhile the small one was sufficient for necessities.

Portable electric heaters could suffice until a full central heating system was installed.

All the requirements for the kitchen had been ordered, and despite the cost I had gone for the very best. There was a six to eight week delivery time, so with Christmas looming it should all arrive early in the New Year. Although I was impatient, it was the perfect schedule to give the builders time to have everything prepared.

I hadn't mentioned it to Paul, but my plan was for us to spend his Christmas leave together in the house. I intended to buy a tree and if necessary, put a mattress on the floor to sleep on. He was due home early on Christmas Eve and I wanted to wake up in his arms on Christmas morning. We were expected for the traditional lunch with my family, but at least we could have a few precious hours alone together in our new home.

Time flew past. There were disasters and unexpected problems. The size of the rooms meant doors were not standard sizes and needed to be specially made. Several coats of paint had been applied on top of others, taking twice as long to strip down, and revealing crumbling plaster underneath. Although Paul was supportive, it wasn't the same as having him actually there to see things for himself. I had been taking photographs regularly from the day the house first became ours, to act as a memory of what we had achieved, and to show our grandchildren. As with any major renovation it was always the ground work that took the time. When I started to despair, I'd pull out the original photos, and even at that early stage was cheered up by the transformation so far, even if we still had a long way to go.

Structurally the house was very sound, despite its age. The important thing was to bring it up to date without destroying its charm. I was restricted to long-distance communication, and only able to visit the site at weekends to chivvy things along, but fortunately the workmen were brilliant. They seemed to have taken the renovations to heart, and were as enthusiastic as I was in creating a masterpiece. Not for them a nine to five, Monday to Friday, get it done and get paid job. I was delighted at the effort and commitment they put in to make things perfect. They worked late without asking for extra payment, and went to a lot of trouble to source the exact materials they needed to retain the character of the original designs.

Two weeks before Christmas the plumbing and electricity were installed, and although the house still looked like a builder's yard, there was light, heat and gas for cooking. I was even more determined that Paul and I should have our first Christmas together in our own home. Although our bedroom still needed decorating, we could use the bathroom, and the small kitchen for the basics. I had ordered a Christmas tree for the lounge, and brightened the rubble with fairy lights. Every Christmas card I received I took to the house, and hung on strings along the unplastered bare walls.

Chapter 4. Christmas guest.

'I can't wait for next week, darling. You and me together in our own home. What more could a girl want? Are you still expecting to arrive early evening, Christmas Eve?'

'Should be. I'll come straight there from the airport. Shame we'll have to do the duty visits on Christmas day, but maybe next year everyone can come to us. When do you finish work?'

'Friday. Then we've got our Christmas party in the evening. I'm driving down to the house Saturday lunchtime, so I'll have the rest of Saturday and all day Sunday to prepare for your arrival. Can't wait. See you soon.'

My car was already loaded up with the basic necessities for the long weekend, as well as special treats and drinks for our first Christmas together. Presents for the family were wrapped, ready to put in the boot when I left. The workmen would be at the house for a while in the afternoon, so I made sure I had their Christmas cards ready. Tucked inside each one was a bonus cheque, a sign of appreciation for all they had done to help make my dream come true.

The week before Christmas was more social than work, but even so I was busy checking and double checking that I had everything I'd need for the weekend. We'd be marooned without a corner shop to dash to for anything I had forgotten, but I couldn't wait. Friday night I enjoyed the work Christmas party with my colleagues, ate, danced, drank and joined in the merriment and seasonal good wishes. Like everyone else I was a bit tipsy by the time the evening finished, and had done my share of flirting and kissing under the mistletoe.

'It's only one o'clock,' one of the younger crowd said. 'We're going clubbing. Come on, you'll enjoy it.'

'Have fun, guys, but I'm heading for home. Merry Christmas, everyone.'

I wanted to catch up with sleep, thinking of the full day ahead of me, but couldn't relax. My mind was too full of plans of seeing Paul, being together in our own home, and celebrating Christmas in the traditional style.

I woke the next morning around eight, but however much I tried to enjoy the comfort of my proper bed, by nine o'clock I was bathed, dressed and packing the car. Included in my arrangements had been the loan of a sofa bed, so I had somewhere to sleep until our proper bed was delivered. The sheets, duvet and pillows had been taken down the previous weekend. Everything was ready and I was off.

My first stop when I arrived at the house was to drop off all my parcels and supplies. The workmen were winding down for the Christmas break, and there were more mistletoe kisses, and grateful thanks when they opened their Christmas cards and saw their thank-you cheques.

'That's very generous of you, Missus. We'll be back on Thursday to cram in the final touches so it's all ready for the furniture delivery in the New Year. Are you sure you'll be okay until then?'

'I'll be fine. Thanks for everything. Merry Christmas.'

When they left, soon after two, I drove into the village for a late lunch at the local family-run restaurant, then found it impossible to resist buying some last-minute decorations from the shop next door. Several of the villagers recognised me, and at every step I was wished a Merry Christmas, and began to really feel part of the community. Heading for home shortly before four, it was already sunset. I was thankful for the welcoming light as I turned on the switch and entered my new home.

It was the first time I had been there alone after dark, and it struck me how isolated it was. Berating myself for being a wimp, I got stuck into finishing the Christmas preparations, as it needed to be habitable and welcoming for when Paul joined me on Christmas Eve. After a late supper, with the clock saying it was already 10.30, it was time for an early night. Making myself comfortable on the temporary bed, I felt restless, but soon drifted off into a deep and dreamless sleep.

Waking with a start in the early hours, I was momentarily confused by my surroundings. The blackness of the night was not like the dark of London, where even in the early hours street lights shone, and people were still going about their business. Reaching for the small torch on the bedside table I glanced at the travelling alarm clock. It was 3 a.m. Snuggling back under the duvet I was drifting off when I heard the same noise that had woken me originally.

It sounded like a cross between a moan and a cry for help. I listened intently. All was silent, but as I decided it must be either the wind or the cry of a wild beast, it came again, louder and more distressed. Perhaps an animal was caught somewhere, in pain. There was no way it could be left to suffer. Grabbing the torch and summoning up my courage, I threw on a fleecy dressing-gown and got out of bed. Turning on every light in the house, I sent a silent prayer of thanks to the workmen who had given up their own holiday time to ensure I had electricity for the Christmas break.

Working my way slowly through every room, I tried to discover the source of the sound. For a while I heard nothing and began to think I had been dreaming when suddenly it came again. By then I was in the old servants' kitchen. For the first time I noticed a door which the plasterers had uncovered. Previously it must have been hidden as part of the wall, and only the renovations had brought it to light.

I slipped the bolt and tugged at it but it remained immovable. It must have been either warped or locked, but as I turned to go back to bed the wail came again, louder than ever. Despite the late hour I was wide awake, and remembered seeing a box of old rusted keys on a ledge, at the other side of the kitchen. My memory hadn't let me down, and I quickly found the box and took out all the keys that might fit. There were about twenty, and after I had tried most of them in the lock, I began to feel foolish.

Suddenly the key I was holding slipped into place, although the door still wouldn't budge. I noticed some rust remover spray the builders had left, and grabbed it to soak the key. Twisting and turning I was on the point of giving up when I heard a click, and with a hefty shove, the door opened. The torch light revealed a flight of steps leading to what was obviously a basement or cellar. Perhaps it had once been a wine or cold storage area. Although there was a switch at the top of the stairs it didn't work, probably because the electricians hadn't yet discovered this area.

All along the wall leading down the stairs was a series of what looked to be the original gas lamp or candle holders. For now, my trusty torch was the best I could do, as I tentatively started the descent. When I reached the bottom I was greeted by an enormous open expanse, with racking along two walls, which housed an array of cobweb-bedecked bottles. My guess had been right; this must have been the original wine cellar of the old house. As I turned to go back up to the kitchen, I heard the plaintive cry again.

Using the torch to examine the dark and eerie corners, cursing myself for being a fool scrabbling about at this hour when I should have been in bed, I saw a movement in a dark corner. I almost panicked and ran, to escape back up the stairs to the comparative safety of the house, as two big, sad eyes gazed at me. I was not a country girl and thought at first it must be a wild woodland creature, but as I grew closer I realised it was a dog. He was shivering with cold and hunger, his bones showing through his emaciated frame, but I could see he had once been a beautiful Alsatian. I should have been apprehensive of a wild animal in such a state, but I approached him, speaking softly to try and reassure him. I knew I had made the right decision when he stretched out his tongue and tried to lick my hand. It took a lot of heaving, carrying, encouragement and time, but eventually I managed to manipulate him up the stairs and into the small kitchen.

The cellar was something to sort out the following day, but for now my new guest needed attention. I had no dog food to hand, but milk, water and bits from the fridge proved how starving he was, as he devoured everything I put in front of him. He wouldn't leave my side so I set up a make-shift bed for him in the living room with an old dressing-gown, and some cover sheets the builders had left. He snuggled down as if he had always slept there, but when I went back to bed he left it to lick me goodnight. It was lucky I had set up the temporary bed downstairs, otherwise he wouldn't have settled with me out of sight. Once I was back in bed he retreated to his make-shift blankets, and we both slept peacefully for the rest of the night.

Waking early the next morning, I felt a sloppy tongue giving me a good morning wash. Already he looked less like a stray, and more as if he had always lived here. I made us both breakfast and then, unable to resist his pleading look, took him for a walk over the fields. His lead was a piece of string and an old belt, but they weren't needed. Apart from wandering off for a quick sniff he seemed to want to stay close to me. Although it was late December it was a beautiful day; bright, bracing and with the winter sun shining its glow over the countryside. It was lovely to enjoy the fresh air after the traumas of my disturbed sleep, and the unexpected results of my night excursions.

Luckily I had brought a few extra dishes with me, so one of my best soup bowls became the dog's drinking bowl, and a tin cooking tray his food bowl. At least he wasn't a fussy eater. When we returned from our walk, he polished off everything I put in front of him. The fact it was prime ham from the bone, chipolata sausages intended to go with Christmas dinner, and the plainest of the biscuits from the gourmet selection box, might have had something to do with it. I made myself lunch, then settled down to catch up with correspondence on my laptop. *Woof*, for want of a better name, took to his bed for a snooze, but still seemed to be keeping one eye on me.

I had tried to phone Paul to tell him about our guest without success, although it was not surprising as he had already told me it might be difficult to contact him for a few days. It made the anticipation of seeing him the following evening to start our Christmas even sweeter. After a while I decided to spend some time exploring the cellar again, while there were still daylight hours left. As soon as I stood up Woof left his bed and became my shadow, walking a few paces behind me. He seemed happy enough until I opened the cellar door, when he started a high-pitched whine which set my nerves on edge. The area must hold bad memories for him, which started me wondering how long he had been there, and how he had ended up there in the first place.

Chapter 5. Exploring.

As I descended the stairs Woof watched, whimpering a warning, but not following me down. An oil lamp from the garden shed cast more light than my small torch, which I had taken as a back-up. I took my time exploring the cellar, but hunted in vain for some previously unseen hole through which Woof could have entered and become trapped. It was a mystery how he had managed to find his way in.

It struck me that the lay-out of the cellar made it the perfect location for a home gym. From the plans of the house, I suspected the outside wall was close to the swimming pool. It would be easy to knock through, put in an exterior door, and make a shower and changing room for when the pool was restored. My mind buzzing with ideas as I turned to go back up the steps, I jumped at the sound of the door slamming shut. At the same moment the lamp spluttered and went out, and for a moment panic set in. The torch in my pocket provided some reassurance, so I tried to calm my nerves by thinking a gust of wind must have caught it, and it would open easily.

'It's all right, Woof,' I called in response to the plaintive cries penetrating through the thick wood, trying to keep my voice steady to reassure him. 'I'm coming up.'

At the top of the stairs I pulled the door. Nothing happened. I tugged again, harder this time. Still it didn't budge. Assuming it had warped with age, I put all my weight and energy into trying to force the door open. The top and bottom quivered, but the middle remained firmly closed. It was as if it had been locked from the outside. Woof had freaked out and so had I. It would be another thirty hours or so before Paul arrived and, being Christmas, there were no workmen around to hear my cries for help. As I was new to the area it was unlikely a neighbour would call to wish us the compliments of the season.

I screamed as the door reverberated under a powerful force on the other side. Hearing Woof's whimper, then another bang, I realised he was actually trying to break the door down. Although it seemed ridiculous, I spoke to him as if he was a human rescuer. Counting out loud 'One, two, three, NOW!' I pulled at the door for all I was worth, at the same split second he used his weight against the outside.

The door flew open throwing me against the side wall before I regained my balance and we collapsed against each in a heap on the floor of the old kitchen. It was only as he licked my face I noticed the blood and cuts on his side, where he had hurt himself trying to rescue me. In his weakened state it must have been agony, but he had given his all to help me escape.

He was struggling and limping badly as I led him back to the new kitchen where I had a first aid box. Although he winced when I bathed his wounds with antiseptic, he seemed to have complete trust in me that it was for his own good. He drank some water, then went to rest in his bed, secure in the knowledge I was close by, and we were friends for life.

He stirred when I carried out some last-minute preparations, but as long as I was in sight, putting the Christmas presents under the tree, he remained watchful but relaxed. Plucking up my courage, I went back to check the door to the cellar. Woof followed me, and immediately started whining as I approached the entrance.

'It's all right, Woof. The door's locked, and the key's back in its place on the shelf. We're safe now.'

Woof seemed to be reassured, and after eating our evening meal together we settled down to watch the small portable TV, before having an early night. The weather had changed again, and now a gale force wind blew, rattling all the windows and doors in the old house. It had turned a lot colder, and I was grateful to the workmen who had ensured the heating was up and running. Although we were warm and cosy, as I drew the make-shift curtains I noticed the first few flakes of snow beginning to fall. It looked beautiful but I hoped it wouldn't delay Paul's arrival on Christmas Eve.

Suddenly Woof started barking and a knock at the door made me nearly jump out of my skin. Taking him with me for moral support, I saw a large delivery van outside, bearing the name of the company from which I had ordered my new bed.

'Sorry, to be so late, love,' one of the men called from where there were unpacking. 'This weather's put us all behind, but we wanted to complete all the deliveries before Christmas, so as not to let people down.'

Within a few minutes they had it installed in the bedroom, and declining my offer of a warming drink they were on their way, with my grateful thanks ringing in their ears. Taking the new bedding from its wrappings, I smiled with satisfaction. My house was beginning to look like a home and my fiancé would soon be joining me. Settling into the new bed to sleep, it occurred to me that Woof was now part of the house, even though he had been here less than twenty-four hours. Once Paul arrived, our small family would be complete.

When we woke the next morning everywhere was white. All around was an orange glow and a serene silence, as if the snow had reclaimed the earth to cover the hardships of the land beneath. Woof was eager to go out, so I wrapped up warmly and took him to explore. After the wildness of the previous day it seemed so tranquil, with the winter sun shining as if to prove it wasn't only summer that could lighten the heart.

I arrived home with my face glowing from the exercise and feeling all was right with the world, appreciating the warmth and comfort as we entered the house after the cold outside. Wanting everything perfect for when Paul arrived, I spent the rest of the day cleaning the habitable rooms, cooking the extras to go with Christmas dinner, and preparing our meal for that evening.

With no guarantee what time Paul would actually make it home, it seemed a good idea to make a light buffet supper. It wouldn't spoil however late we sat down to eat, and an accompanying bottle of wine would make it perfect. I couldn't wait for Paul to arrive so we could start our Christmas properly. Woof seemed as excited as me, and I was only sorry Father Christmas wouldn't have a present for him.

After a light lunch, I intended to explore the cellar again before it was too dark. As before, Woof followed me to the top of the stairs but would come no further. This time, as well as the torch and a lantern, I had taken my mobile and a large hammer and screwdriver. Making sure the door was securely propped open with a chunk of wood as a door-stop, I taped a large piece of cardboard against one edge to stop it being able to close completely, and for good measure took the key with me.

So many precautions seemed excessive, but the sight of Woof lying against the open door also gave me reassurance. He seemed to have decided to add his weight to ensure the door couldn't close and lock me in.

Chapter 6. Discovering secrets.

As I examined the nooks and crannies, Woof watched my every move, and only whined when I was round one of the corners, out of sight behind the wine racks. Although covered with cobwebs, the bottles were fascinating, and despite not being a connoisseur, something about them gave the impression they might be worth a lot of money, as long as they hadn't gone sour with age.

Hunting around, I could find no way Woof might have entered and become trapped. On the point of giving up, my attention was caught by a weird cry. Moving behind one of the wine racks and shining the torch down low, I was surprised to see what appeared to be runners along the bottom of the heavy unit. The metal attachment down on one corner looked to be some sort of latch. I gave it a tug, and tried a sharp bang with the hammer. At first nothing happened, then with a groan it came free, and as I leaned against the side, the whole unit swung out a few inches. Using the torch to peer into the gloom beyond, I could make out a wall beyond the gap, with a sturdy door set into the centre. It was too narrow for me to squeeze behind, but I sensed movement in the darkness. Jumping back, I managed to catch a glimpse of what I thought was a squirrel disappearing through a hole in the rotted wood along the skirting board.

At least it explained how the creature had been able to get in. I assumed Woof had found a bigger opening somewhere, and then been unable to find his way out again. As if he knew I was thinking of him he started howling. It was time to move back into view to reassure him. I'd had enough exploring for one day, so I started back up the stairs, but on impulse grabbed one of the bottles of wine. No doubt it would be sour, but at least I could look up the name and date on the label, and find out more about it.

The welcoming lick from Woof when I reached the door made me realise how grubby I had become down in the cellar. Locking the door securely I cleaned the dirt and grime off the bottle before going for a long reviving soak in the bath. The water was hot and the bath luxurious, even if the surroundings were still bare plaster, waiting the return of the workmen after Christmas to fit the tiles currently heaped up around the room.

By now it was dark, so after dressing in my warm but sparkly outfit for the evening, I gazed out at the night before closing all the curtains. It looked magical with the falling snow outside casting a fairy-tale glow over the surroundings. Switching on the Christmas tree lights, I turned on the TV and tuned into an old-fashioned Christmas show, singing along to the carols as I prepared the turkey for our dinner the following day. At regular intervals I checked my mobile phone for messages, and my laptop in case Paul had sent me an e-mail.

The clock showed it was gone six, and Paul had told me he should arrive anytime between six-thirty and eight, depending on flight connections, and the traffic from the airport. As he'd be unlikely to find a cab to bring him to this remote spot on Christmas Eve, we had arranged a hire car so he could drive himself. He had rejected my offer to pick him up as he hadn't wanted me venturing out, especially if the weather turned bad, so all I could do was sit and wait for him to arrive.

Meanwhile, there was plenty to keep me busy with the full traditional Christmas dinner to cook, even if it was only for the two of us. Well, actually three now, as I was sure Woof could help us out if there was too much. As I was putting the white wine in the fridge to chill, I remembered the bottle from the cellar. After checking the label, I entered the details into a search engine on my laptop. The name came up and described it as a good vintage, probably worth about £40 or £50. Although it was a lot more than I'd normally pay for a reputable supermarket brand, it wasn't going to make us millionaires. There was more information about the vineyard where it was produced, and amazingly, the grapes were grown in England.

Woof, who had been lying quietly at my feet, jumped up and headed towards the front door. At the same moment I heard the sound of an engine being switched off, and a car door slamming. Then the front door swung open. I had time to notice the ground was now covered with a thick, white blanket of snow before I was enveloped in a bear hug from Paul. When he put me down he turned to look at Woof who was waiting patiently for his greeting.

'Who's this then?' Paul asked as he bent down to rub his ears.

'Oh, I forgot. Paul meet Woof. Woof, this is my lovely man Paul.'

With a smile Paul held out his hand. 'Pleased to meet you, Woof. I hope you've been looking after my beautiful fiancée properly.'

I was amazed when Woof lifted up his paw, as if he was shaking hands and confirming that he was keeping me safe. We laughed as Paul patted him, and took my hand to lead me into the front room.

'Anything else I should know?' he asked as he took off his wet coat.

'Only that I love you,' I replied as he pulled me into his arms for a proper Christmas kiss.

'I love you too, babe,' he said, 'but right now what I'd really love is a nice hot shower. Is that possible?'

'The builders have been brilliant. The bathroom's still under construction but there's plenty of hot water. You go and warm up while I finish off in the kitchen.'

Blowing me a kiss, he went upstairs while I put the oven on to warm the hot dishes, and set the table with the assortment of tapas which I had prepared earlier. When Paul came down fifteen minutes later, everything was ready, with the wine waiting to be poured.

'That looks great,' he said. 'The shower made me feel human again. I didn't expect so much to have been done in the house, and had visions of sitting huddled in blankets to keep warm, and eating cold baked beans out of a tin. You must have been a real slave driver to get so much done.'

Opening the wine, he poured two large glasses and passed one to me before raising his in a toast. 'Here's to you, my wonderful wife-to-be, to our new home, the industrious workmen who pulled out all the stops, and our future life together. Merry Christmas Darling.'

'Woof,' said Woof.

'And a Merry Christmas to you too, Woof,' Paul laughed as he kissed me again. We talked as we ate, and I updated Paul on all that had happened while he was away. I explained how I had found Woof, and about the door behind the racks in the cellar. He was interested in the article I had found about the vineyard, but as he read it he noticed something I hadn't. Picking up the unopened bottle from the side table, he examined the faded label carefully, before going back to look at my laptop. He had always been interested in wine and had become quite an expert in his own small way.

'Did you notice the year on this bottle?' he asked.

'No, not really. I was just looking at it when I heard your car pull up.'

'Well, I'll need to investigate, but I have a feeling this is actually a very rare vintage and may be worth quite a lot more than your £50. The other thing is, I think it was actually produced right here in the grounds of this house.'

'Wow. That's amazing,' I said as I took the bottle from him to look at it more closely. 'You mean we might have our very own vineyard in the grounds?'

'Maybe,' he said, 'but we also have our very own bed and right now that's more important.'

Chapter 7. Christmas.

I glanced round at the mess after our meal, and started collecting up the plates and cutlery.

'Leave it,' Paul said. 'We can clear everything in the morning.'

Taking my hand, he said goodnight to Woof, then led me to our bed where we made love for the first time in our new home, before both falling sound asleep.

I woke the next morning around nine to find the sun streaming through the uncurtained window, and turned over to reach for Paul, only to find his side of the bed empty. For a moment I imagined it was just a dream, until the tantalising smell of bacon and coffee brought a smile to my face. Downstairs I found Paul in the kitchen, wearing a Father Christmas apron, a pair of underpants and very little else. Woof came over to greet me, then went back to devouring the breakfast Paul had given him.

'Morning, sleepyhead,' Paul called as I showed my face. 'Go and sit at the table, breakfast's coming up.'

Blowing him a kiss I went into the front room to find all the debris of the night before had been cleared away, and the table laid with a festive red and green tablecloth. Our first proper Christmas together and already it felt perfect. Although the snow was thick outside, the winter sun was again doing its best to break through.

After devouring breakfast, I had intended to have some present-opening time but Woof had other ideas. We gave in to the inevitable, donned warm clothes and boots, and took him for some exercise. The

35

three of us ended up in a snowball fight, and I could not remember ever being so happy.

We wandered as far as the village, and I was amazed at the number of people about, until I realised they were returning from the Christmas services. I felt sorry we hadn't thought to join them, but everywhere we were met with smiles and good wishes for the Christmas season. It seemed we had been accepted in the village as a family, me, Paul and Woof.

I knew we'd be happy here, and vowed that once the renovations were finished, I would get to know my neighbours properly, and become more involved in the village life. Laughing and glowing with our excursions despite the cold, we were nevertheless pleased to return home to the welcoming warmth. As soon as Woof had devoured his doggie treats and drank some water, he curled up in the living room and was soon snoring softly. While Paul went up to shower and change, I turned on the oven and started preparing our Christmas lunch. After he emerged, I went to freshen up and put on a suitable ensemble for our celebration meal.

The sparkle on my dress matched the shine in Paul's eyes as he handed me a glass of Champagne, before pulling me under the mistletoe for a toast to our happiness. As the turkey roasted, we opened the presents from under the Christmas tree, and spent time on our mobiles and the laptop, sending thanks, and catching up with family and friends to wish them the compliments of the season. We ate our meal wearing party hats, giggled over the silly jokes in the crackers, and laughed at the traditional Christmas TV shows. Even Woof was affected by the party atmosphere, and the photos we took of him wearing a paper crown and garlands while devouring the left-overs, became a treasured memory.

Once it was dark we drew the curtains, and the warmth and snugness of the house served to complement the darkness of the winter countryside beyond our haven. Having cleared the remnants of our over-indulgent lunch, we did what people everywhere do on Christmas afternoon - listened to the Queen's speech, dozed and watched television.

I awoke from my comfortable position curled up against Paul on the settee to find him missing. He was sitting at the table, using my laptop, engrossed in something. Noticing I was awake, he turned to smile at me.

'All this good living is turning you into a real country bumpkin.'

Stretching, I moved over to stand behind him, and look over his shoulder to see what he was doing. The screen showed various images that I recognised as our house. There were even plans of the original layout dating back to the 1850s. Fascinated, I noticed the area surrounding the swimming pool had originally been the vineyard.

'This little baby,' he said holding up the bottle of wine I had brought up from the cellar, 'might be worth a lot more than we first thought. It looks as if the original vineyard that went with the house had a reputation rivalling the best French chateaus. Even though the production wasn't enormous, the quality was first class, and its very rarity made it sought after by all the connoisseurs. You never really told me how you came to find it. Was it the only bottle or were there more?'

We sat on the settee and I explained about the cellar, the wine racks, nearly getting locked down there, the hole in the wall, Woof's apprehension about going back to what must have been his prison, and everything else I had discovered. He listened fascinated until he noticed me yawning, which set him off as well. All the stresses of the past few weeks, his horrendous journey home, the Champagne we had drunk, and the joy of finally being together for Christmas had all caught up with us. After making an old-fashioned hot chocolate drink and a very light snack, we decided on an early night.

Paul did venture outside with Woof before we settled before down for the night, but both came back after only a few minutes, shaking off the still-falling snow. 'It's freezing out there,' he said. 'It makes you appreciate how warm and comfortable the house is.'

We bade Woof goodnight, and went off hand-in-hand to our own bed. Our lovemaking, even though it was quick, was sweet and gentle and we were soon sound asleep. I woke early the next morning and went to look out of the window. The sun shone brightly, and although it was no longer snowing the landscape appeared as a perfect winter wonderland with its thick blanket of snow. Sensing movement behind me I turned to see Paul smiling at me.

'Sorry,' I said. 'Did I disturb you?'

'Not as much as you might do if you come back to bed,' he grinned.

This time we were not worn out, and took our time in making love, and enjoyed being together with the whole day stretched before us. It was well over an hour later that we rolled out of bed, and I prepared some breakfast while Paul took Woof out for a quick romp in the snow. They both came in with their faces glowing, and devoured their food as if they hadn't eaten for a week.

Once we had cleared up Paul expressed an interest in exploring the cellar. Taking spare batteries and torches with us as well as the hammer I felt a lot safer with Paul close by, although Woof still refused to come down with us. Using our combined force, we managed to move the unit behind the racks a few more feet. I remembered seeing a can of oil to help ease the rusted mechanism, and went back upstairs to fetch it, leaving Paul to explore. When I went back down I couldn't see him, and for a moment I panicked, calling out his name.

'I'm in here,' he called back. 'Be careful, there's a lot of rotted wood around and it's quite slippery.'

Ducking behind the racks, I went through the gap which was now considerably wider. I shone my torch and was amazed at the sight of Paul in the middle of a narrow corridor. He passed the small hole near the door I had noticed on my last visit, and stood in front of a vast opening, through which the snow in the fields could be seen.

'This was obviously how Woof got in,' he said. 'I thought that other way was too small.'

Together with the light coming through the fissure and my torch, I could see the corridor extended a long way beyond him, until it turned a corner into darkness.

'I'll board this up temporarily,' he said, 'then perhaps the workmen can do a proper job when they come back. We'll also get them to rig up some lighting down here so we can explore properly.'

While he was working I took time to explore more of the cellar, which I had been too frightened to examine on my own. It was enormous, much larger than I had first thought. I guessed that it ran the whole length of the house, and although only part of it was used for the wine racks, there must have been hundreds of bottles stored there. After about half an hour Paul announced he had finished, and joined me in my investigations. He was fascinated by the rows of bottles and picked up several before, feeling decidedly mucky, we ventured back upstairs.

'How about getting some fresh air before we clean up?' he suggested.

Praying we wouldn't bump into any of our neighbours in our dishevelled state, I threw on some boots and warm clothes. Calling Woof, we set off across the grounds and out into the fields beyond.

Woof bounded about enjoying the freedom and churning up the snow which was almost knee deep. When one wet, soggy mess hit Paul, he retaliated by rolling a snowball which he threw at Woof, who immediately caught it in his mouth.

'That's not fair,' I hollered before rolling my own to throw at him. He struck back by aiming one at me, and soon all three of us were involved in a snowball fight. Laughing and trying to avoid another missile, I slipped and fell headlong into the soft wet snow. When he came to see if I had hurt myself, I caught him off-guard and as he bent over me managed to get him with the snow I had scooped up. Barking with delight, Woof joined in the fun and soon we were all rolling about and becoming thoroughly soaked.

It was time we headed back, and we welcomed the warmth that hit us as we opened the front door.

While I went for a bath Paul found an old towel to dry Woof, then I heated some soup for lunch while Paul cleaned himself. We ate off trays in front of the TV with Woof snoozing at our feet. Although it was a simple meal, soup had never tasted so good.

'While it's still light, how about we go for a walk round the grounds?' Paul suggested. 'I haven't seen anything of them yet.'

We put our boots and warm coats on again, but this time we were sensible, without the childish pranks we had enjoyed that morning. As always Woof was at our heels while we walked hand in hand round the garden, until we reached the old swimming pool area. Paul examined the surrounds more closely, then pushed his way through some dense bushes. 'Come and have a look at this.'

Once I had forced my way behind the undergrowth I was able to make out, invisible from the path, two dilapidated wooden buildings.

'It's a bit dark in there,' I said as I forced open the crumbling doors, and peered into the space beyond. 'As they're so close to the pool, I guess they were originally some sort of changing or shower rooms.'

This was borne out when we ventured further inside and managed to make out in the gloom some rusted pipes and mouldy curtaining. Unbelievably, it also looked as if the larger of the two buildings had once held a sauna and hot pool.

'It's not worth getting mucked up again. Let's leave it for another time,' Paul suggested, although I noticed he wrote a quick reminder in a notebook he had brought with him.

'I hope you've stocked up on baked beans and toast,' he smiled. 'I've a feeling that's what we're going to be living on for the next few years with all these extra areas needing restoration.' Seeing my downcast face, he smiled and kissed me. 'Don't look so glum. As the saying goes "it'll be great when it's finished." What do you say to blowing caution to the wind and splashing out our last few pennies in the pub?'

'Do you think we should leave Woof indoors first? I'm not sure dogs will be allowed.'

Woof's face looked as if he understood every word, and he had no intention of being left behind.

'Don't forget we're in the country,' Paul replied. 'He's very well-behaved, and I'm sure they must be used to farmers taking their dogs when they go for a pint. Let's try, and see what happens.'

Woof's happy bark showed I was outnumbered, so I tagged along with the two of them until we reached the village pub. Although it was fairly crowded, the barmaid called out a cheery greeting and didn't bat an eyelid at our four-legged friend. I found a table in an empty corner booth, and Woof settled down at my feet while Paul fetched our drinks. He was gone quite a while, but when he returned he not only had a pint for himself and a drink for me, but also a metal bowl of water for Woof.

'Sorry I was so long, but I got chatting with some locals who wanted to know how we were settling in. By the way, there's no problem with Woof; he's already charmed the customers. I think Anna the barmaid has fallen in love with him.'

Feeling more at ease, I relaxed on the comfortable bench seat and raised my glass in a toast to my two best men. Over the next couple of hours various people came over to wish us the compliments of the season, make a fuss of Woof, and ask how we were getting on in the house. It seemed everyone knew who we were, wanted to know all about the renovations, and were pleased the old house was becoming less of an eyesore. It was good to feel we had been welcomed into the village.

'What do you think about having a housewarming for the villagers once everything's settled? It'd be a way of thanking them for their cordiality.'

'Good idea. I'll sound Anna out, and see what she thinks.'

It had only been a passing thought but the word soon spread, and all who spoke to us afterwards asked to be invited; it was a bit overwhelming how quickly things snowballed. Many seemed to have memories and reminiscences of the house in its earlier days, particularly the older clientele. Several of the old boys mentioned the vineyard, and remembered their grandfathers' stories of the pride in their local vinery, which had once been a world-class producer.

'Hello, you two. We haven't met but I'm Debbie. I run the library, the fount of all knowledge and source of all gossip. If you're interested, we have an extensive collection of memorabilia about the house. I'd be pleased to show you round the archives if you wanted to call in one day.'

'Hello, Debbie. Thanks. That'd be great. I'd love to learn more once the holidays are over, and the building works are progressing again.'

Before leaving, we bought tickets for the New Year's Eve gala dinner-dance, and left happy, with numerous goodnights called out to us. As it was already dark, and we were both a little tipsy, we gratefully accepted the flashlight Anna offered us, and promised to return it within a few days.

Chapter 8. New Year discoveries.

Yesterday had been a full-on day and although we had only been pottering about, by early evening we were both yawning, and felt we were already adapting to the early-to-bed, early-to-rise country mentality. Maybe the amount of alcohol we had drunk had something to do with it. Whatever the reason, after a late supper and settling Woof for the night, we were in bed by 10 o'clock.

The following day was going to be a busy one, with the builders returning to work and all the extras that needed quotes. As I fell asleep in Paul's arms, I couldn't believe how quickly we had settled into our new life. It felt as if this had always been home. The only disturbing thought was that Paul would have to leave again for work, but for now I intended to make the most of every minute we spent together.

I woke early the next morning with a smile on my face when I saw Paul next to me, snoring softly and still dead to the world. Climbing carefully out of bed so I didn't disturb him, I opened the door to let Woof out. As it had turned considerably warmer, the beautiful landscape of the previous magical day had now turned into a grey, slush-coloured winter. The weather made it appropriate to let the diet go to the wind, so I prepared a fry-up for breakfast. Woof followed my every move, waiting to scrounge a few left-overs, but unfortunately for the dog there were not a lot once a sleepy-eyed Paul joined me, and devoured everything I put in front of him.

To make up for it, Paul took Woof for a run while I cleared up the remnants of our meal. Around nine o'clock my two boys returned, at the same time as the builders arrived to carry on their work before the New Year break. When I went to greet them, Paul was already in conversation with the foreman. I overheard him explaining about the things we had discovered over the holiday, and asking for his advice and estimates for even more renovations.

Having managed the project from the beginning, I felt put out when they disappeared to the cellar to look at the work to be done, without inviting me to join them. Feeling like the proverbial "little woman," I started scrubbing and cleaning with a vengeance to relieve my frustrations. Half an hour later I was relieved not to have been with them, when Paul and the builder emerged from the cellar, both with faces as white as chalk.

'Can you find the number of the local police station?' Paul asked quietly. 'There's something downstairs they need to know about.'

'What is it?' I asked, 'What's wrong?'

'On second thoughts, it's probably better if we go there.'

Before I could ask any more questions he and the foreman rushed out. Although I was sorely tempted to investigate for myself, if the police were involved, it was probably better if I waited for his return. There was no sound of the workmen's radio playing or their usual banter, and for about an hour, only banging and hammering broke the silence. Eventually I decided to see if they knew anything.

'I've made a brew if anyone's interested,' I said as I set down the tray. Several pairs of eyes swivelled towards me as I approached, but their formal thank you instead of cheerful teasing made me even more apprehensive.

'Everything okay, Missus?' one of them finally asked. 'Anything you're not happy with? Let us know and we'll do our best to put it right.'

'The work's fine. What I want to know is what's going on? Why have Paul and your foreman disappeared? What did they find downstairs?'

They all glanced at each other before one of them replied, 'Well, we intended to be finished by the New Year, but with the extra things your young man has discovered, I'm afraid it'll take a bit longer and cost more than was estimated.'

For a moment I was distracted and took what he said at face value, then realised there was a lot more to it than extra work and expense.

'We can come to some agreement about that,' I said. 'What I want to know is what's happened? What've they found? Why are you all so serious, and what are you keeping from me?'

After a few seconds of silence, one of the older men spoke up.

'You're a good lass,' he said. 'You've been fair with us and I don't think you're the hysterical type, so I'll tell you. When the boss went down to the cellar with your man, they found some bodies. They were looking at the foundations and examining the layout when they discovered a sort of dungeon. There was a hidden room with about a dozen skeletons chained to the wall. That's why they've gone to the police.'

Chapter 9. Revelations.

At first, I just stared at him in disbelief, although there was a quiver in my voice as I replied.

'Skeletons? In a dungeon? But this house was never the town jail, at least I don't think so. And why would they be chained up? The police wouldn't have just left them there to die. Someone must have known about the room in the cellar. Or are we talking about a mass murderer? Those poor souls. I can't believe we were carrying on with life and all the time they were under our feet.'

'From the little Terry said, the bodies have probably been there for many a year. Maybe, I should have let them tell you about it, but it shook us up a bit even if we haven't seen what they saw. Not something you find every day, and I wouldn't like to be the one to sort it out.'

'Especially if it meant charging extra VAT,' I added.

A couple of the guys laughed, which broke the tense atmosphere and we were able to talk about the findings in a more open way. It helped to pass the time, and various ideas were thrown around until Paul returned with the foreman and a couple of constables in tow, who immediately descended to the cellar. Taking my hand to lead me into the old kitchen, Paul asked what the workmen had told me.

'Only that you found a sort of dungeon with some bodies,' I replied. 'Are you all right? I know it's early, but it seems a brandy is in order.'

I put a large reviver in his hands before sipping at the single one I had poured for myself. Paul downed most of his in one gulp, showing how shaken he was.

'Sorry for being such a wimp', he said as he gave me a hug. 'The only thing I'm thankful for is you didn't discover them when you were on your own. Promise me you won't go into the cellar again until we've cleared out every inch of it.'

'You're not a wimp,' I said hugging him back. 'Anyone would be shaken making such a discovery. Even Woof wouldn't go down there. It was as if he knew something was wrong.'

As if to prove my point the two policemen emerged with faces as serious as Paul's had been.

'I've put in my report to the sergeant,' one said, 'and he's on his way. He asked me to inform you he's been on to forensics, and they should be here within the hour.'

As he finished speaking the doorbell rang, and Paul admitted the local sergeant who went straight down to the cellar to see for himself. When he emerged he appeared concerned, but not as disturbed as the constables had been.

'Good morning, Madam,' he said. 'I take it you're Miss Kingston. I'm Sergeant Marston. Not a very pleasant discovery, but I must warn you the cellar is a crime scene. It's out of bounds until we've finished our investigations. Do you by any chance have a key so we can secure it properly until my colleagues arrive?'

'I do have a key, but I also have a large padlock, which would be stronger. I'll go and find it.'

'Thank you, Madam. That would do perfectly,' he replied. 'Obviously the bodies have been there for some time, but due to the circumstances in which we found them, there will have to be a full enquiry.'

When I came back with the padlock the policemen still looked shaken. I saw that Paul had made them both a hot drink, and holding the brandy bottle over their mugs, I volunteered 'I know you're all on duty but it is Christmas?'

They both glanced as the sergeant who gave a nod, and none of them stopped me as I poured a generous slug into their coffee. After taking a long swig, some colour returned to the faces of the two young constables.

'Thank you very much, Madam,' the sergeant replied. 'The compliments of the season to you and your fiancé.'

The drink seemed to loosen their tongues, and they became less formal. The constable even provided the information that his grandfather, who had also been in the police force, had investigated the house many years before, after rumours about wild goings-on. Nothing had ever been proven but the local villagers still speculated on its secrets.

We were sitting chatting when a knock at the door made us all jump. Paul stood up to admit the forensic team, clad in white coveralls, who promptly descended to the cellar. A few minutes later a police photographer arrived, also clad in protective garments, and followed them down.

For the next hour or so a constant stream of police professionals came in and out. Finally, one of them asked us to remain in the living room for a short while, and pulled the door to behind him. Eventually the sergeant and his constables left, saying they'd be in touch shortly and leaving a contact number for emergencies. As the last of the examination team was leaving, before the door closed behind them, I caught a glimpse of the stragglers carrying what looked like a body bag. Paul went to see them out, but glancing through the window towards the rear door of the large van outside, I saw that the interior was piled high with similar bags.

'Well,' said Paul as he came back into the living room, 'you can't say it's been boring.'

At that moment there was a knock at the door, and Terry poked his head round. 'Sorry to disturb you,' he said. 'We didn't like to interrupt while the police were here, but we thought we'd pop into the village to see if anywhere is open for a bite to eat.'

'I'm so sorry,' I said. 'With everything going on I totally forgot you were still working. Give me ten minutes and I'll make some soup and sandwiches. Is that okay?'

'That would be great, if you're sure. The café is closed for the Christmas break, and we could do with something warming. I'll tell the lads. Give me a call when it's ready.'

Guilty for neglecting the men who had worked so hard to make our home habitable, I set about preparing their meal. Having a task to occupy me kept my mind off the horrors of the morning, and helped put things into perspective.

Fifteen minutes later, when they were enjoying their lunch, Paul and I also sat down to eat. For a while we were silent, and then with our stomachs satisfied we discussed the events of the day. Eventually Paul brought up what had been on his mind. 'Do you want to sell the house and find somewhere else?' he asked.

'If we finish the renovations, we might even make a profit.'

I thought about it for a few minutes but was able to answer truthfully, 'I know what you mean, but despite all that's happened today this is still our house. I want to stay here and see this through. What about you? How do you feel?'

'When I first made that discovery I wanted to run,' he replied honestly, 'but I think you're right. That all happened a long while ago and this house has so much going for it. I want to stay too.'

Without thinking we moved into each other's arms and hugged for a while.

'We'll make this house happy again,' I told him. 'We can overcome the past by having so much love the previous history won't stand a chance. This is our home, and it will be good again. When our grandchildren come to visit, we can tell them how our pleasant memories overcame the bad ones.'

'Well, if we're going to have all these grandchildren, I think we'd better get some practice in,' he smiled.

Taking my hand, he led me off to our bedroom and firmly locked the door behind us. Afterwards, we even managed to doze off for an hour or so. When I woke and glanced at the clock I saw it was already gone five, and dark. I remembered the workmen were still there, so quickly dressed and went downstairs to make coffee. I was in the old kitchen when the foreman popped his head round the door, and asked if I wanted to see what they had achieved that day.

At that moment Paul appeared and we went together to inspect the workmanship. Despite all the interruptions of the day the transformation was amazing. The bathroom was cleared of all the rubble, the tiles on the walls looked fantastic, and the room was good enough to appear in the latest edition of "House and Home."

'We'll be knocking off now, Miss Kingston, if that's all right with you. All we need to do tomorrow is finish off the new kitchen, and you can have your house back to yourselves. Well, apart from the cellar and the swimming pool surround. With what's been happening, I expect that might have to wait for a while. Give us a ring when you get the all-clear, and we'll come back and sort that out. I'll send you our estimate in a few days, then you can decide what you want to do about it. See you in the morning.'

'Thank you so much,' I replied as we saw them out. 'You've been great, and we're really happy with everything you've done. See you tomorrow.'

Somehow the house felt empty after they left. Paul turned on the TV and flicked through the channels until he came across a local news programme. Unbelievably, there was already a mention of the discovery in our cellar under the story-line of "House of Horrors." There wasn't much detail, just the fact that an undisclosed number of bodies had been recovered from beneath the house while renovations were taking place. A spokesman for the police had confirmed they had been there for around a century, and the new owners of the property were not under any suspicion.

The only other thing it mentioned was that the house had at one time been called *Alderslay*.

While I settled down to watch an old Christmas film, Paul fetched his laptop and started researching the house name. After a while he called to show me the information he had found. 'Hey, look at this. It details the history of the house right from when it was first built. There's even more on here than the villagers were telling us about.'

There was some up-to-date information, including hints that the house had once been used for nefarious purposes. I remembered the invitation from the librarian, and we decided to spend part of Saturday finding out more.

Although it was dark, Paul took Woof for a final run around the grounds while I prepared our supper. After all the traumas of the day Paul insisted we open one of the two remaining bottles of wine I had brought with me. We thought of opening the one from the cellar, but decided to stick with something that, although it might not be so valuable, at least would be drinkable. Once we had finished our meal we settled on our old, lumpy settee to discuss our plans for the rest of the holiday season. We were not sure how much involvement we'd have with the police, or whether we'd need to be available in case they wanted access.

'Supposing we stay around the house tomorrow, while the workmen are finishing off, and then spend Saturday at the library,' I suggested.

'Good idea. While we're in the village we can call into the police station to see what's happening, and then stock up with some supplies.'

We had originally planned to take a quick trip back to the flat on Sunday, to collect some of our possessions before returning to the house, giving us the rest of Sunday and all day Monday to sort it out before we went to the New Year's Eve do. Paul had to be back at work the following Wednesday, so he'd need to leave Tuesday night to catch his flight. I had intended to go back to the flat after he left, even though I didn't start work again until the Thursday.

Suddenly I remembered Woof. There was no way I could take him back to the flat, or leave him alone in the house when I returned to London. Decision made, I told Paul I intended to stay on at the house when he left and commute from there. He wasn't keen on the idea, especially in view of all that had happened but I was adamant. It'd be good experience for when we both moved in permanently.

Chapter 10. Making the move.

Originally, we hadn't planned on moving until the end of January or early February, but as the builders had completed so much, there was no reason why I shouldn't relocate earlier.

'I'll arrange a week off in January,' said Paul, kissing my neck, 'so I can help move the rest.'

With everything settled, we slept well and woke early to find the sun streaming through the windows. Most of the snow had melted, and although it was still cold, the air had lost the bitter chill it had at Christmas.

'Let's take Woof for a quick walk before breakfast,' I suggested, grabbing his lead and preparing to face the elements.

'You're mad,' Paul laughed, struggling into a thick coat as the dog pulled me towards the door. The snow in the fields hadn't yet thawed, and Woof had a wonderful time catching the snowballs we threw him, and getting thoroughly soaked.

'That's what you call invigorating,' Paul shivered as he dug out the old towel to dry Woof when we returned to the house. 'I'm starving. How about a fry-up?'

'Your wish is my command, your highness, but the washing-up is down to you.'

As we finished clearing the dishes away, there was a knock at the door, even though it was only shortly after eight.

'I expect it's the workmen,' I said, but was surprised when Paul led two policemen into the sitting room.

'We thought we should bring you up to date,' the sergeant informed us. 'Forensics have confirmed that the, er, people we found have been dead for around ninety years. Although the investigation will continue, we won't need to bother you at all. However, I'd prefer it if you didn't go down to the cellar for the time being.'

'I don't intend to,' I shuddered, 'but thanks for letting us know.'

'Have you any idea how long the cellar will be out of bounds?' Paul asked. 'There's no immediate rush, but eventually we intend to renovate down there, as well as restoring the entrance to the swimming pool.'

'It shouldn't be more than a couple of weeks, then it's all yours. By the way, I take it you've now moved in permanently.'

'Actually, I'll be abroad until February, but my fiancée has decided to remain here after the holidays.'

'I'll be at work during the day,' I put in, 'but you can have my mobile number in case you need to contact me.'

'That's fine, Miss,' he replied. 'I'll give you my card with a direct contact line. You can call me anytime, day or night if you have a problem.'

'Thanks, Sergeant,' Paul answered. 'I'll feel happier knowing there's someone around she can contact while I'm away.'

As Paul let the policemen out, the workmen turned up, closely followed by a large lorry delivering our new kitchen. He helped the driver unload while I worked out what to bring back from our trip on Sunday. Around mid-morning I made tea, but felt at a loss as to what to do next. I'd only be in the way in the new kitchen, and I couldn't sort things out until the workmen had finished.

'Paul, there's not much I can do round here. I'm going to make a quick trip back to the flat. Some of the smaller things will fit in the car, so there'll be less to bring on Sunday. Anyway, I need something decent to wear for the New Year's Eve party. All I brought with me for the holiday break were a few essentials.'

'You mean we've got to make our own tea?' he joked. 'Actually, that's a good idea. Drive carefully.'

Pleased to be doing something useful, I grabbed my car keys and set off. It was a pleasant drive through the country lanes, and the overhanging trees had kept them relatively dry. My thoughts switched between pleasure at the way the house was being rejuvenated, and repulsion at what had been hidden beneath my feet. Would I really feel comfortable alone on a dark, winter's night? Knowing I'd have Woof for company and protection lightened my mood, and within a short time I was pulling up outside the flat.

Although I'd not been away for long, it looked small and dingy compared to the spaciousness I'd enjoyed recently. As we'd rented fully furnished, nearly everything for the house had been bought brand new. The bed and major items of furniture had already been delivered, leaving only our clothes, books and other personal items to be cleared out from my old home. Bert and Mary, the old couple who owned the house lived in the ground floor flat, so I popped down to formally give them notice. They knew we intended to move, but the actual date had been left open.

'Gina, my dear, how lovely to see you. We heard you moving around upstairs and guessed you were packing up. Come in and have a cup of tea. You must be parched. Is Paul with you? How was your Christmas? How are things coming on with the house?' Mary said as she enveloped me into a hug.

'Give the poor girl a chance to get in the door,' Bert teased. 'Hello, Gina. Have a seat while I put the kettle on. We'll have no peace until she hears every little detail, so you'd better make yourself comfortable and stay for lunch.'

I didn't mention our grisly discovery in the cellar but enthused over the house, the village, our welcoming neighbours and our new house-guest, Woof.

'That's lovely. I'm so pleased it's all working out for you,' Mary said. 'We'll miss you but our granddaughter wants a place of her own, and she's been dropping hints the flat would be ideal. How would a month's notice suit you?'

'That's perfect,' I agreed. 'If I return the keys at the end of January, it'll give me a few more weekends to clear out the rest of our things.'

With the formalities settled, I returned upstairs to sort out what I needed to take back with me, and was piling up the car when the two men from the top flat arrived home.

'Happy New Year,' Jeremy called. 'How's the house?'

'Hello, you two. It's wonderful, but I didn't realise how much paraphernalia we'd accumulated. It seems never-ending,' I replied.

'Give us five minutes to change,' Clive offered, 'and we'll come down and give you a hand.'

'That'd be great. Thanks,' I replied as they disappeared inside.

Between us we soon had it all stowed away in every nook and cranny of the car, and it meant I could leave a bit earlier and avoid the worst of the rush hour. I said goodbye to my old neighbours, and headed for home. "Home." What a lovely thought. Paul came out to greet me as I arrived, and as it was already nearly six, I was surprised to see the builder's van still there.

'Good grief, woman, just as well it's a big house,' Paul laughed. 'However did you manage to load all that yourself?'

'Jeremy and Clive helped me. If there'd been room, I'd have kidnapped them to help unpack it all again. How are things going here? I see the van's still outside.'

'They've been working like Trojans. You couldn't have found a better bunch of lads. They're clearing up now, but have offered to come back tomorrow morning to put the final touches. It should only take a couple of hours, then it's all done. Come and see.'

Paul propelled me towards the new kitchen, but covered my eyes as we reached the door. As he took his hands away, I saw six faces watching me. The transformation was amazing. Although all the preparatory work had been completed before I left, seeing the final result took my breath away. The cupboards and white goods had been installed, the central counter and breakfast table completed, with the boxes of new saucepans and dishes stacked neatly in one corner.

'We thought you'd prefer to unpack those yourself,' the foreman smiled. 'I know what my wife's like if I try to interfere when she's organising.'

'It's fantastic. I can't thank you enough for everything you've done. You've been tremendous.'

He blushed a deep red as I gave him a big kiss on the cheek. The others all laughed, teasing him, so I went round and gave them all a similar thank-you.

'Hey, you hussy,' Paul laughed as he took my hand again. 'Come and see this before you make me jealous.'

The old conservatory had already been demolished, but as we went through the side door at the back of the kitchen, we emerged into the now completed extension, with the new washing machine plumbed in ready.

'Wow, how marvellous to have so much storage!' I exclaimed, opening the various cupboard doors.

'Yep,' agreed Paul. 'Plenty of space for the hoover, mops, buckets and all the cleaning things, so they won't clutter up the kitchen.'

Another small room led into the garden, and held a rack to take muddy boots. There was even a low-level sink where we could wash them off, to save traipsing in the dirt. This was the only area not completely finished, and there were still a few boxes of tiles and skirting boards scattered around.

'Sorry we couldn't finish it completely tonight, Miss,' the foreman said. 'If it's all right with you we'll be here early in the morning, and we should have everything done by lunchtime. Weather permitting, the conservatory should only take about three or four days, and we'll have the swimming pool area finished before the spring. I've given your young man the designs, so let us know when you're ready and I'll get everything ordered. Right, now we'd better be off, or my wife will be locking me out. See you in the morning.'

'Goodnight and thank you so much for all you've done for us. You and your wife must come to dinner one night to let me make it up to her for stealing her husband for so long. See you tomorrow.'

After they left, Paul helped me unload my car. 'Shall I cook my special curry while you sort out your bits and pieces?' he asked.

'Good idea. I had a big lunch but all this hard work has given me an appetite.'

I left him to cook while I unpacked the various boxes and it was well past nine by the time we had eaten and cleared the dishes. After a relaxing bath, seeing my own clothes hanging in the new wardrobes made our house really start to feel like home.

Paul had put away the CDs and books, and I couldn't resist playing some of our favourite music. We sat together on the settee drinking hot chocolate, looking at the plans for the conservatory, and discussing the remaining work. Surprisingly neither of us mentioned the events of the previous day. Instead we concentrated on exactly what we wanted for the proposed conservatory. I was adamant it should be rosewood, with plenty of glass to make it light and airy.

'We could have a diving board over the pool,' he suggested, 'and perhaps one of those thatched kiosks for a bar, with a few serving wenches to bring me cocktails, or put sun tan lotion on my back.'

'This is England, you idiot, not the Mediterranean. And I don't think the water is deep enough for diving. What do you think? Should we have a fixed ladder, or stone steps to get in?'

Eventually we reached an agreement which suited us both, then found ourselves yawning.

'Time for bed, I think,' Paul said as we finalised the plans to give to the builders the following day. Having survived a long but satisfying twenty-four hours, we slept soundly in the house which was now truly our home. The next morning, in my sleepy state, I couldn't make out why things looked different. Then it struck me. The few simple belongings I had put in the bedroom made it feel complete. It might only have been a favourite picture on the wall, or the ornate looking-glass mirror I had always loved, but seeing them there made it feel permanent. With a smile on my face I stretched to find Paul awake and watching me.

'Morning, darling,' he said. 'You look happy.'

'I am,' I replied, cuddling up to him. 'Welcome home.'

He looked serious for a moment then asked quietly, 'Things haven't put you off then?'

'It gave me a start for a while but it happened a long time ago. I think overall this house has more happy memories than sad ones, and now the renovations are more or less finished it really feels like home. I think we're going to be happy here. By the way, the washing room was a lovely surprise. Thank you.'

'I'm glad you liked it, Darling. Now, how about showing me just how grateful you are.'

So I did.

As the workmen were due early, we reluctantly left our bed and prepared to face the world. They arrived shortly after eight thirty and stuck straight into finishing off the final touches. By midday, after discussing our plans for the conservatory, they were ready to go.

'We'll be in touch once the next stage is ready to begin,' the foreman called as he climbed into his van.

'What do you fancy for lunch?' I asked Paul as we went inside. 'There's not much left.'

'Let's splash out and hit the pub. Then we could stock up with supplies and even spend some time in the library. What do you think?'

'Sounds good to me,' I replied and before long we were in the car heading for the village.

Despite being remote, we found a well-stocked mini supermarket, with goods mainly fresh and locally produced, rather than packaged in plastic. We bought a leg of lamb for the freezer, potatoes, vegetables, rice, pasta and other staples, and couldn't resist prime steak and fresh salad for our meal that evening. Even so, we gorged ourselves on the homemade lasagna in the pub before making our way to the library. The librarian recognised us immediately, and offered to make us coffee.

'Follow me,' she said as she led us to the archives, where she had set out the relevant tomes containing the details of our house. We spent a happy couple of hours going through the particulars, and noting down things of special interest.

'Sorry to disturb you, folks, but it's gone five, and I thought I'd better warn you we'll be closing shortly.'

Time had flown. Thanking her for her help we headed home. Woof greeted us as if we had neglected him for years and, after we'd bribed him with doggie treats, he settled down happily as we spent an hour or more browsing and collating the information we had gathered from the library.

I stretched. 'Shall we go for some fresh air?'

Woof agreed wholeheartedly so, grabbing a torch, we set off for an invigorating walk. The peace of the countryside and the beautiful surroundings brought tranquility to our hearts, while Woof expended his energy chasing rabbits and non-existent shadows. Despite all the traumas of the last few days the house felt like a welcoming haven when we returned around seven. The warmth, both physical and mental, cast a welcoming glow and I felt truly glad to be home. Although the old servant's kitchen had been perfectly adequate, somehow, using the newly laid out original one for the first time felt extra special.

Paul set the table in the living room using the new cutlery, and I dug out the plates from one of the boxes to make it a special memory for the future. On impulse, he opened the bottle of wine from the cellar, although we had a back-up supermarket plonk in case it was undrinkable. After a few tentative sips and sniffs we realised it was actually superb, and the years had enhanced, not diminished, its flavour and aromas.

'That steak was excellent,' exclaimed Paul, leaning back and rubbing his stomach.

'Probably the fresh, local produce,' I replied. 'Or perhaps because it was our first meal in our new home but I agree. It was the best meal I've ever tasted.'

Even using the pristine dishwasher for the first time was fun, and it worked perfectly. I was like a kiddie in a sweetie shop, wanting to try out everything.

'Come on, let's relax in the living room,' said Paul eventually, and I allowed him to drag me away.

Chapter 11. Learning the history.

We had a brandy with our coffee, and returned to browsing the mass of information about the house which included confirmation of its original name. I downloaded copies of news stories, and added dates to the house's history to expand on what Paul had learnt from the locals. The wild parties thrown by the grandson of the original owner had spread over several years from about 1910 onwards. During that time there were several reports of girls from the village mysteriously disappearing. Although they were never found, it seemed they had all been young and pretty. The reports indicated they were respectable girls of good character, and not the type to run away or get into trouble.

The villagers' homes and livelihoods had been dependent on the squire, and at first there was no hint he might have been involved. Gradually, as more girls disappeared without trace, the mood of the articles changed. Hints and innuendoes appeared, together with criticisms of the way the estate was run. Eventually there was outright condemnation, resulting in the fire of 1920 in which the squire died, aged fifty-five.

In the following years the house and surrounding cottages fell into disrepair, and the village became almost a ghost-town as people moved away. As the last squire of Alder had no legal heirs, the house was neglected for a decade until it was commandeered for the war effort. The bombing had also meant a lack of suitable housing, and being some way out of London, the village became revitalised. After the war the house returned to its semi-derelict state until it was bought by the property developer in 1951. The village had continued to prosper, and the new hotel brought employment to many locals.

We had become so involved in the history that I hadn't noticed the time until Paul said, 'Don't forget we've a full day tomorrow. Best we make an early start to collect the rest of our things from the flat, and be home before dark.'

The sun streaming through the make-shift curtains reminded me there was still a lot to be done. Opening the back door for Woof, I realised how deceiving the sunshine had been. Although it was a beautiful day there was an icy wind blowing. Even Woof had only a quick run, before returning to the warmth and comfort of the living room. How would he react to being locked up all day while we went back to the flat? I considered leaving a door open, but even in our remote location that might be asking for trouble.

'I'm a bit worried about how Woof will cope, being alone all day while we're out,' I said to Paul when he came down while I was preparing breakfast.

'I'm sure he'll be fine, love, but maybe it'd be better for him to get used to the idea. After all, you'll be going back to work soon, so he'll be left alone then.'

I had totally forgotten about work. The last few days had been so surreal I knew it'd take me a while to adjust to a normal routine.

'You're right,' I said, 'but don't let's think of that now. When I go back I'll only have two days before the week-end. I can't wait to organise the house properly.'

Paul pulled me into his arms for a hug before he asked, 'Are you sure you're going to be all right on your own? I so wish I could be with you to help, but I must finish my contract first. It does worry me though being so far away, especially after all that's happened.'

Not wanting to think about him leaving, I pushed him away as I joked, 'Who said I wanted you around? You'd only get under my feet, and I'll be fine with Woof for company. How many rashers of bacon do you want?'

Before we left, I fed Woof and explained we'd have to leave him for a while, but would be back before dark. It seemed he was listening to every word and understood me as he looked so dejected. As he followed us to the door, I almost changed my mind, but remembering Paul's words about starting as we needed to go on, I gave Woof a hug, before getting in the car and driving quickly away.

Being the Sunday morning after the Christmas period the roads were empty, and we arrived at the flat much earlier than I had anticipated. We tried not to make too much noise as we packed up the rest of our possessions, and carried them down to the car. After a couple of hours of hard work, we felt we were getting somewhere when there was a knock on the door. It was Bert our landlord, with strict instructions from his wife that we were to join them for a bite to eat.

'We're fine, honestly, but thanks for the offer.'

'No arguments. It'll be more than my life's worth if I go back without you. You've ten minutes, then it'll be on the table. Don't let me down now.'

'Okay. Tell her we're really grateful. We'll be down in a bit. Can't have her mucking up her kitchen by massacring you after all that time spent cooking,' Paul laughed.

Mary had prepared a lovely meal and we were ravenous after all our hard work.

'We're really taking advantage of your hospitality, but that was delicious,' I complimented her.

'Good. I hate waste. Much better to see empty plates. I'd have been upset if there'd been anything left so I'm pleased you enjoyed it,' she responded.

Her remark reminded me of my store cupboard upstairs. 'We can't take it with us as the car's already overloaded. Is it of any use to you?'

'But you might need it if you pop back.'

I thought I had insulted her by offering her our left-overs. 'Any other visits we make will be fleeting, so it'll only go to waste,' I replied. 'I hate to chuck it in the bin.'

'Well, we do have our church fete coming up. I'm running a dry-goods stall, and I was a little worried there weren't enough donated goods to sell,' Mary replied.

The matter was settled. As she had a key to the flat we could leave it there until they were ready to collect it, and obviously we refused when she offered to pay for the items. They were such a lovely couple.

'We'll miss you so much,' I said. 'Keep in touch.'

As we kissed them goodbye Paul said, 'When the weather's better we could pick you up one Sunday, and take you to the house for a meal, to thank you for all you've done for us.'

'That would be lovely. I so want to see your new home and meet Woof. You've got our phone number. Let us know once you're settled and we'd be delighted to come.'

We went back up to my old flat to finish cleaning up and I put the remaining contents of the kitchen into boxes, and labelled them with stickers for the fete so they'd know it wasn't rubbish we'd left behind. Paul crammed everything else into the car, and with a final goodbye to Bert and Mary, we drove home, and arrived just as it was getting dark. I had left a light on, and the glow made it feel welcoming. As we opened the door we were almost knocked over by an ecstatic Woof, who greeted us with sloppy kisses and boundless energy. Although he seemed loathe to leave us, he bounded into the garden to relieve himself before returning to greet us again. It was a good omen that he already seemed to be house-trained. Woof bounced around getting under our feet as we unpacked the car.

'How about we leave the rest until tomorrow?' Paul suggested. 'He deserves a run and I don't think he'll settle until he's had one.'

'Good idea. Do you want walkies, Woof?'

The answer was a resounding yes. We put on warm clothes and set out, with Woof showing his enthusiasm by haring off, before coming back to check we were still close then running off again. By the time we walked back our faces were glowing from the cold, but it felt good to feel the fresh air. All three of us had worked up an appetite, but as Woof's meal didn't entail cooking he ate first. I had put the leg of lamb in the oven as soon as we arrived home, and despite our big lunch we devoured our Sunday roast as if we hadn't eaten for days.

It seemed we had already adapted to country ways. Maybe it was the exercise and relaxed holiday mode, but we were eating twice as much as normal. We were also going to bed earlier, but sleeping soundly and waking refreshed to face another exciting new day. I knew all this would change once we got back into the work routine, but meanwhile I intended to enjoy every minute of it. It would feel lonely without Paul around, but I still had Woof and could count the days, hours and weeks until Paul was back with me permanently. Despite our long day I wanted to spend time sorting the boxes, and we worked together as a team for a couple of hours. Eventually, I noticed Paul yawning.

'We've done enough for one day,' I said, and he agreed.

Expecting a late night, we didn't rush to get up the following morning, but found something better to do during our lie-in. I was really going to miss having Paul around when he went back to work. At least we had the party to look forward to that night, and I was determined to make the most of it. Paul pitched in to help me unpack the rest of the boxes until I had everything in its proper place. The living room would look less empty once the new dining table, chairs and settee arrived in a few weeks' time. The old settee was destined for the conservatory once it was finished, but meanwhile there was room for both.

When the weather improved I intended to plant a herb garden and set out flower beds. Paul was going to convert one of the old outhouse buildings into a proper garage and restore the driveway. He also had plans to replace the entrance gates, and had even considered installing a proper security system, with an access phone communicating with the house. Once the renovations for the swimming pool and changing rooms had been completed, we'd be able to spend the summer enjoying the fruits of all our hard work. Suddenly I shivered although the house was warm. I had almost forgotten about the cellar and its grizzly contents. For the time being it was still securely locked and out of bounds.

'You tired, love? Are you sure you still want to go tonight?'

'No, I'm fine. Perhaps a ghost walked over my grave.' I shuddered again at what I had just said. 'I was thinking how much there is still to do. The entire garden and the grounds, the swimming pool and I suppose the cellar eventually.'

'I thought you might still be worrying about that. Before I go tomorrow, I'll spend a couple of hours down there boarding it up properly.'

'Tomorrow! I can't believe the time has gone so quickly. I'm really going to miss you.'

'You could always go back to the flat for a few weeks. We could sort out something about Woof. Maybe someone in the village could take him in for a while.'

Hearing his name Woof got up from his snooze and padded over to rub his head against my arm.

'Don't worry,' I laughed, hugging him. 'You can stay here and look after me. We won't leave you. Well, only for a couple of hours tonight while we go out. Okay?' As if he understood every word, he gave me a sloppy lick then went back to resume his snooze.

For a while we pored over the plans for the conservatory. As the house was detached and we didn't intrude on to any neighbours, the builder had already obtained the necessary planning permission. Despite the extra cost we were going for the larger option. After all, we had the space, and it wasn't something we'd be doing every year. We had agreed on an L-shape. With the bulk of the building to the side of the kitchen, and the narrower part across the back wall stopping at the kitchen windows, we wouldn't block out any light. There would be a side door from the end of the bay, leading onto a patio area in front of the kitchen, with large sliding doors opening off the main plot. We both liked the idea of having mainly glass, which meant we could have the woodwork in a rich dark shade, in keeping with the age of the property. As I was browsing online for blinds and wicker furniture Paul drew my attention to the time.

'Okay. I'll phone the builder on Wednesday and give him the go-ahead to order what he'll need,' I said as Paul packed away the plans. 'Now I'd better go and transform myself into the Belle of the ball.'

'Better get your skates on, Cinderella. The pumpkin will be here soon,' he laughed, blowing me a kiss.

Chapter 12. New Year, New life.

Although it was only a short walk to the pub, Paul had booked transport to take us to the inn and back.

'I can imagine you in your gladrags dancing with your sandals covered in mud,' he laughed.

We were ready and waiting when the bell rang, although Paul looked so gorgeous in his tuxedo I was tempted to forget about going out. As he opened the door, I realised he meant carriage literally. Instead of the expected taxi, a horse-drawn landau waited, with a driver complete with top-hat and riding crop perched on the high seat. Lanterns shone from each corner, and blankets covered the richly-padded bench in case we felt cold. It was the perfect start to what turned out to be an unforgettable evening as Paul helped me to climb in. He rarely showed his romantic side, and I felt like royalty as we drew up outside the inn, which was ablaze with twinkling illuminations. The main bar was heaving with people, but we were directed through an archway leading to the rear, and into what was almost a ballroom, beautifully decorated with an enormous Christmas tree in one corner, and hundreds of tiny lights creating a magical atmosphere.

As we entered I heard the sounds of a band warming up, and noticed the large central space, presumably reserved for dancing later. I was surprised to see the tables set with crystal glasses, and cutlery on pristine white tablecloths, as I hadn't been expecting a sophisticated evening. Wine coolers brimmed with ice, while an assortment of streamers, poppers and other party favours covered the centre.

'May I take your coats?' a waitress dressed as a pixie asked as we entered.

'Champagne?' another of Santa's helpers offered.

'Hello, and welcome. Happy New Year. You're on table ten, I believe. Follow me and I'll show you through,' another smiled, without even asking our names or checking the list pinned up on a board behind her. Several people were already seated, including Debbie the librarian with her partner, and the constable with his wife. They introduced us to the other couple, and shortly afterwards we were joined by our foreman Terry, with his wife and another couple of their friends.

Drinks flowed freely, and by the time we had eaten our first course we had become firm friends. While we were being expertly served a delicious salmon mousse the band played a selection of Christmas and traditional tunes. This was followed by a succulent mix of roast meats with potatoes and vegetables, all cooked to perfection. Before long we were tipsy but enjoyed a troupe of dancers and acrobats who, considering the space they had to work in, were absolutely amazing. They were followed by a comedian who had the audience in stitches, until around ten o'clock the compere announced a short break before the band returned to start their next set.

A DJ played dance music, rock and roll and other party favourites, and before long nearly everyone was on their feet trying to burn off some calories, then, exhausted after all the energy we had expended, we had a break. We chatted and laughed as we enjoyed a delightful cheesecake with rum and coconut ice cream, followed by cheese and biscuits and coffee.

Later we took to the dance floor again, this time to romantic, late night music under dim lights. In the arms of my lovely fiancé, knowing he would share my bed that night, I felt all was right with my world. As midnight approached, the indefatigable waitresses brought more champagne for a New Year toast. John, the owner of the pub, called for quiet.

'It's a pleasure living in such a friendly community with such delightful neighbours, including our newcomers, Paul and Gina. In the short time they've been here, they've revealed themselves as perfect additions to the "family". We wish them a long and happy life in the village.'

I could feel myself blushing as we all raised our glasses to wish each other a happy and prosperous New Year, before linking arms in a huge circle on the dance floor, to join in the traditional singing of Old Lang Syne, just as the clock struck midnight. Soon everyone was kissing everyone else. It was traditional and fun, but I couldn't help noticing a striking redhead I hadn't seen before, grabbing Paul and giving him a kiss that was anything but platonic.

He looked embarrassed and hurriedly disengaged himself to give an elderly lady sitting close by a kiss on the cheek. She smiled broadly as I approached, and Paul stretched out his arm to draw me close to his side. I noticed the redhead watching, but it was the elderly lady who saved the day. She glanced at the other girl before smiling broadly at me and saying, 'Sorry, my love. I saw him first.' Then she pulled Paul down towards her, and gave him a noisy, smacking kiss on the cheek.

'Aren't you going to introduce me to your new girlfriend?' I asked Paul, nodding towards the old lady.

'I would,' Paul replied, 'but it was love at first sight and I didn't even have a chance to find out her name.'

Laughing, the old woman replied, 'It's Mrs Simpson, but in the circumstances you'd better call me Betty.'

'Lovely to meet you, Betty,' I said as I pecked her cheek. 'I'm Gina and this is my fiancé Paul.'

'I know who you are, my dears,' she replied. 'Don't forget this is a small village where everyone knows everyone else's business. How are you settling into the old manor? I hear you've done wonders, but it must have been hard work.'

'We're getting there,' Paul answered. 'We still have all the gardens and exterior to sort out, but most of the rooms are organised, thanks to Gina. I haven't been around to help much, but I'm looking forward to being here permanently once my contract finishes.'

'Oh, yes, you're working abroad, aren't you? It must be hard for you, Gina, trying to manage everything without your man around. I suppose I'd better let you have him back, providing I get one more kiss for luck.'

Paul obliged, and bidding Betty goodnight, we made our way back to our table. For a while we chatted until Terry mentioned he had seen us talking to "that woman."

'I'm not one to spread gossip but you take care,' he said to me quietly. 'She can cause a lot of trouble, that one.'

'You mean Betty?'

'Oh, no. Salt of the earth is our Betty. Anything you want to know about the history of your house, she's the one to ask. You wouldn't believe she's well into her eighties, and her family have lived here all their lives. Her father and grandfather both worked for the old lord, and rumour has it they were instrumental in rallying the villagers against him.'

Terry turned away as his friend said something to him, and later I realised I had not found out about the mysterious, trouble-making redhead. The band played romantic, late-night numbers, and I enjoyed a couple of smoochy dances with Paul, before realising it was nearly one in the morning. As the party broke up, we joined in the toast to our wonderful host and his staff before saying our goodbyes. There was no sign of the redhead, but we did catch Betty to say goodnight as she was leaving with a young man who she introduced as her grandson.

Our landau drew up, and with the nip in the air we were glad of the blankets to cover our knees. The ride home with the bright stars sparkling above us was pure magic, the gentle clip-clop of the horse's hooves in the silent night something I will remember all my life. We were brought back to reality as we opened the door and Woof dived at us with no thought for our evening finery. As it was so late, Paul let him have a run in the grounds, promising him a proper walk in the morning. When he returned, Woof settled down as if he was a doting parent, waiting for the children to come home before retiring. Yawning but happy, Paul and I followed his example.

Chapter 13. Unexpected bonuses.

Despite our late night we both woke at a reasonable hour. I was content until I realised it would be the last time we would share a bed for a couple of weeks. The same thought must have occurred to Paul as he took me in his arms, and we didn't get up until after ten. It was not as cold as it had been the previous night and a weak winter sun tried to break through the grey clouds. After a few minutes Woof nudged Paul as if to remind him of his promise.

'Okay, Okay,' he laughed reaching for the lead and a ball. 'Never let it be said I don't keep my word.'

'I'll come with you,' I said. 'We could all do with some fresh air and exercise.'

Later, as we drank out coffee, Paul turned to more practical matters.

'I'm going down to the cellar to finish securing it properly,' he said.

'If you're there, I might come too,' I replied, determined to overcome my apprehension, although I still had bad feelings about it.

We took several lamps with us, and as we descended the stairs I realised I was holding my breath. Woof positioned himself against the open door, but could not be persuaded to come down. I had almost forgotten about the wine, and although initially I kept close to Paul, eventually I left him to examine the bottles in more detail. The reassuring sound of him hammering gradually restored my confidence as I wandered around picking up bottles from the racks, then called out to tell him I was popping back upstairs.

Woof greeted me like a long-lost friend, and I gave him a pat before collecting a notebook and a wet sponge. He wasn't happy when I went back down a few minutes later, but resumed his previous watchful position. At the bottom of the stairs I could hear only silence.

'Paul, where are you?' I called, my voice sounding shaky.

For a moment there was no reply, then he appeared from my left, making me jump.

'Sorry, love,' he said, 'I didn't mean to scare you but this place is enormous. I've finished boarding up the first holes we found, but when I followed the corridor it goes all the way round. There are several other areas where the wood has rotted, but I've made everything safe now. What have you been up to?'

'I thought I'd have a look at the wine bottles, and see if they'd be worth anything. It might help to try and cover the extra money we've been spending. I want to clean the labels, and make notes about the different names and vintages. They're so filthy I'm trying to decide whether to cart down loads of buckets of water, or take the bottles upstairs to wash them.'

'I've got a better idea. Why not use the running water from the tap in the corner? Come, I'll show you.'

He took my hand and led me round the curve to show me a hidden sink. As he turned the tap, the water spluttered out. Although it was rusty it flowed freely and after a while ran clear.

'That's brilliant,' I said and then wondered whether it had been put there to provide water for the poor girls who had been locked in their prison. A shiver ran down my spine.

'Are you cold?' Paul asked, putting his arm around me.

'It's nothing. I'm a bit chilly but want to finish off cleaning the bottles first,' I said, not wanting him to worry.

Between us we washed the shelves and soon had the whole of one run spotless, so the clean bottles could be put back after I had noted the details on the labels. There were still row after row we hadn't touched, and we estimated there must be at least five hundred in all. Even if we were only able to sell them for a few pounds each it would help towards the expense of renovating the cellar, which we hadn't allowed for in our original costings.

'That's enough for today,' I said, picking up my notebook to go back upstairs and be greeted by an exuberant Woof. While I fed him and prepared an early dinner, Paul cleaned up and packed for his flight that evening. An hour or so researching our wines, and all too soon it was time for Paul to leave. I would miss him so much and it was hard to keep smiling as we said our goodbyes.

He tried to hide his emotion by turning to Woof and saying, 'You make sure you take care of her until I return.'

We ended up laughing as Woof barked his confirmation, then came to stand protectively next to me as if he understood every word. The hire car had already been collected, when a beep from outside told us the cab had arrived. Paul picked up his flight bag, then with a final hug and goodbye kiss he was gone. For a while I felt bereft, but pulling myself together researched potential buyers for our wine. I finished unpacking the remaining boxes we had brought back, before having a light supper and taking myself off to bed.

At first I slept soundly, but around three a.m. I woke from a disturbing dream. I had been down in the cellar, but this time trying to escape from an unknown but frightening entity. Struggling to get up the stairs, my legs felt as if they were stuck in some kind of glue. However much I struggled, I could only move forward in slow motion. The creature was getting closer and closer and I was in a panic when a loud bark woke me, and I discovered Woof licking my face to bring me comfort. Normally he slept soundly downstairs in his own bed, but it was as if he knew I needed him and had come into my bedroom to make sure I was safe. I gave him a hug, and after a while heard him pad back downstairs. For the rest of the night I slept soundly.

Making myself breakfast it felt odd to be cooking just for one, although Woof was only too pleased to help me out with the left-overs. With Paul no longer around, it was down to me to take Woof for his morning run, and we set out for a long ramble across the fields. We ended up near the village, and I took the opportunity to stock up on provisions for the week ahead. I could barely lift the bags and regretted not bringing the car. That problem was easily solved when the shopkeeper offered to deliver everything if I could wait until around four that afternoon.

When I arrived home, a message from Paul put a smile on my face. He had landed safely, but was missing me already. I sent a reply telling him I was missing him too, and described our jaunt and the shopping expedition.

Around three there was a knock at the door, and I assumed it was the delivery coming early, so was surprised to recognise the sergeant who had inspected the cellar's grizzly contents. Once he had made himself comfortable, he gave me an update.

'It's been confirmed all the bodies removed were young girls,' he said, 'ranging in age as far as they could tell, from about fourteen to eighteen or nineteen years old. Forensics confirmed they all died around one hundred years ago, and although the investigations will continue, there's no reason why you shouldn't renovate the cellar, if you're so inclined.'

As he left, the shopping delivery turned up, closely followed by Terry the foreman, wanting a quick chat about our plans for the conservatory.

'You've just missed the police. We've been given the all-clear for the cellar,' I explained.

'Fine. How about I call in Saturday morning to examine the cellar properly, and see what needs to be done?'

Due to go back to work, and unsure how long the journey would take, I was apprehensive about leaving Woof alone. The following morning I found myself explaining to him I had to be out all day, but promised to return that evening. After an easy drive to the station, I managed to find somewhere to park and as the train was on time, arrived at work earlier than usual.

The day started slowly with everyone catching up with their tales of the holidays, and the afternoon quickly passed as we became immersed in clearing up the backlog. As soon as my train stopped at my station I dashed for the car, and broke a few speed limits to reach home quickly. The house was in total darkness and I made a mental note to leave lights on in future. Woof was already barking before I opened the door, and for a moment my heart sank, wondering what I might find. Everything was fine though as he jumped all over me. Giving him a big cuddle, I explained about having to go to work every day, but offering reassurance I'd always come home. As usual he cocked his head to listen, then hinted he was hungry.

'How about a quick walkies first?' I asked.

That seemed to meet with approval, so after changing my work shoes and collecting a torch, we set off. It was fully dark, and although he went off to investigate enticing smells, he never strayed too far from my side. Half an hour later he had been fed, and while my dinner was cooking, I turned on my laptop, pleased to see replies from connoisseurs and experts interested in our wine. It seemed a good idea to compose a general information leaflet explaining how it had been left untouched for so many decades, and adding a warning there was no guarantee as to its quality.

I could confirm that to the best of my knowledge the labels were genuine, and the wine was produced on the estate we now owned, that we were in the course of cataloguing the entire stock, and ask that anyone interested should contact me with their offers. After sending the details to some of the main distributors I had discovered on the Internet, I was astounded when a few hours later I found around twenty responses with various bids. Never mind the few pounds we had been expecting, some of the offers were nearly one thousand pounds for a single bottle.

It was unbelievable, but before raising my hopes too high, I realised we had to be open, and make it clear the wine might have gone sour. It gave me the idea of having an "Open House" day for prospective buyers to visit and see for themselves once the cellar was organised. Terry had promised to call Saturday morning for a proper inspection. We had already decided to go-ahead with the conservatory, and I could kill two birds with one stone by confirming we wanted him to start work on the cellar at the same time. With a bit of luck, it would be finished by the time Paul's contract ended in mid-February.

All of a sudden, my mind was buzzing with plans and dates, so I used my computer to jot down notes, and provisional diary dates with reminders. All I had to do was overcome my fear of the cellar, and accept it as part of our home once the refurbishments were completed. Needing to prove something to myself, I plucked up my courage and grabbed a torch, but as I reached the door Woof started whining, and I chose to believe it wasn't fair to leave him alone. Feeling a fool, but also letting the sensible part of my mind convince me I could accidentally get locked in again and no one would know, I decided to forget about it until Paul's next leave when we could go down together.

That night the terrible dream returned. I was in the cellar which was filled with a red glow although I knew it was night-time, and there were no lights on. Slowly moving my head, I could see the candles spluttering in their sconces on the wall. My hair was matted and filthy, as were my clothes, which were in the mid-19th century style. Trying to pull my arms down to cover my modesty where my dress was torn, I could only move the left limb. Looking round in pain, I could see my right arm was shackled to a ring set in the wall above me. I assumed I had been unconscious, my head ached and there was blood on my arms, and dried stains on my dress. A sound close by made me freeze, until I realised it was someone moaning. As my eyes became accustomed to the gloom, it was possible to make out the shape of another girl in a similar position to my own.

'Hello,' I called quietly. 'Who are you?'

At first there was no answer then I heard a whispered, 'Betty. I'm the blacksmith's daughter. Who are you?'

'I remember you, and your beautiful long tresses. I'm Georgina. Why are we here? What's happened to us?'

'I know you too, Georgina. You are as fair-haired as I am dark. Did you not work for a while at the manor as a housemaid?'

'Yes, but some of the squire's gentleman friends tried to take too many liberties, so I left to help my father. But how did we get here?'

'I only know I was walking home when three ruffians grabbed me. They put a smelly old sack over my head, and dragged me into a back room of the manor house. His Lordship was there with some friends, and they tried to make me do horrible things with them. When I refused they beat me, until I used my nails and nearly took out his eye. Then I woke up to find myself here.'

'I had a similar experience with his Lordship's friends. He was so angry when I left, he refused to give me a reference. It didn't matter because I could work with my father, but later he sent a message to apologise. He instructed me to come to the manor for my dues, but not to tell anyone, as he was so embarrassed at the treatment I had received. He gave me a glass of mead, and the next thing I remember is waking up here. I believe he put a drug in it, as I still feel so dizzy.'

Our conversation was interrupted by the sound of the cellar door opening, and at the top of the stairs we could see the dark shadows of several men coming down towards us. I screamed, and woke to find Woof licking my face again. What a horrible dream! The clock showed it was only 5.30, but there was no way I could go back to sleep. After a long bath, I cooked an enormous fry up, which made me feel more human. Although it was still dark, I took Woof for a run to help clear my mind. By the time we returned it was light, so after feeding him and changing my clothes I left early for work.

Although busy, every now and then my mind recalled the vision of my nightmare. So vivid and detailed, it felt like déjà vu, and I found it hard to concentrate. As I had come in early, at 4.30 my boss sent me home as he thought I was coming down with something. I was only too pleased to take up his suggestion, and shortly after half past five, I was opening my front door. Despite all the problems with the cellar it still felt like home, especially when Woof greeted me like a long-lost friend. Quickly changing my shoes, we went for another run before I locked the doors for the night.

As it was the week-end, I treated myself to a glass of shop-bought wine to go with my evening meal. With a doggie treat for Woof, we settled down contentedly to enjoy our evening. The next day Terry was due to come and sort out the conservatory and cellar. I wasn't sure whether to let him go down alone, or if I would have the courage to accompany him, but decided it was something to worry about when the time came.

I was closing down my laptop after working on ideas for the house-warming and wine fest, when a message popped up from Paul. He was sorry it was late, but had been working all hours to try to catch up after the Christmas break. He asked how I had found the journey to work, and if Woof had behaved himself. I didn't mention my dream, but told him about my ideas for organising an open day for prospective wine purchasers. I reminded him of the plan for a house-warming for the locals, and about Terry coming the following day, and said I missed him. After a few minutes I received a reply saying he didn't know how I had time to miss him with all that was going on. He couldn't wait until he was home to help, and sent me a big goodnight kiss. I went to bed with a huge smile on my face, and slept dreaming of pleasant things with Paul by my side.

Saturday was another cold but beautiful day. I woke rested and ready to face the world, and took Woof for an early bracing run, returning home starving. The way I was going I would soon weigh twenty stone, but the fresh country air and exercise made me feel alive. When Terry turned up, I made coffee while we chatted about the conservatory.

'All the supplies have been ordered, my lovely, and I can start as soon as they arrive. They should be here by the end of the month, or early February at the latest, if that suits you.'

'Perfect. What's the chances of it being finished by mid-February? That's when Paul's contract finishes, and I'd love to surprise him.'

'I'll do my best. Now what about the cellar?'

'Well…' Loathe to talk about it, I updated him with my ideas for displaying our wines, and the need to make the cellar hospitable.

'That's a great idea. I promise I'll make it a place to be proud of when you're showing the connoisseurs round,' he said. Taking a deep breath, I grabbed a torch and we descended the stairs together. The atmosphere didn't feel so oppressive, perhaps because I had someone with me. Terry carried on making notes, measuring up and looking at the practicalities, while I cleaned bottles and organised shelves. It was reassuring having him around, especially when he commented on the number of bottles on the racks, and confirmed my idea of having an open house for the wine sales was a good one.

Mid-morning, we stopped for a welcome coffee break.

'The first priority is lighting, so I'll arrange for an electrician to come mid-week,' Terry said between sips. 'I'll also have the walls rendered and the old rubbish cleared out.'

The thought of having a blank canvas was exciting, but I didn't want it to become a dumping ground, and still had the idea of converting part of it into a gym. Although I would be at work, I was happy to leave Terry to it, and made a note to go into the village that afternoon to have a spare key cut.

'Should be easy enough to knock down part of the outer wall, and make easy access to the pool. Shall we go out there now, and have a look from that side?' he suggested.

'Much of the pipe work in the two cabins will need replacing, but most of the rest is just cosmetic renovations,' Terry said. 'I'll get a plumber to come when the electrician's here, so they can work in tandem.'

The possible extra costs concerned me, but he promised to drop in his itemised quotes on the following Monday, so we could see what we wanted doing first. After he left, I told Woof I wouldn't be long, and drove the short distance to the village to cut the new key. After stocking up with supplies for the week, rather than heading straight home, I decided to treat myself to lunch. The pub was busy, and after ordering the pork and apple pie with chips and roast vegetables, I looked round for a table.

A voice called, 'Come and join us,' and I was delighted to see Betty, sitting with the young man I recognised as her grandson. We chatted about what a great New Year celebration it had been, and my plans for the house until her grandson stood up, saying, 'If you ladies will excuse me, I've some things to do so I'll leave you to it.'

Once he had left Betty became more serious, and gently probed into how I was finding the house, and my experiences there. At first, I was light-hearted and told her about the wine store, how great the new kitchen was, and what we wanted to do with the pool and conservatory. It was she who brought up the subject of the cellar. She was such a good listener that without thinking, I found myself revealing my dreams and apprehensions. For a while she was silent, then it struck me that despite her age, her hair was still long and black, although speckled with grey.

'Yes dear,' she said in response to my unasked question, 'My mother was also called Betty and from the pictures I've seen, you're the spitting image of her poor friend Georgina.'

'What happened to her?' I whispered.

'I don't know,' came the reply. 'That was the night of the fire. Afterwards, Mother told me she thought she would die, but some villagers found her and cut her free. She didn't remember much after that, except waking up safe in my grandfather's house. I often wonder what happened to the other girls and if they too survived.

'The lord had perished and the villagers had closed ranks, so it was difficult to find any actual facts about what happened. There was an official investigation, of course, but even though the police chief's daughter was one of the girls who had gone missing, I don't think we'll ever find out the full truth. Maybe it's a coincidence you have the same name as my mother's friend, but it's strange you had such a vivid dream, if you have no connection.'

I felt my skin crawl as I explained about being named after my maternal great grandmother, although I was brought up by adoptive parents as my own died in a car crash when I was only a few months old.

'Another funny thing I remember being told was that Georgina always had a dog with her. He looked like a wolf, but however gentle he was with her, low betide anyone who tried to harm his mistress. He was another one we never saw again after the great fire, although rumour circulated he mated with a bitch from the village, and had pups. It was all a long while ago and I'm an old lady, so don't take too much notice of my reminiscences. Lovely to see you again my dear, we'll talk again soon.' With that Betty stood up and left.

Chapter 14. Dreams and realities.

Woof greeting me at the door reminded me of the surreal conversation, and how ancient history and reality were blurring into one. Could it be that my great grandmother had actually been Betty's fellow prisoner in this house? Was that why I felt as if I recognised it the first time I saw it? Was Woof actually a descendant of the dog who had been Georgina's constant companion? Why was I having such vivid dreams that seemed to tie in so closely with what had actually happened? Even though I thought my imagination was running away with me, I wished Paul was there so I could voice all those questions. He might laugh, but at least he'd listen and understand my fears.

As it was only dusk, I took Woof to have another look at the area surrounding the swimming pool. The water seemed dark and murky, and I made a mental note to have someone clean it, and to find out about on-going maintenance. While there, I decided to have a quick peek into the two ramshackle outhouses that had once been the changing rooms. Although they were dingy and depressing, Woof showed none of the reticence about entering that he had about going near the cellar, and for a while we poked around.

By torch light it seemed to be only the old pipes that needed replacing. With a cosmetic overhaul the two rooms could make an ideal changing area. It occurred to me that in the winter a hot-tub and sauna might be a luxury for dispelling the winter blues. If we could knock through an entrance from the house we wouldn't even need to go outside if the weather was bad. Realising I was getting carried away again without thinking of the costs involved, I went back to the house to think about supper.

After reviewing all the expenditure so far, and estimating the likely costs to complete the rest I was surprised to realise it wasn't much over our original budget. Partly because of the reduced price I had been able to negotiate for the house itself, we still had money in the bank, even after settling all the current bills. With Paul and I both earning we could turn our house into a wonderful home with every imaginable amenity. Any money we might raise from the sale of the wine would be an added bonus.

The days and weeks passed and I settled into a routine. Terry turned up with the electrician, and they installed proper lighting in the cellar. They repaired all the crumbling stone work, replaced the rotted wood and made a proper entrance via the outhouses to the pool.

Meanwhile, I took the opportunity to wash off the grime and categorise the remaining bottles. What a difference their handiwork made to the cellar. The pale blue paint on the walls gave it a bright and peaceful look, and the strip lighting and side lamps did away with gloomy corners. In such a large area, even the rosewood I had chosen to match the conservatory didn't make it look ominous. Terry had a key, so while I was at work, he and his team got on with rebuilding the outside structures by the pool, and replacing all the pipework.

Going the whole hog, I decided on a hot-tub as well as two showers in the building backing onto the cellar. The other structure was left empty until I decided what to do with it, although it was fitted out with running water and electricity. Then I had the brainwave of converting it into a kitchen. It would be perfect for storing food and drinks for barbeques in the summer. Knowing what our weather was like, it could also supply an alternative venue if the heavens opened, and we had to run for cover from the elements.

I ordered a large freezer and sink unit, and had the fridge and oven moved from the old kitchen. Terry installed everything, and put up cupboards in the same rosewood to match the brand-new exterior. By the time Paul was due back on a week-end leave at the end of January, it was nearly complete. The hot-tub was due for delivery the following week, together with the materials for the new conservatory. Meanwhile Terry and his men worked on preparing the foundations. That left the old interior kitchen, which I wanted to make into a study.

The interest for the wine snowballed, and I set a date early in March for the open day. I could use the new kitchen to provide refreshments, and the direct access into the cellar meant I wouldn't have people traipsing all over the rest of the house. By then the conservatory should be finished, and as Paul was due a week's holiday before starting his relocated job in London, it was ideal timing. Meanwhile I looked forward to him coming home late the following Friday evening, so I could show him everything. I wanted it all to be perfect.

Thankfully I had no more dreams, apart from ones involving paint, wood and decorating. I had seen Betty several times, but as if by mutual consent, we did not mention her family memories of the cellar. Several of the villagers had also become close friends, which reminded me of the need to organise the house-warming. I hoped to arrange it for late April or early

May, and with a bit of luck, the weather might allow us to have a barbeque outside.

I continued to carry out research on the house, both at the library and online. The more I read, the more fascinating it became, although the old photos were a far cry from the first time I had seen it in such a dilapidated state. As I looked around, I couldn't help but be proud of my comfortable and appealing beautiful home. As my constant companion, I found myself asking Woof's opinion. He'd look at me with his big brown eyes, cock his head to one side and give me either a quizzical look, or a positive one. Perhaps I had been spending too much time on my own if I felt a dog was actually giving his views.

Even so, when I was deciding on the heavy curtains for the living room, he signalled he wasn't keen on my first choice. My second suggestion of a dark gold brocade met with his approval, and once they were hanging at the windows, I realised he was right. Oh, boy, was I losing it or what? I needed human company. Thank goodness Paul was due home that week-end. Provided Terry and his boys had finished by Friday evening, we would have the house to ourselves. I couldn't wait.

Chapter 15. Village gossip.

The week passed slowly at work, even though we were busy. I skived off promptly and most nights managed to catch the earlier train by the skin of my teeth. Even though I knew Paul wouldn't be arriving until late on Friday I wanted the weekend to start as soon as possible.

'Pleased I caught you,' Terry had said on Monday night. 'The hot tub should be here tomorrow, and all the fittings for the conservatory Wednesday. We won't be finished by Friday, and we're not working this weekend, but everything will be done by the first week in February, as I promised.'

It made me realise how much of their own time the boys had given up to achieve my deadlines. Not many workmen worked several weekends on the trot, and they deserved some time off. They were still ahead of schedule, and my pencilled-in dates for the wine day and house warming could now be confirmed without problem. On the Friday, Terry was just leaving as I returned with Woof after our run. Paul was not due home until late and would have eaten on the plane, but I wanted time to feed Woof and eat my own supper before he arrived. I had a few nibbles prepared in case he was still hungry, and had bought a bottle of his favourite brandy for us to enjoy a night-cap.

There was still plenty of time so I sent out some invitations to the connoisseurs to confirm the date for our tasting day. They included directions to the house, and a brief background of the history of the vineyard. Over the weeks I had finished cataloguing our wine stock. Now it was a case of deciding the order of the day, what hospitality should be provided, and anything else needed to make the day a success. The date was set for Sunday 6th March, as Paul would be around the week before to help with the organising. Although not sure how many might actually turn up, I'd need more glasses, so I made a note to ask in the pub if I could borrow some.

Originally, I had thought of doing the food myself, but then remembered meeting someone in the village who ran a catering service, and decided to approach Penny to find out how much she would charge. I needed to firm up on the number of visitors, so it seemed a good idea to ask for their confirmation by the end of February, and to add a £10 entrance fee. Apart from the money helping towards the catering costs, it might make the visitors less likely to cancel at the last minute. With plans in place I sent off invitations, and sat back to await results. It might all be a waste of time if no-one was interested but I couldn't help feeling enthusiastic now everything was coming together. An auction basis would be a silly idea if only two or three people turned up, but my spirits and confidence were high.

Glancing at the clock, I saw it was already gone nine. I expected Paul between ten and eleven, depending on the flights, and my excitement mounted at the thought of seeing him again after nearly four weeks. Although I had received regular e-mails and messages, it was not the same as having him here in the flesh. To pass the time I took Woof for a quick run so when Paul arrived, we'd have the evening to ourselves without interruption. The air was fresh and a full moon made the night magical. Even when a face loomed up from the darkness it didn't scare me as Woof hadn't given any sign of being apprehensive. I recognised Anna the barmaid from the pub, out with her boyfriend, walking his Labrador. We fell into step while the dogs sniffed and chased shadows like old friends.

'Wow. Look at the time,' I said after a while. 'We didn't intend to stay out this long. Paul's coming home tonight, and I want to be there when he arrives. It's been a long four weeks.'

'But he was here last week, he was in the….er, well, you don't want to keep him waiting. Bye then. See you.'

Anna gave me a funny look, and I saw her whispering to her boyfriend as they walked away. It was puzzling, but she must have mixed up the dates. When we arrived home, I gave Woof his final late-night snack, dimmed the lights, and put on some romantic background music while I waited. Around 10.30 a cab drew up and I rushed out to welcome Paul. Woof was ecstatic at seeing him again, although Paul himself was subdued. Assuming he was tired after working so hard and the long flight, I left him in peace while he went upstairs to have a shower and unwind.

'Sorry, love,' he said when he came down, 'it's been full-on since I left and I'm exhausted. I'm not really hungry, but I wouldn't say no to a drop of brandy. So, tell me. What have you been up to?'

While he sipped his drink, I regaled him with my plans for the wine day, and the provisional ideas for the house-warming, and was pleased when he noted the dates in his dairy. Although I wanted to show him all the improvements since he had been away, knowing he was worn out we agreed to leave it until the morning, when he could see it properly in the daylight. He yawned and I suggested we go to bed. It wasn't a totally selfless thought as it crossed my mind we could catch up with our love life, especially as there was no need to be up early the next day.

Within five minutes of getting into bed he was snoring softly, and realising I was being selfish I snuggled up in his arms and tried to sleep. That night the dreams returned. I imagined myself restrained in the cellar, but the face gloating over me was Paul's. I woke the following morning unsettled and tetchy. It should have been a wonderful home-coming, but somehow it had all gone sour. Realising he was missing from the bed, I went downstairs to find he had already cooked breakfast, and was looking much more cheerful.

'Sorry about last night. You've been bursting to show me everything they've done, so eat up and I'm all yours,' he said as he put the plate in front of me. He had been tired the previous evening, and I had expected too much. My journey to work and back was a lot easier than his, with the stress of getting to the airport, flying home and then the long cab journey to reach our remote house. Today would be different, and I couldn't wait to show him the work Terry and his gang had completed.

'Wow, what a transformation,' Paul said as we looked round the cellar. 'Great idea about making an entrance between here and the pool. Who thought of that?'

'Me,' I responded rather smugly. 'Come on, I want to show you how the outhouses have been redesigned.'

'Is there no end to your talents?' he joked. 'Your ideas for the wine opening day sound great too.'

When we went over the costings for the renovations, he saw we were still well within budget and didn't even raise an eyebrow at costs for the hot-tub, shower rooms and barbeque kitchen.

'You've had some brilliant ideas, and I'm sure you'll be happy here.'

It was an odd comment to make. Everything I had done was intended for both of us to enjoy together. When I tried to talk to him about the house warming he agreed in principle, but dropped some hints that he might not actually be around for the Spring. For a moment I felt panic until he explained there was another contract up for grabs, which entailed him returning to work abroad. Nothing was settled, but the money on offer was almost too good to turn down.

'What about the London job?' I asked. 'Have they changed their mind, or what?'

'To be honest, being stuck behind a desk doesn't have me jumping for joy. There are always going to be problems starting from scratch, especially in different countries, but that's what gives me a buzz.'

Despite his enthusiasm I knew something was wrong, but couldn't put my finger on exactly what it was. Maybe work was taking it out of him, maybe the enormity of the house project was too much to take in all in one go, maybe he was tired, maybe he didn't love me anymore. I don't know where that last thought came from, but it suddenly sprang into my mind. As if noticing my concern, he grabbed my hand, kissed me soundly and suggested we took the dog with us for lunch at the pub. Thankful for his lighter mood, I called Woof and we set out. Although it was cold, the sun was shining brightly and I enjoyed the fresh air and peace of the countryside.

When we reached the pub, he settled me at our usual table in the corner with Woof lying quietly at my feet. Paul returned with menus, our drinks and a bowl of water for the dog, while we decided what we were going to eat. As he went to order, I chatted to a few neighbours. He was gone a long while, and I assumed he had been talking to people at the bar. Needing the toilet, I told Woof to stay and headed for the ladies at the rear. The pub was now crowded, but as I worked my way through, I caught sight of Paul. I wasn't certain, but he seemed to be in close conversation with the red-head from the New Year's Eve party.

'Sorry to have been so long,' he said when eventually he returned. 'You know how these country people love to chat.' Before I could ask him who he had been talking to, the waitress brought our meals, and we tucked into the food before it got cold.

Chapter 16. Discussing the future.

When we had finished and the plates had been cleared, I plucked up the courage to ask Paul if everything was all right.

'You've been very quiet. Is something worrying you?'

'No, I'm fine. I was just tired after the flight.'

'Maybe I've been spending too much on the house? I know I've been extravagant but it'll be worth it in the long run. What do you think?'

'It's nearly finished now. Go ahead and tell the builders to do whatever you think it needs to complete it.'

I probed him about his new job offer, and told him if it was what he really wanted I'd support him all the way. He smiled and leant over to kiss me as he said it was all up in the air at the moment, and might not even be a possibility.

'Anyway, I'll definitely be around for the week of your Wine-fest. It'll be interesting to see how much the bottles in the cellar are worth.'

I picked up on the number of times he said "your" instead of "our" and it worried me. Perhaps because he had not been around for most of the renovations he didn't think he was involved, but I had always thought of it as "our" home and wanted him to be happy with the things I did to try to improve it for both of us. It struck me as odd that he seemed to be at ease with the villagers when he had spent so little time here.

'By the way, was the redhead you were talking to the one from the New Year's Eve party?'

'What redhead? I was only chatting to some of the locals.'

Eventually he agreed there was a girl called Gloria who had been at the bar, although he hadn't really noticed her much. *Methinks the gentleman doth protest too much*, I thought. If he hadn't noticed her, how did he know her name and why not be open about it. I wasn't normally the jealous type, but on this occasion the green-eyed monster reared its ugly head. Perhaps I was reading too much into it. It wasn't worth spoiling our precious time together during his leave, so I dropped the subject. We moved onto safer ground talking about the wine, the open day, the renovations and my plans for a party for our neighbours in a few months' time.

The crowd was thinning out, and as we left I made a point of looking around to see if Gloria was still at the bar. She was nowhere to be seen, and after calling our goodbyes we set off for home. When I opened up my laptop, I was astounded to see nearly forty replies asking for further details and expressing an interest in the wine sale. Around half of these also wanted confirmation of where to send their entry fee, which seemed a good omen for the day itself. I sent off replies immediately, and phoned the caterer to confirm she was available for the actual day, and to ask for her quote for approximately thirty people.

With Paul acting so oddly I had forgotten about asking the pub for extra glasses, but this problem was solved when the caterer confirmed she would be able to supply all our requirements. Within the hour she had phoned me back with her quote, which I accepted. The exact numbers would be confirmed a week or so before the actual date, but meanwhile it seemed as if everything was going to plan.

Paul did some research to decide how best to organise the various bottles, while I thought about how to set up the pool kitchen, as I found myself calling it. We decided to put a large table down in the cellar for people to rest the bottles when they took them from the shelves to examine them. If we were to offer tasters, we needed to decide which bottles to open for the hospitality.

'You realise you have to make sure anything you serve is drinkable. It'd be a disaster if their first taster put them off,' he said.

'I know. That's been worrying me too, but what can we do? We can't open every bottle to taste it, or there'd be nothing left.' Again, I picked up on all the times he said you, instead of we.

'Leave it to me. I know a wine producer. If you want, I'll contact him and ask for his opinion.'

He made the phone call and I was relieved when he told me his friend would drive over the following day, arriving about eleven-ish, if I could rustle up lunch for when they had finished in the cellar. That wasn't a problem, but the fact our final few hours together were to be spent in company upset me. Although Paul was right in getting the wine checked out, it felt as if he was inventing reasons not to be alone with me. I was subdued but left Paul to his research while I finished sorting and re-arranging the final few boxes of possessions we had brought back from the flat.

It was gone 7.30 when Paul rose and stretched, telling me he needed some exercise after sitting for so long and was going to take Woof for a run. He didn't ask if I wanted to go too, and well over an hour later I was starting to worry until I heard his key in the door. When he said he was ready for an early night, I misinterpreted his meaning but by the time I joined him in bed, he seemed to be asleep. He roused when I climbed in next to him, but after a chaste goodnight kiss turned away from me and was soon snoring quietly.

That night it took me a long while to doze off, with so many thoughts running through my mind, but I put the reason down to my worries about the wine sale. Just before I slept, my subconscious queried why I wasn't able to relax. All the major problems had been overcome, and the upheaval during the renovations hadn't affected my sleep. The dreams returned, but I couldn't remember the details until I woke to find Paul shaking me and saying I had been screaming in my sleep. Although it was only shortly after six, I decided to get up. Paul didn't come down until I called to say breakfast was on the table. Once he had eaten, he went back to his laptop telling me he had some things to catch up on before his friend Geoff arrived. Following his example, I caught up with my correspondence and for a while we worked in silence. Around mid-morning Paul rose and stretched.

'I think I'll take Woof for a quick run,' he said.

Before I had a chance to collect my coat, I heard the door slam and I was left on my own. Something was definitely wrong, but as Paul only came back a few minutes before Geoff arrived, I had no time to talk to him. Geoff was charming and greeted me warmly, telling Paul what a lucky man he was to have such a beautiful fiancée. He was probably nearing seventy, but flirted outrageously with me and it felt good to have someone pay attention after Paul had been so cold. Geoff made sure he included me in the discussions, and asked for my ideas on how the day would work.

'The bottles are in the cellar Geoff, if you want to follow me down,' Paul said, once the pleasantries were over, making me feel like the proverbial spare part.

'Of course. Lead the way, fair lady,' my knight in shining armour replied, before taking my arm to escort me down the stairs. He was amazed at the size of the cellar, even though he was aware of the history of the house, and knew some of the vintages which had been produced in the years when it was an active vineyard. Paul took over when they got into an in-depth discussion of the various varieties, so I left them to it while I went through the new door into the cellar kitchen. Looking round I planned how to arrange it for the refreshments.

It seemed logical to welcome the guests in via the rear entrance, give them a glass of wine then show them through to the cellar. Once they had examined the goods, I'd take them into the kitchen for light refreshments. Would I have enough chairs? I added them to my list of beg, borrow or steal. The caterer was supplying all the necessary cutlery and napkins, but I would need somewhere to place the refreshments, as well as a table in the cellar to hold the bottles while they were being examined. I was ready to go back upstairs when Geoff came through to see the kitchen.

'Is this where you intend to have the reception?' Geoff asked. 'Ideal. How many are you expecting?'

'I've had twenty people sign up already, so I was thinking of catering for about thirty. I might be over-estimating but I've only just put out the details, and even if some don't turn up, fingers crossed, there'll be more. I need to check about hiring a table for in here, and another one for the cellar to display the bottles. Actually, it all depends on your opinion. If the wine's no good, then it's all off. What do you think so far?'

'I'm 99% sure it's perfect. Although it's been there a long while it was professionally stored, and the temperature in the cellar's just right. I'd say it was originally built by vintners who knew exactly what they were doing. As the saying goes, "the proof of the pudding is in the eating," so we intend to open one bottle to make sure. As for the rest, it's down to the buyers to make their own decision as to whether it'll be worth paying the price. Providing the one we try is satisfactory, I'd suggest organising at least part of the day on an auction basis. There are one or two exceptional bottles which I think could bring a very good price. As for the rest, see what you're offered, and decide on the day if you're satisfied with the price.'

'That sounds great,' I replied, 'but I've never run an auction and wouldn't like to make a mess of it.'

'I'd be happy to help,' Geoff replied. 'By the way, instead of hiring tables have you thought of asking a carpenter to build you some as a permanent structure? You have plenty of space and they'd be useful once the wine day's over.'

'I hadn't thought of that. I'll get onto Terry and see what he comes up with. Thanks for all your advice. Now I'd better think about feeding you. Come upstairs when you're ready.'

I phoned Terry while it was in my mind, and he promised to pop round Tuesday evening to measure up, but was sure it would be a fairly simple job. Paul and Geoff came up carrying two bottles of wine, one red and one white, and Geoff asked me to put one in the fridge to chill, and then opened the red to allow it to breathe.

We retired to the living room and I decided to dig out my best crystal glasses. Although I was not a connoisseur, both wines tasted superb to me and even Geoff pronounced them as top class. Then he asked to see my record of the ones I'd listed, and after asking permission, proceeded to write a suggested price next to each one. Now and again he consulted his record book, but seemed knowledgeable about most of the vintages. He earmarked eight for auctioning, and suggested a reserve price for each.

I had to blink when I saw the figures. Even the ordinary ones were listed at between fifty and one hundred pounds. The exclusive ones started at the thousand-pound mark. Geoff suggested I have plain crackers, water and a sorbet available during the wine tasting itself to help clear the palate, and leave the actual buffet food until after the sale was complete. He suggested some bottles for the tasting and advised me to estimate around ten samples per bottle. Assuming my anticipated numbers of about thirty were correct, three red and three whites should be allocated with a few in reserve in case numbers increased.

He was confident the expense of around five hundred pounds, plus the additional catering costs, would be well covered from the expected sales. It reminded me he hadn't mentioned his own fee for running the auction and providing his expert advice.

'I'm only too happy to offer my services, my dear,' he smiled, 'but if you find yourself with one of the cheaper range bottles unsold, I'd be only too happy to take it off your hands.' He was such pleasant company, the fact Paul had hardly contributed to the conversation went unremarked. Around four Geoff said he must take his leave, and once Paul had shown him out, he called to say he was taking Woof for a final run. Again, they were gone for nearly an hour. Upon his return Paul went straight upstairs to have a shower and collect his bags for the flight. When he came down, I tried to ask if anything was troubling him.

'No, everything's fine. I thought Geoff's visit went quite well.'

Before I knew it, his taxi was at the door and with a quick kiss, he was gone.

Chapter 17. Suspicions.

In some ways it had been a good day but I was still concerned how quiet Paul had been all weekend, and how he seemed to have taken every opportunity not to spend time alone with me. We hadn't even made love, and it would be over a month before I saw him again. Meanwhile I had plenty to keep me busy, and with work the next day, decided to have an early night. I slept as soon as my head hit the pillow but then woke around one a.m. to find myself wide awake, with no idea what had disturbed me. For a while I lay in bed, looking at the shadows, and although my ears were straining for any noise, all I could hear was the blowing of the wind outside.

I jumped when the bedroom door slowly opened and a black shape appeared. It was only Woof but even as I gently scolded him, I realised he didn't usually come into my room during the night. It was as if he too was aware of something, and had come to bring me comfort and company. I gave him a hug and we stayed together providing mutual support. He drew close, and rested his head against my arm lying above the covers. After twenty minutes I drifted off to sleep again, and when I woke the next morning Woof was back in his own bed, snoring softly.

He woke when he heard me go into the kitchen, so I opened the back door to let him out while I got ready. As usual, I explained it was Monday so I had to leave him for a while, but would be back later. He nodded his understanding, and it occurred to me there had been more conversations between us than with my boyfriend this weekend. The ridiculousness of the situation helped lighten my mood, and I blew Woof a kiss before setting off for work.

I stayed late as I hoped to get away early the following day to see Terry, and make sure the arrangements for the tables, hot-tub and conservatory were all going to plan. In the end I didn't leave until nearly quarter to seven, and was worried if Woof had been all right on his own for so long. By the time I arrived home it was nearly eight and the house was in darkness. Turning on all the lights I called out to Woof, only to be met with silence. My heart sank as my imagination ran riot, until after a few minutes the dog slunk up to me with his tail between his legs.

'What's wrong, sweetheart?' I asked as I gave him a cuddle. 'I was worried about you.' When I went into the kitchen I saw the reason for his distress. There was a little packet on the floor to greet me, and he looked embarrassed.

As I reassured him, I felt relief it was such a minor problem, and realised it could be easily solved by asking Terry to fit a dog flap into the conservatory so Woof could get out while I was at work. Once I had cleaned up in the kitchen, I grabbed Woof's lead before even thinking about my supper. Outside, his high spirits soon returned as if he knew he had been forgiven, and I found myself laughing at his antics after a stressful day. We were both ravenous when we reached home, and after eating I settled down in the living room with him content at my feet, as if he knew he was no longer in disgrace. I spent a couple of hours catching up with people on my laptop, and even sent a message to Paul, but received no reply.

In the morning I woke refreshed and eagerly anticipated the completion of the renovations. Woof looked miserable when I said goodbye, but seemed reassured with my promise I'd be home early, and that he'd soon be able to get out on his own. Work was a nightmare, but shortly after four I felt I could escape without feeling guilty. When I arrived home, I found Terry had already opened the back door for Woof.

'Tea's up, Terry,' I called ten minutes later. 'Thanks for letting Woof out. Is there any chance you could put in a dog flap? It's not fair to keep him cooped up inside all day.'

'No problem at all,' he replied. 'All the basic parts for the conservatory have been delivered, but I can easily source and fit a flap. No extra charge. Count it as a present to Woof for keeping me company today.'

As if he knew exactly what Terry was saying, Woof gave him a lick by way of appreciation. We both laughed as he barked his thanks.

'We'll be over early in the morning if that's all right with you,' Terry said. 'Don't worry about Woof, he'll be fine with us, and hopefully by early next week he should have his own private entrance. We did a lot of preparation work today so you'll see results soon. I'll be off now. See you tomorrow.'

'Well, Mister,' I said to the dog who had been listening attentively, 'you'll have company for the next few days but I suppose you still want your walkies?'

A resounding *Woof* of agreement met my remark and we took off before it got too late. Returning via the back of the house, I was surprised but pleased to see the hot-tub in its packaging in a corner of the shower room, but then remembered Terry had said he was expecting delivery that day. The fitted table was already in place in the kitchen and although it needed finishing off, it looked great and matched perfectly.

Although Woof had been quite happy in the shower room and kitchen, I couldn't persuade him to follow me into the cellar. Giving up the idea, we entered by the front door and he happily settled down in the living room. It was only then it occurred to me that the door at the top of the cellar stairs would have been locked, so we couldn't have gained access into the house through that route. I checked my phone, hoping for a message from Paul. Still nothing, and I tried to convince myself he was busy, or in an area with no connection. I spent time revising my final plans for the wine day and checking I hadn't missed anything, but eventually, with still no word from Paul, I locked up and went to bed.

I didn't sleep well, but it was not a nightmare disturbing me. Whatever excuses I tried to make, my subconscious knew the change in Paul was cause for concern. Perhaps work worries, or the amount we had spent on the house were causing him anxiety, but deep down I felt it was our relationship burdening him. Maybe he wasn't ready to settle down, and the pressures of buying the house had pushed him before he was ready. However much it hurt, we needed a proper discussion when he came home on his next leave, so I could find out exactly what was on his mind.

I overslept, and was still clearing up when Terry let himself in with the key I'd given him. He looked embarrassed when he found me still there.

'Sorry. Didn't mean to intrude. You're usually gone by now.'

'No problem, Terry,' I replied. 'Forgive me if I don't make you tea but I'm late already. Got to rush.' With that I dashed out and managed to catch my train just before the doors locked. When I arrived home on the Friday evening it was dark, and I was too exhausted to explore the house to see what progress had been made, but Saturday morning I woke early to make the most of my free time. Around 10.30 there was a knock at the door and I opened it to see Terry standing there. At first surprised he hadn't used his key, I realised he knew I'd be home.

'I'm not staying long,' he said as I welcomed him in. 'I thought I'd show you what's what downstairs if you've got a few minutes.'

'Sure, Coffee?'

'Maybe afterwards. Let's see what you think first.'

In the outhouses, he showed me the finished kitchen. They had even put up shelves to match the table, and everything looked perfect. Then he led me to the room next door. I stood and stared in amazement at the transformation. From a crumbling, decayed wreck it had been transformed into a luxury spa room, fit to grace the grandest hotel. In one corner the hot-tub had been installed with a wooden slatted surround. Along one wall were matching storage shelves, and lockers in the same timber. On the other side Terry opened two matching doors to display a pair of showers units, complete with rich brass taps and shower heads. There were even wooden curtain poles with brass rings attached.

'You'll want to choose your own curtains,' he said, 'but apart from that it's as good as finished. I'll show you how to work the controls, then have a final check on Monday to make sure there are no problems. There's a manual control for the extractor fan, but once the sparks finishes setting up the connections it'll come on automatically when you start the shower.

'You can use it before then if you want, but it'd be better if you left it until we've made sure everything has been double-checked. Do you want to see the conservatory now? We've only got the basics in place, but it'll give you an idea of what it'll look like finished. You can tell me where you want the power points and light switches.'

With Woof bounding along behind us, we went into the grounds to the conservatory plot at the back of the main kitchen.

'Take care where you tread,' Terry warned. 'It's still a building site out here.'

The foundations were in place, with timber packed neatly along one side, as well as bubble-wrapped packs containing glass panels, covered with a tarpaulin. I called to Woof to stop him exploring, but had to laugh when we saw he was showing particular interest in a package marked "dog flap". It was as if he knew that was to become his own personal door. Stepping carefully across the floor base, I visualised where things ought to go and where the sockets should be placed. Terry made several helpful suggestions and we didn't realise how quickly the time was passing. Having promised his wife he'd be home for lunch, he finalised a few details and took his leave.

I needed bread and a few other items from the village, so decided to combine a pub lunch with a bit of shopping. I completed my purchases while Woof sat quietly waiting outside the shops. Although it was bright and sunny, we were both pleased to escape the chill wind and reach the warmth of the pub. As soon as she saw us, Anna, the barmaid, came over to make a fuss of Woof before taking my order for beef and ale

115

pie, with onion mash and vegetables, and a glass of red wine to wash it down.

On her return she smiled and said, 'Pie for the lady, water and kitchen speciality for the young man,' as she placed a bowl of mixed left-overs, including sausages, chops and cubes of beef on the floor for Woof. With a quick bark of thanks, he devoured the lot before taking a long drink of water from the other bowl.

'Anna, I should pay for Woof's dinner,' I told her when she came to clear the plates.

'Don't be daft. It'll only go to waste. Was everything to your satisfaction, sir?' She laughed when he gave her a lick to confirm his thanks, before settling down to let his meal digest. Catching sight of us, Debbie from the library came over, and we chatted about how she'd found more details of Alderslay, and I promised to call in the following weekend to go over the information with her.

'How are the renovations going?' she asked.

'Everything's going great,' I told her. 'I was even thinking of having an open day for the neighbours in a couple of months. What do you think?'

'I'm sure they'd love it. It'd give them a chance to officially welcome you and your fiancé to the village.'

She had to get back to work, but her comment made me think of Paul again, and the thought crossed my mind whether he would be around to share the party. As if on cue, I glanced up and caught sight of the redhead, Gloria, walking past my table on the way to the ladies. She looked as if she had drunk more than a few, and staggered against my table. Righting herself she seemed to recognise me and slurred, 'Well, if it isn't little Miss Perfect with her constant companion. What a shame she has to rely on the company of a dog while her man plays away. How is the gorgeous Paul? At least he'll be back next week so we won't be so lonesome.'

'Actually, he's not due back for a couple of weeks yet,' I replied, annoyed I'd risen to her bait. I watched her leave the toilets and take the shorter route back to her companions at the bar, which made me wonder if she had only come my way to rile me. I noticed Woof's hackles had risen, in stark contrast to his normal friendly manner, especially with Anna. He moved closer as if to defend me, and his tail was down instead of gently wagging as normal.

'You're right, Woof,' I said as I bent down to stroke him. 'She's not worth it. Are you ready to go?'

As usual he seemed to understand every word and jumped up straight away. For a moment I was worried when he headed towards Gloria. The dog was so intelligent I wouldn't have put it past him to approach her and give her a piece of his mind. Instead, he ignored her and walked to the end of the bar where Anna was finishing serving a customer. She bent down to give him a pat.

'I wish all my customers were as polite as you, boy,' she smiled. 'You've come to thank me for your lunch. You're very welcome, any time.' Grinning at me, she joked, 'And you're welcome to bring Gina as well. Any friend of yours is a friend of mine.' With a glance towards Gloria at the other end of the bar she said, 'Pity all my regulars aren't as nice as you two.'

'Thanks, Anna, for a lovely meal and for looking after us so well. See you soon.'

'See you next week, maybe Saturday when Paul's home?' Anna called as she turned to serve another customer.

I realised she was the second one who had mentioned Paul being home next weekend. He'd told me he wouldn't be back until the beginning of March, over two weeks away. How odd they thought he'd be back sooner. I decided if I didn't get a message from him that night I'd phone him the following day, despite the cost. Being Sunday, he should be at his lodgings, so it wasn't as if I'd be disturbing him at work.

As if he'd read my mind, I found a message from Paul on my phone. He said he was missing me and looking forward to his week's leave and the wine party, and hoped all was going well with the renovations. He even mentioned he'd hoped to come home for a weekend before then, but work was so busy it had proved impossible. Apologising for leaving all the arrangements to me, he'd signed off with his usual kisses. I was so pleased to hear from him that for a while I forgot this was the first I'd heard of a possible extra visit, although everyone else seemed to know about it. Maybe he'd mentioned it to the workmen when he was here, but had asked them to keep it secret to surprise me.

I replied saying I was missing him too, updated him on what a wonderful job Terry and his boys were doing, and said I couldn't wait until March when he'd be able to share it all with me. Checking my other e-mails and my online bank account, I was delighted to see that of the visitors to the wine day who had confirmed attendance, twenty had already sent their entry fee. I spent the rest of the evening acknowledging their entries, and providing a brief outline of timings

118

and the format for the day. Although there were still some weeks to go, everything seemed to be running to plan, and it looked as if the event would be a success.

It had been a funny day; a mixture of good and bad. I had been pleased with the work Terry had completed, the welcome from Anna in the pub, the message from Paul and the response to the wine day. Against that were the nasty comments from Gloria, and the underlying inference that Paul had been back to the village without coming home, or even letting me know. On balance I decided Gloria was a troublemaker, and had probably told Anna a pack of lies.

Chapter 18. Dreams and practicalities.

The nightmares returned again that night. This time they didn't take place in the cellar but around the swimming pool, which in my dream had been fully restored. Although it was dark, I was swimming lengths when I heard a splash. I recognised Paul's face, but as he came closer I could see it was an old man. He was joined by a younger guy, while a woman with red hair stood on the side screaming encouragement as they tried to force my head under the water.

Fighting back, I was going down for the third time when there was a splash close by, and I was hauled to the surface of the thick, red water and dragged to the steps at the side. I managed to crawl up them and lay spluttering and coughing as I tried to regain my breath. Hearing a commotion behind me I turned, horrified to see the three people using sticks and chains to beat the wolf who had been my rescuer. He was snarling and screaming in pain but determined to keep them away from me. I tried to go to his aid, when a crowd appeared wielding pitchforks and other farming implements, and drove the terrible trio back into the darkness.

As I reached the wolf, the night sky lit up with a red glow and I could smell burning. Despite warnings from the villagers that he was a wild animal, I was sure the wolf would do me no harm. I bent to check his wounds and he licked my face as I gently tried to help him. Then I woke to find Woof next to my bed, whining softly. It was three in the morning. Gradually my heart stopped racing, and once I dozed off again, Woof went back to his own bed.

Although I had decided everything was fine between Paul and me, I spent a restless night. Perhaps, subconsciously, it had been playing on my mind. It was cold and raining as I settled down with my notebook and laptop to browse for shower curtains, towels and other bits and pieces to finish off the shower and hot-tub room. As I needed to measure the drop for the curtains I went down through the cellar to the outhouses, rather than go via the back way and be soaked. As usual Woof showed his reluctance at following me down the stairs, so I left him to go on my own.

Despite feeling nervous, it was necessary to get used to going that way, rather than go outside every time I went to the out-buildings. This time it was easier as the newly installed electricity made it less gloomy, and the decoration gave the impression of an airy basement rather than a dungeon. Feeling more confident, I moved through to the shower room, but jumped when a dark shadow appeared. It was only when I heard him bark that I realised Woof had raced outside and gone the long way round to meet me there. He seemed to have no fear of the downstairs kitchen or shower rooms; it was only the stairs to the cellar that caused him concern.

Once over the shock I found myself talking to him as I measured up.

'What do you think Woof? Should they reach to the floor, or shorter? Plain or pattern? What about the colour? Any suggestions from the male perspective?'

After half an hour I had all the measurements, and went through the dividing door to the cellar, intending to return the way I had come. I called to Woof and very hesitantly he started following. He almost turned and ran back the other way, but speaking softly I encouraged him to stay by my side. I could almost read his mind as he looked backwards and forwards. He was torn between self-preservation and staying to protect me, but I put my arm around his neck, and gently but firmly encouraged him to accompany me into the cellar. We made very slow progress, and the trauma he had suffered being locked down here when I first found him was obvious. Gradually we crossed the floor of the cellar, and eventually reached the bottom of the stairs, where he raced ahead and waited for me at the top.

'Good boy, Woof. Well done,' I said as I gave him a hug. Although he was eager for me to open the door and get back into the house, at least we'd made progress. Having to encourage him had given me confidence to go down alone after the horrific discoveries of the previous few weeks. Finally, the house was truly becoming mine, and the terrible history of the past might not be forgotten, but could be disregarded.

Woof settled happily at my feet as I browsed the Internet for the perfect accessories for the shower room, and eventually found some that would be suitable, although they were not exactly what I wanted. Tempted to place the online order straight away, I remembered there was a shop in the village selling bathroom supplies. I could go there the following Saturday and see what they had, and even if it wasn't what I wanted, I'd still be able to order online and have time for the items to be delivered.

That night I slept soundly, and woke early to face the usual working week. A quick look at my phone showed no messages from Paul, which in a strange way was a relief. Whatever the problems between us, I wanted to speak to him face to face to find out his feelings, and not rely on ambiguous messages which might be misinterpreted. Most evenings when I reached home Terry was still working, although he normally left shortly afterwards. On the Friday I was able to leave work early, and found him waiting to see me. It was difficult to tell who was more excited, him or me, as he showed me the results of the week's labours. Both of the outhouses had been completed, the hot-tub and showers had been tested and were working perfectly, and I was determined to try them out the following day.

The conservatory had been finished and the raffia furniture set delivered and installed. Even though it was cold out, the underfloor heating made it a perfectly warm and cosy room. While I was examining everything, Woof took himself off outside. Terry had installed the dog-flap and even showed the dog how to use it, so it seemed second nature to go out that way when he needed to. There was a lock for overnight, but during the day I could leave it open without compromising security. When Terry gave me his final bill I was ready to pay him straight away, but once he had seen I was satisfied with his work he insisted there was no rush. He wanted to make sure everything was satisfactory before I paid him.

Ecstatic with the way the renovations had been done, I determined to give him a good bonus by way of thanks. Who would have thought it possible the derelict, ramshackle ruin I had fallen in love with all those months ago, had been transformed into the wonderful mansion now greeting me at every turn? The only thing spoiling my pleasure was whether Paul would be with me to enjoy the transformation. Although I had no hard evidence, I could picture myself living there with only Woof for company. Even telling myself not to be silly, I knew it was more than just my over active imagination running riot.

My plans for the wine day were more reliant on Geoff being available to help out, than Paul being present. As it was the end of February, there was only a week to wait until Paul came home, and I'd know for sure how things stood between us.

The forecast was for icy winds with rain later, so Woof and I set off early to the village. The shop I was looking for was close to the pub, and as we approached I heard Anna call out a cheerful good morning. Woof bounded up to her, knowing she'd make a fuss of him.

'And how's my favourite young man today?' she asked, bending to stroke him. 'You're out and about early, Gina. Shopping?'

'Looking for shower curtains. Sorry, Woof, your muddy paws won't be welcome with all that clean linen around,' I said, tying him up outside the shop. He was most displeased, and Anna suggested she take him to the pub while I browsed in peace.

'He won't be any trouble,' she assured me, 'and I'll be glad of the company. You can do your shopping and pick him up when you've finished. We'll be all right together, Woof, won't we?'

Woof barked in agreement and the matter was settled. He gave me a nod goodbye, then trotted off happily with Anna. Knowing he was in good hands, I took my time browsing the shop, amazed at the range of stock. I not only bought the perfect shower curtains, but ordered drapes for the living room windows, blinds for the conservatory and a range of towels and bedding. Jackie, the owner who served me, promised to have them delivered later that afternoon, and for the fitter to come on Saturday morning to install the blinds and curtains.

Taking advantage of Anna's hospitality, I called into a couple of others shops to make the most of my freedom, but as I headed back to the pub the rain started, and I barely managed to get in the door without being totally soaked. Woof was comfortably ensconced at the end of the bar, with a big bowl of kitchen specials and some water in front of him. When he saw me, he came over to say hello, then resumed his meal as I went to talk to Anna.

'I hope he hasn't been any trouble,' I said as I approached her.

'He's been as good as gold, haven't you boy,' she replied ruffling his fur. 'Not only that but we had a couple of troublemakers in a while ago. He followed me when I went to tell them to leave, and after taking one look at him they decided to skedaddle. I've never heard him growl like that before, so I'm glad he's my friend. He makes an excellent guard dog. Then a lady came in with her two toddlers. They were poking and pulling him about, but he didn't bat an eyelid. You wouldn't believe it was the same dog; he was such a big softie and let them get on with it. If we were allowed to have pets permanently I'd kidnap him,' she smiled, 'but the odd night, or even a week won't be a problem if you need a doggie-sitter. Now, what can I get you? The chicken in lemon sauce is particularly good today.'

'That sounds fine,' I said, 'and a large glass of white wine to wash it down. Will you have one, Anna, as a thank you for looking after my best boy?'

'Another time perhaps. Talking of best boys, what time's Paul due home today?'

'He's not back until next week. Which reminds me, you're the second person who thought it was today. What made you think that?'

Anna blushed scarlet, then mumbled something about getting mixed up, before excusing herself to serve another customer at the other end of the bar. Feeling uneasy I found a table, and Woof followed to sit at my feet, having finished his gourmet meal.

Betty came in, and waved hello. She stopped at the bar to talk to Anna, and both glanced in my direction before she came over to join me. Maybe my imagination was running riot, and she was merely placing her lunch order before telling Anna where she'd be sitting.

'May I join you?' Betty asked as she sat down at the table with me. 'It's nice to see you again. How are you? How's the house coming on?'

'It's nearly finished,' I replied. 'There's only the swimming pool area to do later in the spring, but everything else is ready. I've been buying curtains and blinds which they're fitting this weekend, so by the time Paul gets back he'll see the full effect.'

'Trust a man to keep out of the way until all the hard work's done,' she laughed. 'So how long is it since you've seen him?'

'It's been over four weeks but he should be back next weekend, then he's got a week's leave so he'll be here for the wine tasting day. After that he should be relocating to London so he'll be around a lot more.'

'So, he hasn't been back since the end of January?' Betty asked. It seemed a strange thing to say so I just nodded. She was quiet for a moment then asked softly, 'Do you feel you belong here, Gina, with or without Paul?'

There was concern and apprehension on her face but I knew she was asking with the best of intentions.

'Yes. Obviously, I'd prefer to have Paul with me to share the house together, but if, for some reason, that wasn't possible, then yes, I'd stay on. This is my home now.'

'I'm happy to hear you say that, my dear. Sometimes things don't turn out as we expect, but in the long run it's usually for the best. Well, I'd better be off now, but don't forget if you ever want a chat you know where to find me. A small village is always full of gossip but sometimes there's no smoke without fire. Be happy.'

With those cryptic remarks she was gone. A moment later Anna brought my meal, as if she had been waiting for Betty to finish her conversation.

'Didn't Betty want something to eat?' I asked, seeing her carrying only one plate.

'No,' Anna replied, 'she often pops in to say hello. I think she has an appointment with the hairdressers this afternoon so she's already had her lunch.'

I ate my meal alone, my mind buzzing with all the innuendos flying around, although nothing tangible had actually been said. Looking up, I saw Gloria, sober this time, heading towards the empty table next to mine. When she noticed me, she turned away to look elsewhere, but taking my courage in both hands, I called out to her.

Reluctantly she accepted my invitation to join me at my table. With a sweet smile on my face, and without mentioning Paul, I introduced myself merely as Gina, and said that, as the newcomer to the village I was eager to get to know everyone. For a while we chatted generally about the house and the renovations until she seemed to relax, and even admitted that she was distantly related to the original Lord of the Manor. It seemed a safe subject to get her to open up, and I told her of my interest in discovering more about the origins of the house.

After her initial distrust she warmed to the subject, and provided me with a lot of information about the history of the building, and stories related to her by her grandfather. Apparently his father had been the one to suggest they produce wine from the vines in the grounds, and he had quite a reputation in his time as an expert vintner. I told her about the open day we were arranging, and without thinking she mentioned Paul had told her he'd be back this weekend. Blushing scarlet, she realised she'd put her foot in it, but I carried on chatting as if I hadn't noticed.

I even lied and said, 'He told me when he saw you last week, you mentioned your family had been involved in growing grapes.'

Without realising she'd been tricked, she volunteered she'd bumped into him in the pub on Saturday and they'd started talking. My worst fears had been confirmed but I made no comment.

'Did I say last week?' she babbled. 'It might have been the week before, or even a few weeks ago. It's so easy to get mixed up.'

It was too late. To change the subject, I asked if she'd ever related her grandfather's stories to her own children.

'Oh, I don't have any,' she said, 'and I'm unlikely to, since my divorce five years ago.'

Soon after, she made an excuse to leave and even though my heart was breaking I smiled.

'I look forward to seeing you again before too long.'

It didn't confirm Paul had been unfaithful, but if it was innocent why hadn't he told me about meeting up with her? Why had he been in the village last week without coming home? How had other people seen him when I hadn't? Although I loved Paul, the house and the village, I was starting to feel like an intruder in my own environment, with secrets kept from me at every turn. With a heavy heart and my mind buzzing, I paid my bill, gave a distant wave goodbye to Anna, called to Woof and set off for home.

By the time I opened the front door after a bracing walk my mind had cleared, and I felt strong enough to face whatever the future might hold. Even so my feelings were mixed; part anger, part resignation and part curiosity. Although it was only early afternoon, I wanted to take to my bed to wallow in self-pity and see if the morning offered any explanations.

A knock at the door brought me out of my reverie, and I opened it to find a smiling young man who announced he was there to fit my blinds. Seeing my reticence, he said he could call back next Saturday if it was not convenient. Pulling myself together I told him I hadn't expected such quick service, but was happy for him to go ahead. I went to make him tea while he set to work, and an hour or so later everything was in place. Seeing the finished blinds and curtains looking so delightful helped to lift my mood.

Later I was relaxing, catching up with friends, when a message popped up from Paul: 'How are things? Not sure I'll get back Friday night as arranged. Work stuff. You know how it is. I need to finish things before the move to the London office, although that might have to be delayed for a few weeks unless I can sort out a few problems. I'll let you know.'

Would he even be there for the wine fest? At first I felt angry and upset, then realised I could manage quite well without him. Before sending a reply, I checked that Geoff was still available, advising him Paul might not make the day, and apologising for contacting him at the weekend.

Within a few minutes he replied, 'Looking forward to it, and don't worry, we'll cope. If it suits you, I could come Friday evening and stay in a local hotel, so I'll be on hand first thing Saturday morning to make sure there are no last-minute hitches.'

I replied, 'That's perfect, and as I have plenty of spare room, you should stay here at the house. Thanks again for your help. I'll confirm details later in the week.'

In the mood to ensure everything would be organised for the Saturday, I contacted the caterer, receiving a positive response, and sent messages to the thirty attendees, giving them final directions and times. Surprisingly some replied immediately, and running through my check list, I felt confident there was nothing more to be done but cross my fingers and hope for the best.

I eventually replied to Paul, 'What a shame, but everything's in hand. Let me know closer to the day if you're coming or not.' Reading the message after I'd pressed SEND, it struck me how curt it sounded, but it was too late. I hadn't even asked when he'd be "coming home," just when he'd be coming, as if he was one of the invited guests.

That night the dreams returned. I was in the cellar, surrounded by friends enjoying themselves, when a man in a red mask, dripping with blood and brandishing a bottle, appeared. He tried to attack me, but was overpowered by the others who ripped off his mask. It was Paul! I woke up sweating, but with an icy chill running down my back. Perhaps it was the insinuations of the day, finishing with Paul's email, but it was horrible to think this man I had once loved could be threatening me, even if in a dream. Before I drifted off to sleep I realised my thought had been "once loved" instead of "loved." Did I still love him? Only time, and seeing him again, would tell.

On Sunday I didn't bother rushing until I found Woof tugging at my duvet. Throwing on a dressing gown, I went down to open the back door and he rushed off, coming back five minutes later looking relieved, and hinting it was time for breakfast. Rather than going back to bed, I slobbed around, preparing a fry-up. With nothing special to do, I was looking forward to a lazy day. Famous last words.

Chapter 19. Getting organised.

I hadn't yet tried the hot tub but now seemed a suitable opportunity. Grabbing a towel, I made my way down to what I had christened the Spa room, and investigated the controls. It was fairly simple to operate and fifteen minutes later I was wallowing in luxurious hot bubbles with Woof looking as if he'd love to join me. Half an hour later, I felt relaxed and refreshed, and decided to get dressed and go for a walk.

The fabulous new blinds and curtains made me proud of my beautiful home. The basement kitchen was exactly right to welcome my guests for the wine tasting. I ventured into the cellar and Woof even followed me, although he still seemed on edge. Although a far cry from the dingy, threatening building where I'd first found him, he needed time to get over his horrible memories of being trapped in there. Was it really only a few months ago? So much had happened in such a short space of time; I'd discovered a derelict building, fallen in love with it, and possibly out of love with the man in my life. I'd made new friends and possibly a few enemies. With the house of my dreams and the perfect loyal companion by my side, I had the excitement of the new venture to look forward to, and all my life before me. Soon it would be spring and time to sort out the swimming pool for the summer.

It stuck me although the house was now truly our home, "our" referred to Woof, and not my so-called fiancé. As if he could sense my mood, at that moment another message arrived.

'You okay? You didn't sound your usual self.'

I was tempted to reply, 'What do you think? Tell me the truth about your clandestine visits to the village.' Instead I took a deep breath and sent 'I'm fine, everything has been arranged for the wine day, and don't worry if you can't make it. We'll talk properly next time you visit.'

Even to my ears it sounded harsh, and my finger hovered for a moment before I pressed SEND. Let him worry for a change. I needed to get on with life, with or without him. My thoughts alternated between feeling my heart was broken and being determined to prove I didn't need him. For a while I pondered the practicalities of our split, which already seemed a forgone conclusion. Perhaps I had been looking at our relationship through rose-coloured glasses, but if he wanted out why hadn't he said something? Was the redhead his new love, or a convenient excuse?

Determined not to think about him I focused on practical matters. The most important problem was the monetary aspect. Even though the house was in my name, some of the purchase costs had been paid by Paul, so he had a right to his share. If he turned awkward, he could insist on selling the house to repay him. I realised losing my home concerned me more than losing him, and I started investigating mortgage companies, to see what sort of funds might be available if I could buy him out. Even if I was over reacting it wouldn't hurt to have options available.

That night, Woof didn't return after a few minutes as he usually did before I locked up. Worried, I grabbed a torch and set out into the grounds to look for him, and found him near the swimming pool with his hackles raised. He glanced up when he saw me, but continued to peer into the darkness near the back door to the cellar rooms, growling softly. I touched his neck, more for my comfort than for his.

'What's wrong, boy? What is it?' I jumped as a black shape darted across our path and ran off into the distance. 'You daft lump. It's only a cat, or maybe a fox,' I told him, laughing at my own nervousness. Taking hold of Woof's collar, I persuaded him towards the front of the house. He came reluctantly, continuously glancing back even though the animal, whatever it was, had long gone. I double and triple checked all the doors and windows were locked before settling down to watch a film on television. Woof still seemed restless, and I pondered if it was more than the night creature disturbing him.

I realised that although he'd glanced at the animal as it ran past, he'd immediately returned his gaze towards the door before I'd dragged him away. I checked the cellar was safely locked but then, disconcerted, found the padlock and added that for good measure. Woof followed me on my rounds, and seemed to agree with my decision to take extra precautions. When I returned to the living room he settled down more like his usual self, snoozing at my feet.

Surprisingly I slept well, and woke with the alarm to find the winter sun trying hard to break through the clouds. Reassuring Woof I'd be back by the evening, I set off for the station to catch the earlier train. Settling in my seat, it struck me there'd be no workmen around to keep him company and he'd be on his own until I returned from work. My thoughts kept returning to him during the day, even though the office was hectic and kept me occupied. As I had been in so early, I didn't feel guilty about catching the earlier train home, and by five thirty was back at the house. Woof had obviously been out through the dog flap in the conservatory, as he came bounding up to greet me as soon as I drove through the gate. I was as pleased to see him as he was to see me, so after dumping my work bag we set off for a final walk before it got too dark.

That set the pattern for the following days, and Thursday arrived almost before I knew it. During the week there had been various phone calls and e-mails from mortgage companies, confirming that unless he was unreasonable about his share, buying Paul out was well within my means. I had also received several e-mails and phone calls from Geoff, the caterer, and several more people who wanted to attend the open day. Paul messaged to say that unfortunately he wouldn't be able to get back on Friday as we had arranged, and hinted that perhaps I should cancel the wine day. I replied with another curt response saying not to worry, everything was organised and I was going ahead, ending up by telling him Geoff was helping out, and Woof and I were well. As if he was a stranger or business partner, I promised to let him know how things went, and suggested we could discuss the future properly whenever he was able to get some leave.

At work on Friday morning, I received a message from Paul wishing me well for the following day. 'I'm hoping to come to the house next Friday evening. Is it OK with you if I stay the weekend?'

I noticed he didn't say "home" and appeared to be asking permission. It hurt that his feelings had changed so much, and resentment raged as I sent a quick reply saying that would be fine and left it at that. As usual on a Friday there was a last-minute panic at work, and I barely managed to catch the early train home. As Geoff was due to arrive at approximately the same time as me, I had confirmed I'd meet him at the station shortly after five, and drive him back to the house for the night. He was waiting as my train pulled in, and surprised me by wrapping me in a bear hug. We chatted like old friends as we made our way to the car, and his enthusiasm was infectious as he told me what high hopes he had for the sale.

'It's going to be a resounding success,' he said, 'and with a bit of luck very profitable by the end of the day.'

Very diplomatically he avoided mentioning Paul. It was as if he knew something was wrong and this project was now dependent on just the two of us.

'By the way, I forgot to mention earlier,' Geoff said, 'I've roped in my friend Steve to give us a hand. I hope you don't mind. He'll be joining us tomorrow morning to offer advice, and help with the sale. The numbers have grown so much I realised it'd be beneficial to have another expert on hand. You'll be busy playing hostess, and a second specialist will definitely increase the possibility of more sales.'

I was a bit worried about the cost implications of paying for another professional, but before I had a chance to broach the subject Geoff himself brought it up. It was as if he could read my mind, even though we'd only met once before.

'Steve's a local whose family I've known for years. Although he's a good deal younger than me I have the greatest respect for his knowledge, both as a wine expert and as an historian. Through his family Steve has expertise not only of the trade, but also of the history of the house and its original vineyards. His local know-how will add to the romance of the origins of the produce and help increase the sales, although the quality of the vintages themselves should be sufficient.'

By the time we reached home I felt as if I had known Geoff all my life, and had no misgivings about his involvement, or having him sleep under my roof when my partner was away. As I opened the door my instincts were confirmed. After greeting me with his usual enthusiasm, Woof showed a similar response to my visitor and welcomed him like a long-lost friend. They say animals have a natural intuition, and if that was true then Geoff was someone I could trust completely. It was a pleasant evening with the three of us together, and after we had finished eating, I showed him the spare room where he was to sleep.

'That's fine my dear. Thank you. Steve should be here around ten to check on final details, and acquaint himself with the surroundings.'

I woke from another nightmare, although I couldn't remember any specifics. My subconscious seemed to tell me I was safe with a protector keeping me from harm. The next morning I drifted for a while in a state of half awareness. Perhaps having someone else in the house made me feel more secure? Somehow, I knew it was more than that. Although I was unsure of my future with Paul, I was surrounded by people who had my interests at heart, and was confident everything would turn out for the best.

The following morning, I prepared a proper English breakfast and with perfect timing Geoff appeared as I set out the plates. After a hearty meal to set us up for the day ahead, I left him clearing up while I took Woof out. When I returned, I found the kitchen spotless but no sign of Geoff, and discovered him already hard at work, setting out the bottles and checking the stock. He seemed to have everything well under control, so I left him to it. Half an hour later there was a knock at the door, and I opened it to see the most gorgeous man standing in front of me. For a moment I gaped at him until, with a devastating smile, he said, 'Hi. You must be Gina. I'm Steve, come to give Geoff a hand with your open day. Pleased to meet you.'

Chapter 20. Wine and new opportunities.

I managed to recover enough to offer him a coffee.

'That'd be great, but if you don't mind I'll check in with Geoff first,' he smiled. I opened the door to the cellar and heard Geoff call hello as he went down to greet him. Woof had welcomed Steve in a friendly manner, but stayed with me. About ten minutes later the door bell sounded, and this time it was the caterer. I gave her a hand unloading her car with the supplies for the refreshments.

By eleven everything was well organised; the food was set out, the glasses sparkling and ready for the tasters, and the bottles suitably labelled and beautifully displayed. There was even a board set up listing the particulars of the superior vintages, and giving details of the reserve prices for the sale which was scheduled for two thirty. Chairs with numbered boards on each seat had been arranged inside the cellar, ready for the auction. By then everyone was ready for a break, so we all went back up to the kitchen for a coffee, and Geoff explained his plans for how the afternoon would run.

'The guests are due from twelve thirty onwards, and I suggest Steve and I take them round the cellar to give them a chance to examine the stock and ask questions. The more ordinary bottles have been labelled with prices, and can be sold immediately to anyone willing to pay the suggested price; first come, first served. I've put out a small table and chair in the downstairs kitchen, and recommend that, as the hostess, you, Gina, should be responsible for taking the money, and marking off the sales on the list I've left there. Penny will be by the food table to serve refreshments and give you moral support.

'Shortly before two, the guests can be directed back into the cellar where Steve and I will give a brief outline of the history of the wines, and the rules of the auction. You might like to give a short welcoming speech, Gina, and then we can start the actual sale, with Steve acting as auctioneer. I'll keep a note of the buyers and sale prices, but it might be as well if you also kept a record so there can be no ambiguity.'

'How long do you thing the auction will last?' I asked, half scared witless, and half excited.

'It should be finalised within about half an hour, then if we serve more refreshments while they chat it's likely to be over by sometime after three.'

We were in total agreement with his plans, and I felt reassured at the way he was running things. It had been like a company board meeting, but at the same time I didn't feel as if Geoff was taking over. He seemed to have been at pains to ensure everyone was appreciated for their particular talents. Steve had made one or two quiet comments, and I noticed Penny had greeted his every word with enthusiasm. Looking between the two of them I could understand why. Steve was not only gorgeous with his dark, floppy hair and tanned colouring, but seemed a pleasant, intelligent man and as far as I knew Penny was young, free and single.

Geoff was checking last minute notes, but catching my eye he glanced at the two of them, then gave me a wink. It was as if he knew what was going on, but I couldn't help wondering if he thought the sparks were between Steve and me, and Penny was chasing rainbows. Perhaps I was letting my imagination run riot; after all I was still technically engaged to Paul. Thinking about him made me realise that apart from his message saying he was unlikely to be able to make the open day, I still didn't know for certain when I'd be seeing him again. Time was getting on, and Geoff suggested we go downstairs to be prepared, in case of early arrivals. We took up our various positions and, dead on cue, shortly after twelve thirty the first guests arrived. At first I was nervous, but with the support of my companions soon fell into the swing of acting as lady of the manor, and making them welcome. After the first trickle the other guests arrived in floods, and we were soon engrossed in coping with them. It was a good atmosphere and everything seemed to be going to plan, with the visitors appearing enthusiastic about the goods on offer.

Almost before I knew it, Geoff was calling for attention and asking people to make their way into the cellar for the final auction. Glancing down at my notebook and the overflowing cash box in front of me, I was astounded to realise how much money we had already taken on the sale of the mundane wines, even before the auction had begun. There was more than enough to pay off the caterer and my helpers, and still leave a healthy profit on the day. I locked the box away, and after checking Woof was okay made my way into the cellar to be greeted by a round of applause. Somewhat taken aback at the enthusiastic greeting, I was dumbfounded for a moment as Geoff led me to the makeshift podium.

'Ladies and gentlemen, it is my pleasure to introduce Gina, our hostess. On behalf of the guests,

I'd like to extend our thanks for the excellent hospitality.'

Once the applause died down, I took a deep breath before beginning my speech.

'What a wonderful introduction. I'd like to thank you all for coming, and especial thanks to those of you who have already purchased some of our wines. I really hope you'll enjoy them. I'm now going to hand you back to Geoff to take over the proceedings for the auction, and wish you every success in your bids for the more expensive vintages.'

As I sat down, I was genuinely amazed at the cheers and applause that greeted my impromptu words. It seemed everyone was satisfied so far. Pleased, and relieved that my part was over, I was able to relax as Geoff took control. He introduced Steve as the auctioneer, giving me the opportunity to observe him without being too obvious as he described the first lot. Although it started slowly Steve had a natural charm, and with his encouragement the first bottle sold for £120. Remembering I was supposed to be making notes on the sales, I jotted down the details of the paddle number and price. The second lot took off much more quickly, and after a short battle between three bidders was sold for £245. Again I made a note, and after that the action became fast and furious. I realised that Geoff had organised the less popular wines first, to get the ball rolling.

The sixth sale was a batch of three bottles sold as a set, and I listened in amazement as the starting price of £300 rose rapidly until it finally sold for over £1,000. The tenth and final lot of two bottles of the same type, but with three years between their vintages started at £1200, and seemed to be the ones for which everyone had been waiting. I could hardly keep up as the bidders tried to outdo each other, until eventually they sold for over £4,000.

My hand was shaking as I wrote down the details of the winning bid. To a round of applause, I realised Geoff was winding up the proceedings and thanking everyone for coming. He led the winning purchasers over to my table while the others were encouraged to partake of the refreshments. As we confirmed details and prices it struck me how totally lost I'd have been without his and Steve's help. I hadn't given a thought to how to collect the money, but Geoff produced a small, hand-held credit card machine. While he processed the payments, Steve boxed up the bottles in cases he had brought, and helped load them into the various cars. Meanwhile Penny was kept on her toes and I went over to help her. Within the hour all the visitors had drifted away, many leaving me their business cards and asking to be kept informed about the next sale.

Penny packed up her belongings which Steve helped her carry out. I saw her talking to him animatedly and was surprised to feel a twinge of jealousy, as she was obviously attracted to him. She came back to collect her earnings and was happy with the extra tip I gave her. That left Steve, Geoff and me. When everything was cleared up downstairs, I sat with them in the living room to have a coffee and discuss how the day had gone. Both thought it had been excellent, and Geoff confirmed my figures that the day had brought in a fraction short of £13,000.

Embarrassed, I asked, 'We never did agree on a figure for your services, so how much is your cut for making it such a success?'

I should have been more formal in agreeing payment beforehand, but unless they were totally unreasonable I'd still make a good profit.

'Well, my dear. If you're agreeable, I'd like to take up your offer of a bottle of wine,' Geoff suggested.

'That's fine with me too,' Steve agreed, as I looked towards him.

'But what about cash?' I asked, wanting to clarify exactly what they meant.

'I'm sorry,' Geoff said, 'I was going to ask how you wanted paying. I can write you a cheque now, or arrange a direct transfer into your bank, whichever you prefer.'

'No, I meant what about the cash to pay you for your time and expertise. I really couldn't have done it without you.'

'The wine will be more than enough,' Geoff smiled. 'You do realise that at a professional auction the ones we have our eye on could be worth anything up to £500 on a good day. We did have some expenses, but we wouldn't like you to feel you've been cheated, so I want to make it clear exactly what they're worth.'

'You've been more than fair with me,' I replied. 'It hadn't occurred to me how they'd get their purchases home, and I hadn't the faintest idea of the prices for each lot. If you're satisfied, then I am more than happy for you to take your pick from the cellar.'

'That's sorted then,' Geoff replied. 'Steve, you collect them while I pay our lovely hostess the rest of the takings.'

'Sure,' Steve said and I gave him the key to the cellar. Meanwhile Geoff took out his cheque book and after asking me to confirm the figure from my own records, handed me a cheque for the monies he had collected via credit cards. When Steve came back up clutching the two bottles, I was still staring at the cash and cheque in amazement.

'You do realise you haven't even made a dent in the total stock down there,' Steve said. 'You don't want to flood the market, but if you held a similar day every six months or so, you could make at least as much as you made today, and still have enough to last for several years. As your reputation grows so the prices will rise. Anyway, we don't want to push you into anything, but if you do decide to hold another open day, I'll be more than happy to help out. I'm sure Geoff will be too. Isn't that right Geoff?'

'Definitely,' Geoff replied. 'I agree with Steve. An auction twice a year would be perfect timing. You still have some wonderful vintages down there. You should seriously think of resurrecting the vineyard and start growing again. It's been a long but successful day, so if I can prevail upon Steve to give me a lift to the station, my train's due in half an hour. Thank you, my dear for the wine. My intention is to store it as a future investment, but I have a very strong feeling I will be unable to resist sampling it. My golden wedding anniversary is in a few weeks, and it'll make a perfect toast for my wife and I to celebrate our happy years together.'

With that he gave me a hug and a fatherly kiss goodbye. Steve came to shake my hand but then also gave me a hug, and a kiss on the cheek. As they left he slipped his business card into my hand, and I noticed he had written his personal mobile number on the back.

When they had gone the house suddenly felt empty after all the excitement of the day. Woof gave me a lick and I realised I had been neglecting him. Throwing on my coat and walking shoes I picked up his lead, and he bounded after me as we headed for the fields.

Chapter 21. Beware the Ides of March.

Although it was only early March, the evenings were becoming lighter and the first signs of Spring were appearing. Wild daffodils and crocus pushed their way through the undergrowth, waiting to greet the sun. After his day without company, Woof made the most of it, examining every scent, sniffing and chasing around in the woods. The fresh air felt so good, I stayed out much longer than I intended, until the deepening gloom made it difficult to see him and we headed home.

Deciding the day deserved a glass of a good red to go with my mixed grill, I ventured down to the cellar to select one. Rather than deplete the best stock, I made for the cheaper ones which I had labelled but not sold. Surprisingly, Woof accompanied me and ambled around as if he had lost some of his fear.

'What do you think, Woof?' I asked, dithering between the bottles.

He poked his nose at one as if to say *"This one is good."* A wise choice; it was delicious with a delicate aroma. When we had finished eating I settled down to go through the events of the day, still not quite believing the amount on the cheque Geoff had given me. For a moment I wondered whether it would actually be honoured; after all I had only met him once before. He and Steve could be conmen on to a good thing, taking advantage of a naïve woman on her own. They could easily have taken the money collected from the sale and left me with a dud cheque.

I had no way of contacting them apart from mobile telephone numbers which could be blocked or changed. Although Paul had professed to know Geoff, with the situation as it was between us he could quite well be in on it. I had heard nothing from Paul for a few days, but if the cheque did clear at the bank, by rights he was entitled to a half share. Although the house was in my sole name the original purchase had been a joint project, so he'd morally be entitled to a proportion of any profits from the wine. As if he had read my mind a message popped up on my phone.

'Hello. Hope everything went well, and you weren't too disappointed. Are you still free this weekend if I paid a visit? There are a few things we need to talk over. Let me know if that's OK. Paul. X'

It wasn't the sort of message you'd expect from a fiancé, forced by necessity to spend time apart from his loved one. I debated whether to tell him exactly how much the auction had made, and if I should let him know it was feasible it would become a regular occurrence. After giving it some thought, I decided that was the type of information we should discuss face to face.

'Hi. Everything went very well. Geoff and his assistant were invaluable. Really professional and helpful. Let me know when you'll be arriving. If the timing's right I could pick you up from the station.' Hovering over how to finish, I ended up putting my name without any endearments.

I sent off replies to friends and family who had asked how things had gone, saying how amazing the day had been and briefly mentioning Steve and Geoff, only to receive an immediate response from one of my more astute friends.

'Hey! Tell all. You told me Geoff was getting on a bit, but who's this mysterious Steve? I want to know all the juicy details, so don't try to fob me off, I know you too well.'

As if he knew he was being discussed a message arrived from Steve.

'Hi Gina. Thanks for the very generous donation of the bottle of wine. It was great meeting you and I hope you were satisfied with the way the day went. This is my e-mail address in case you ever need it. It would be terrific if you kept in contact, either by e-mail or by phone on the number I left with you. Cheers. Steve.'

I couldn't help comparing his friendly message with the impersonal communication Paul had sent. Before I could think too deeply, I sent off a quick reply reiterating my thanks for all his help, and saying I looked forward to seeing him again as soon as time and circumstances allowed. My mind was in a quandary. I needed to see Paul and find out whether we had a future together. If not, I wanted to settle things, both financially and emotionally, so we could get on with our lives, together or apart, whatever the future held.

Geoff's suggestion for revitalising the vineyard was worth considering, so I spent some time online looking up basic information. Running a vineyard was not something I could do on my own, which brought my thoughts back to Steve. Everything was in limbo until I was able to see Paul, so I contented myself with sending thank you messages to the visitors who had attended, and especially the ones who had made purchases.

Needing to unwind after all the excitement of the day, I decided to have an early night. At first I slept well, but in the early hours of the morning woke from another nightmare. It revolved around the cellar where I had descended to find a maniac smashing bottles. In my dream I realised the man was Paul, although he was dressed in clothes from a hundred years ago. He was screaming like a madman 'Mine, all mine,' and as I approached, my gaze was caught by the sight of several girls chained to the wall. Their old-fashioned garments torn and dirty, most of them looked starving and close to death, as if they had been kept prisoner for many weeks.

Suddenly the man noticed me. His eyes burned black and cold, and a look of pure evil crossed his face as he approached me, wielding the machete. I wanted to run but my legs felt stuck in quicksand, and I watched in horror as he came closer and closer. My mouth opened to scream but nothing came out. As I trembled, thinking I had breathed my last, something rushed past me, and the sight of a wolf grappling with the man pulled me out of my stupor. I ran forward and pushed a plank of wood between the animal and the machete, before it sliced him in two. The timber shattered with the force of the blow. The wolf was already wounded and bleeding from previous attacks, but at least my intervention had stopped him from being killed. He continued to fight as I looked round for something else to stop the maniac.

I woke up, sweating and shaking. Rising from the bed to fetch a glass of water, I nearly fell over Woof, who was standing watching me. He flinched as I hugged him, and I noticed my arm was smeared with blood. How could that be? It was only a dream, so it was impossible my real live dog had been injured. Examining him gently I could find no trace of the source, the only visible scars the now-healed wounds from when I'd rescued him from the cellar all those months ago. Although he normally slept downstairs, I didn't try to move him away when he settled down next to my bed.

Knowing he was nearby helped me relax, and after a while I drifted back to sleep, not waking until gone eleven. I threw on my dressing gown, and found Woof by the locked back door, waiting for me to let him out. When he came back looking relieved, I examined him thoroughly to find the cause of the blood, but he showed no sign of any injuries and only moved away to remind me he was hungry.

The TV morning news was the usual stories of wars, politics and the state of the economy, interspersed with showbiz gossip. Flipping through the channels, I came across the same local programme I had found before. It caught my attention when I heard the word Alderslay, the ancient name of the house. It was creepy how they were broadcasting events almost as soon as they happened.

'*In more local news, a wine sale was held at the property known as Alderslay yesterday,*' the presenter announced. '*Following the completion of renovations, a successful auction of some of the original bottles from the estate proved very popular. Although there are no details of the exact sums involved, it has been rumoured there is a possibility the new owners might restart the production of the quality grapes for which the vineyard was once famous. No announcement has been made of the actual plans, but the idea has already received strong support in the village.*'

Signing off with 'Stay tuned to Village Gossip to hear the latest local news before your neighbours,' it cut to the adverts. I listened for a while to the commercials for businesses in the area then switched off. How had they managed to find their information so promptly? Then I realised in any small village word always spreads quickly, and it had been common knowledge for some weeks that I had intended to hold an auction. The date had been known, and the programme hadn't given any specific details, so the item could easily have been prepared in advance.

Even so, I felt apprehensive about venturing into the village so soon after it had taken place. Woof poked me to remind me of his presence and giving in to the inevitable, we set off together. A light breeze helped to blow away the last remnants of my horrible dream, and I felt full of the joys of Spring. My instincts from when I had first decided to buy the house were the right ones. Despite all the trials and tribulations of the renovations I counted myself lucky I had found such good workmen and not been ripped off by cowboy builders.

My home was wonderful. I had found Woof as the perfect companion and made friends in the village. As for the problem with Paul, well, *que sera, sera*. Within a few days we'd be able to sort things out once and for all. Then I could move on with my life. As that thought crossed my mind, I stopped dead. Why was I so certain we were no longer a couple? He had not actually said or done anything to make me think we no longer had a future together. He had been caught up with work, unable to get home for the weekend we had arranged. That had happened several times in the past, and although I had been disappointed, I had known he was working for our future. It had meant the next time we saw each other was even more special. Tired of my thoughts going in circles, I broke into a stress-breaking run. With Woof chasing and jumping excitedly around me we ended up in the village, both panting from our exertions.

'I'm thirsty after all that exercise, Woof. What about you?' I asked once I had my breath back. 'Shall we stop at the pub for lunch?'

An enthusiastic tail wagging showed he was in complete agreement. He raced ahead, eager to see his friend Anna, but stopped and changed course for the back entrance through the pub garden. Surprised by his change of direction I followed until he stopped by the gazebo close to the back door. It had been set up as a place for smokers, mainly enclosed against the elements, with heaters, comfortable benches and dimmed lighting. As I went to move on, I saw two people inside who appeared oblivious to the outside world. Not seeing any lights from cigarettes, I smiled at the realisation it was the perfect place for a lovers' tryst.

At that moment the man looked up and I found myself staring into the face of my fiancé. The woman adjusted her clothing and as she turned, I recognised Gloria smirking at me. Paul appeared as shocked as me. He pushed Gloria's arm away as she clung onto him, said something to her then came out to meet me.

'It's not what you think,' he blustered. 'Don't get upset. I can explain everything.'

I looked straight into his face as I replied in a quiet voice, 'I'm not upset, Paul. She's welcome to you but we do need to talk. There are things to sort out.'

He looked surprised at my lack of emotion then asked, 'Can you give me an hour? I could come up to the house. There's not much privacy here.'

'Make it an hour and a half. We're going for lunch first and I don't want to have to rush back.'

With that I turned and walked into the pub. After a slight hesitation, Woof followed. I could feel Paul's eyes on me but refused to turn around. My voice sounded cold but my emotions were in turmoil. In my heart I had been expecting it, but it still made me sad to know it was true, and not a figment of my imagination. Anna looked up from serving a customer and glanced in dismay at the door through which I had just entered. In some ways having my suspicions confirmed made it easier than living with uncertainty and gave me the strength to move on. I waited until she had finished serving then said, 'Don't worry, Anna. Everything's fine. Woof and I fancied some lunch. What would you recommend today?'

I didn't imagine the look of relief spreading across her face as she gave me a genuine smile.

'The chicken and white wine pie with sauté potatoes is really tasty, and maybe a glass of Chablis to wash it down?'

'Sounds good to me,' I replied. Bending down to make a fuss of Woof, she asked in a professional voice what he'd like from the menu and listed various left-over items he might enjoy. She nodded as if he had replied then suggested a large bowl of water, special tap vintage to accompany his meal. Woof wagged his tail in agreement, and I smiled as she stood up and asked, 'May I join you for a chat once I've organised your lunch?'

'Of course. And I'm sure your four-legged friend here would be delighted.'

We both laughed as Woof gave a short bark confirming his agreement. Anna went off to sort our

154

order and I went to my favourite alcove booth. I noticed Debbie the librarian hovering as if she wanted to speak to me, but wasn't sure if she should intrude.

'Hi Debbie,' I called. 'How are you?'

Realising I was happy to have her company she sank into the chair opposite me. 'I only have a few minutes before I go back, but I wanted to find out how the sale went. It sounds as if it was a brilliant day. If you want any help in resurrecting the vineyard, I've got some information and contacts you might find useful.'

I was amazed at the efficiency of the village grapevine. A very appropriate thought in the circumstances, which made an ideal name for the new wine range. I realised if my brain was already working on names, I was more than half-way committed to the project. My enthusiasm showed as I explained how the day had gone, and how satisfied I was with the end result. She was delighted when I said I was considering making it a regular event, and she thought the whole village would be pleased and benefit from the publicity.

'Look, we must get together soon. Take my phone number. Got to dash now. Bye, See you soon.'

As she left, Anna appeared, carrying my and Woof's lunch. A few minutes later she returned with her own meal, and we chatted idly while we ate. She seemed as well informed as Debbie about the auction and when I mentioned making it a regular event and producing on a regular basis, she confirmed the news would be welcome in the village. Woof was snoozing contentedly at my feet as she poured us both another glass. I realised that neither Paul nor Gloria had come into the pub since I had been there, although I presumed that had been their original intention. Wanting to get things into the open I asked, 'By the way, Anna, have Paul and Gloria already had lunch or should we save them some wine? I forgot to ask Paul when I spoke to him just before I came in.'

She looked at me for a moment before saying, 'Obviously you know then. I'm really sorry, Gina. I didn't want to interfere but at the same time I didn't want to gossip. I like you a lot and thought Paul was being a scumbag, but it wasn't my place to tell you. You might have known already and thought I was trying to cause trouble. You looked as if you were holding it together but for all I know you were crying yourself to sleep every night. I've been worrying about it for weeks.'

'I'm so sorry, Anna,' I replied. 'Paul shouldn't have been so selfish as to put you in that position. I think I've known for a while, but with everything going on at the house, the open day and him working away, we haven't had time to talk properly. Actually, I can't stay too long as he's coming over soon so we can sort things out. Between you and me, Paul has a stake in the house but I feel so settled here I'd hate to have to sell up and leave. I love my home, the village and the friends I've made here. It all depends if Paul is prepared to be reasonable. Financially it could work if I repaid his initial investment, but despite the success of the wine sale, it wouldn't be viable if he wanted more than his fifty percent. We'll just have to wait and see.'

Anna looked thoughtful for a moment then reluctantly gave her opinion.

'You might not be aware of this, Gina, and it's only a suggestion, but being in a village pub you gain a good idea of how the locals think. They have a few drinks and it all comes out. I can tell you honestly that the villagers have taken to you and want you to stay.

They love what you've done to the house and feel you are really part of the community. Funny enough, we didn't get the same vibes about Paul. Some of the older ones especially, compare him to the old Lord of the Manor. Sorry, I'm letting my mouth run away with me. All I really wanted to say is you have a lot of friends here if ever you need anything. Just let us know.'

'Thanks, Anna. I appreciate your honesty. I'll keep that in mind and it's really nice to know I'm welcome here despite being an outsider.'

'I'm glad that's out of the way,' she replied. 'By the way, do you know anything about cooperative trusts? I might be jumping the gun but I have a friend who's a solicitor and we were talking generally about the estate and wine producing. He mentioned if finance was a stumbling block there's a way of offering shares, so the investors can hopefully get a share of the profits. I don't know all the ins and outs but I'm sure many of the villagers would be interested. After all, the more publicity the village gets, the better chance they have of making a living from tourists and visitors. It could be win/win all round. Anyway, I don't want to push you into anything. You have enough on your plate at the moment, but if you do decide to go ahead with the vineyard, he'd be more than happy to give you the details. Oh, well, better get back to the grind. Lovely to talk to you, and I'm truly sorry for the way things turned out with Paul. Anytime you want to chat I'm always here. See you soon and good luck.'

I had a lot to think about and was overwhelmed at the support I had unexpectedly received. The idea of a cooperative sounded worth looking into, but first I had to sort things out with Paul. Realising how long I had spent in the pub, I needed get a move on or he'd be back at the house before me. Anna wasn't in sight when I went to pay the bill, but when I pointed out they hadn't included the bottle of wine the waitress told me it was on the house. Suddenly Woof disappeared behind the bar, and I called him worried he might be causing a problem. He reappeared, as if he had only gone to say goodbye to Anna, who showed her face in the door and waved a dishcloth as a farewell greeting. We set off home at a slower pace and I had only started topping up Woof's water bowl when I heard the chime of the front door bell. It was Paul. Why hadn't he used his key?

Chapter 22. Revelations.

The clock ticked loudly in the awkward silence while we drank coffee. This was ridiculous. Taking a deep breath, I said what was on my mind.

'Let's cut to the chase. What are your plans? What are you expecting from your share of the house?'

Paul looked surprised as he replied, 'I thought you'd ask me how long I'd been back and where I was staying.'

'Okay. When did you get back? Where are you sleeping?'

'You seem to have a pretty good idea already, so I might as well tell you everything. I'm really sorry, Gina. I think the world of you and never intended to hurt you. You must believe that.'

With a sudden instinct I asked, 'Was this going on at New Year? You seemed happy enough then but maybe I was being blind.'

With a sad smile he replied, 'It was a long while before that,' which did give me a shock. 'Let me explain from the beginning. You know I lost my parents when I was a baby and was brought up by relatives?'

'Yes, you told me that when we first met. What has that to do with it?'

'What I didn't tell you was that I was brought up around here. I even went to the infants' school on the outskirts of the village. I knew Gloria when we were teenagers and our families are distantly related. Her great grandfather worked on the estate and was responsible for the vineyard here.'

159

'Yes, I know. She told me that.' This time it was Paul's turn to look surprised.

'Did you also know that this house originally belonged to one of my ancestors?' Paul asked next.

'No. Presumably that's why you spent your childhood here? Why didn't you mention it when you first saw the house? You must have known.'

'You were so excited and to be honest, I didn't think the purchase would actually go through. After that, events snowballed with all the renovations, and you were so happy here I didn't want to upset you. I thought when I was away so much and you were on your own you would change your mind. I was pretty sure the move to the London office for my job wouldn't come off for a couple of years, and by then you'd have sold up and found somewhere more suitable. It was purely a coincidence the first time I bumped into Gloria, but meeting up with her again made me realise I wasn't ready to settle down here. I was going to tell you after the wine sale. I thought you'd cancel when I said I couldn't make it.'

He stood and went towards the window. 'You're a strong woman. I should have realised you'd make a success of things with or without me. Gloria is the head of the village grapevine so I heard all about it. By the way, I'm not serious about her but she made it obvious she was up for it, and I was weak enough to let her persuade me to stay with her for all my weekend leaves.'

'If you know all about the sale then you know how much it made,' I said as he came back to sit beside me. 'There's also your share of the house to consider. Unless there's no other option, I don't want to sell, but it depends on how you want to play it. I'd like to settle the financial side as quickly as possible, so I know whether I'll have to put my home on the market.'

'As far as the money from the auction day goes that's all yours. You organised everything so you're entitled to the profits. If there are any decent wines left, I wouldn't mind a couple of bottles but apart from that you can do what you like with the rest. I heard you were thinking of making it a regular event, and I wish you luck with it. There's no other way to say this so I'd better just come out with it. I've decided to settle abroad. The flat I'm renting near my job in Europe is coming up for sale and I want to buy it. By the way Gloria doesn't know this yet, although she's been dropping hints about moving out to join me, but actually there's a girl I work with I've been seeing for a while. I've told her there can be nothing formal between us until I've sorted things out with you, but she's prepared to wait.'

With a shake of the head he continued. 'I'm really sorry, Gina. I should have come clean a long while ago but I didn't want to hurt you. I still care for you a great deal and wish you all the luck in the world. I'm happy to settle for repayment of what I originally put up for the house. You've been paying for all the renovations anyway so even if it's worth more now, that's down to you. I need cash to purchase the flat I was telling you about, but property there is a lot cheaper than here. If you can come up with say half of it now, then we can sort out some arrangement for you to repay me the rest over a period of time.'

'That sounds very reasonable,' I replied. Although I was surprised by his news, in a peculiar way it wasn't unexpected. My heart should have been broken, but instead of being angry at the way he had treated me, I was pleased he hadn't dropped me for Gloria, and relieved things were out in the open.

'Thanks, Gina,' Paula said. 'I understand if you want to put everything on a formal footing, but we can keep it informal if you like. Whichever you prefer, and then I'll get out of your life and we can both move on. After all, the house is in your name still, and it'd be expensive to prove how much I put in. Although I know I've hurt you, I hope we can still be friends and sort this out amicably.'

Woof stirred and I stood up to let him out, wondering how to reply.

'Well, I think that covers everything I have to say,' he said tentatively, 'apart from how sorry I am. I'll leave you to think it over. I'm here until Friday week so it would be nice to know what you intend to do before I leave. Give me a ring if you want to meet again to discuss anything.' With that he gave me a brotherly kiss goodbye and left.

For a while I sat pondering, going round in my mind if I had done anything wrong and whether I should have realised sooner. Eventually I gave up thinking, and grabbed Woof's lead before it became too dark. The fresh air helped to clear some cobwebs, and when we returned, I settled down with my laptop to work out figures. Paul's offer to repay the rest over time was fair although, ideally, I wanted to repay him in full and have nothing more to do with him.

Before I could let the sadness overwhelm me, I allowed my usual practical side to take over. The plans to rejuvenate the vineyard would need to be put on hold for a while but I could live with that. There was also the question of the remaining bottles in the cellar. He had implied it was mine to do with as I liked, but I wasn't sure if he realised the possible value of the stock.

First things first. I needed to arrange a mortgage to repay him the first tranche, then organise a proper valuation of the wine. The obvious thing was to contact Geoff and Steve, and my heart gave a little leap now I had a genuine excuse to see Steve again. Expecting Paul to be home, I had taken the week off work so I could use the time sorting my life out and looking to the future. I spent the evening researching mortgage criteria and working out how much I could realistically afford each month to pay Paul off as quickly as possible.

Now that my concerns with Paul had actually become a reality, I realised I was not as upset as I'd expected. Rather than bemoaning my lost love, I was more concerned with the practicalities of removing him completely from my life. My research had made me optimistic I could raise the necessary funds, and the possibility of working with Steve on another sale gladdened my heart. Time to catch up with some sleep.

I couldn't believe it was only three in the morning when I glanced at my bedside clock, as I felt wide awake. I tossed and turned for a while then went to make myself a hot chocolate, hoping it would help me doze off again. Woof woke and padded after me, although he seemed grumpy I had disturbed his rest. The noise of the kettle drowned out most sounds but when I turned it off, I thought I heard banging from the cellar. I listened for a moment. All was quiet but as I took my drink back to bed the noise came again.

My pounding heart almost blocked out any other sound, but there was no way I would sleep until I knew what had disturbed me. Picking up the breadknife and a torch, I called to Woof then quietly unlocked the cellar door. I didn't put on the lights but after giving my eyes a chance to adjust, crept down the stairs. Beyond the rows of wine bottles, I thought I saw a shadow moving in the darkness, and wondered if another wild creature had found their way into the cellar. Moving quietly to the end of the row, I switched on the powerful torch to shine into the eyes of the intruder. This was no animal, but a man. Frozen with shock, I watched as the figure fled towards the doors leading to the outhouses. Woof took off after him, and without thinking I chased after them both. It was a stupid thing to do but Woof gave me courage. I caught up to hear Woof barking madly, but the doors were firmly locked and bolted from the other side. Throwing on every switch to bathe the area in light, I shone the torch down to where Woof was now scrabbling madly at the ground, trying to reach something.

Chapter 23. Intruders.

There was nothing to see except the stone flags of the flooring. I hunted everywhere but there was no sign of anyone, and no way they could have escaped from the cellar. Woof was still sniffing and pawing at the same spot and I went back to examine it. Bending closer, I noticed one area where the grouting between the tiles didn't cover the gaps. Pushing him to one side, I noticed what I had missed before. One of the tiles was slightly lower than the others. The pressure from my foot made it sink slightly, revealing a mechanism underneath. I slipped my fingers under the catch and the trap rose slowly, until it was totally vertical and the gap was big enough for someone to squeeze through. Beyond the opening, a ladder sloped downwards into what was obviously a sub cellar.

Shining my torch down, I glimpsed an indistinct figure hurrying away from the glare of the light. Even with Woof in support I wasn't brave enough to venture down alone, so after slamming the trap door shut, I dragged a heavy table on top of it. I dashed back up the stairs, calling to Woof, and locked the cellar door firmly behind me. I scrabbled through the file of papers on the living room table, found the card the sergeant had left when they had first discovered the bodies, and dialled the number. Luckily, my call was answered straight away.

'Hello. It's Gina. From Alderslay. Sorry to disturb you at this hour of the morning, but there's an intruder in the cellar. A man. At least I think it is. Under the trap door. I've locked him in.'

Saying it out loud made me feel silly and wonder if I was imagining things.

'Stay where you are. We'll be with you in ten minutes,' and the line went dead.

For a while I paced up and down until I saw the lights of a car pulling up outside. Not much more than five minutes had passed although it seemed much longer. I recognised the sergeant and the constable with two other men I hadn't seen before.

'Do you feel up to showing us the trap door, Gina?' the sergeant asked. 'We can find it ourselves but it would be quicker if you directed us to the exact spot.'

'Yes, of course,' I replied. 'Come on, Woof.'

With him at my heels and three policemen following me, I unlocked the cellar door and went down the steps. The fourth man stayed at the top, presumably to cut off any possible escape route. They didn't really need me as Woof went straight to the spot. The men moved the table and as I opened the catch and lifted the cover, I caught sight of a shadow moving out of the glare of the spotlight. One policeman stayed with me while the other two descended. What if I had called out four policemen in the early hours of the morning and all they found was a trapped animal or bird? After all, that was how I had first found Woof imprisoned in the cellar.

Then I heard the sounds of a scuffle and a moment later a voice called up the stairs, 'Pete, ask Alan to escort the lady to the living room and then join us. We've restrained the intruder but we need a photographer and forensics down here.'

'On it, Guv,' Pete called, then as he took me upstairs, he had a quiet word with the man guarding the door. 'Tell you what, Miss,' the one called Alan said as he led me to the living room, 'my old Mum always said a cup of tea helped to steady the nerves. Would you like me to make us one?'

'That's OK. I'll do it.'

Woof hovered between following me and staying to give his assistance. Eventually, he joined me in the kitchen while I made the hot drinks. At least they had found something, although I didn't know what, so it was a relief not to have called them out without good reason. Ten minutes later there was another knock at the front door. I opened it to find a female forensics expert and male photographer waving their identification. When I directed them to the cellar, Alan greeted them as if they were well acquainted. As I took the extra cups into the living room, one of the policemen pulled the door closed behind me, but not before I saw a shadowy figure in handcuffs being led away. Through the window I noticed a black van pull up, and the prisoner was handed in before the two original policemen returned.

'Tea, perfect,' Pete said as he took a cup and sat down. He was soon joined by Alan and the sergeant, who also seemed to be happy to see a hot drink. I put out a fruit cake I'd bought in the village, and all three of them devoured it with gusto. It felt odd to be having a tea party at four in the morning, but I assumed they were well used to the nocturnal hours. Shortly afterwards the other two joined us and expressed their thanks for my hospitality.

'What did you find down there?' I asked. 'I saw you taking someone away. Who was it?'

The others looked towards the sergeant who cleared his throat and finished his tea before explaining. 'I'm afraid I can't divulge the gentleman's identity at the moment but there is something else I can tell you. I know you're not the hysterical type, but it's only fair to warn you we discovered more bodies in the sub-cellar. It looks as if they died at about the same time as the others we found. Can you confirm that, Jen?'

The lady looked surprised as his openness, but explained in what was a court-reporting voice, 'From my examination of the skeletons shackled to the walls, I would estimate they had been there for approximately the same time as the others found on the premises. They were all females, aged between fifteen and twenty. At this stage I can't be certain, but would suggest they had been incarcerated and either beaten or starved to death. Tests will tell us more but it's likely they had been drugged, either before or after being brought here.'

'Those poor girls,' I said. 'How many were there altogether? Who was responsible? Have you any idea?'

'Well,' the sergeant responded, 'only the rumours we heard from our parents and grandparents. It was always assumed that the old Squire was responsible. I mean the grandson, Henry, not the original one. It was believed he perished in the fire, but who knows? Until you started renovating, no one knew about the wine store, and now you've found this sub-basement. Perhaps there were other exits and he managed to escape. His body was never found and until now we never knew these poor girls were still down there. Anyway, Miss, we've caught your intruder and will let you know the outcome of our questioning in due course. Will you be at home tomorrow? We need to arrange for those bodies to be removed. I won't make it too early; you need to catch up on some sleep. Will about three o'clock tomorrow afternoon be suitable? Or I should say, this afternoon?'

My watch told me it was already well past five, and dawn was breaking. 'I have some things to sort out tomorrow,' I said, 'but I'm sure I'll be home by three. Goodnight, and thanks for coming so quickly.'

Chapter 24. Moving on.

I saw them out then made sure all the doors and windows were securely locked before going back to bed. My mind was buzzing, but I needed sleep. Making sure Woof was settled, I went to bed and pulled the covers over my head to block out the breaking daylight.

Surprisingly, considering the events of the night, I slept like a log and woke refreshed. Woof too seemed full of beans, eager to explore the beautiful spring-like day. I treated myself to a proper English breakfast with Woof tail-wagging and nose twitching at the smell of bacon.

I decided to go into the village early, make an appointment with the building society to see about a mortgage, and find a solicitor to get things with Paul put on a proper legal footing. That reminded me I needed a professional valuation for the wine. Once the police had removed the bones from the sub cellar, I could phone Steve for advice.

It seemed an ideal opportunity to give the builders a call and see what needed to be done down there. They could also give me an estimate for restoring the swimming pool so the further costs could be included, and I could see what was viable.

In the end, I dialled Steve's number before I did anything else. He answered after only two rings and I felt nervous as I explained who I was.

'Hey, Gina. Good to hear from you.' His rich throaty laugh reassured me as he recognised my voice immediately. Although I didn't go into details, I briefly explained the need for a professional valuation of the wine stock as part of the settlement with my ex-fiancé.

He was quiet for a moment and I wondered if I had pushed too far. 'I'm sorry things haven't worked out with Paul,' he said, 'but I want to help in any way I can. I think of you as a friend so it would be better if someone else did the actual valuation.'

'Oh. OK,' I replied, hoping the disappointment didn't show in my voice.

'Sorry, that didn't come out as I intended. I know someone who'll be perfect. It would be better if it was independent. Let me take your mobile number and I'll get back to you. Are you around today?'

'I've some things to sort out later, but I'll wait to hear from you then.'

'Great. I'm looking forward to seeing you again. Bye for now.'

As I put the phone down, I wasn't sure if I was pleased or apprehensive at the way the call had gone. Maybe I was reading too much into one meeting with an attractive man, and his interest in me was purely professional although he had mentioned us being friends. Oh well, time would tell. For now I had other things to organise. Even so, I double checked I had my mobile as I called Woof and set off towards the village. At the building society I explained about needing to see an advisor to discuss a possible mortgage.

The helpful lady at reception explained, 'The consultant is currently with a customer, but if you could wait ten minutes or so, I'm sure she'll fit you in.'

'Thanks, that's fine,' I replied. 'I need to check my dog is okay. I'll be back in a minute.'

'You don't need to leave him out there,' she said, noticing Woof tied up outside. 'Jenny's a dog fanatic, so you're welcome to bring him inside to wait with you.'

I was starting to appreciate the differences between living in London, and a country village where animals were accepted as a part of everyday life. Woof was as good as gold and settled at my feet to wait patiently for our appointment. Only five minutes later, Jenny, a tall, plump lady in her fifties showed her customer out and bent down to make a fuss of Woof, who responded by greeting her like a long-lost friend. She led us into her office, and only after she had asked my dog's name did she ask mine. After that she was all professionalism, and I found myself explaining everything as she listened carefully, then outlined the options open to me. In between patting Woof, she made copious entries on her computer, and her enthusiasm was infectious.

'Well,' she said, a short while later, 'I wish all my clients were that easy. It won't be any problem to offer you the full amount you requested, or even more if want. All I need for now is the documentation proving your ID. As soon as you drop them in, I can let you have a formal offer on the spot.

'Now, you mentioned needing a solicitor to sort things out legally with your ex-boyfriend. If you don't already have one I would recommend Jackson, Brown & Co. in the village. Bernard's not only an old friend of mine but has excellent local knowledge and is also something of a wine buff. He specialises in partnership settlements and has an exceptional reputation, not only here but also in his London practice. It's entirely up to you, of course, and you're free to consult anyone you wish. If you already have a solicitor, send me their details and I can get the ball rolling.'

'Actually, I don't have anyone in mind and it would be good to use local expertise. If you let me have his address I can pop along now and make an appointment to see him.'

'I can do better than that,' she smiled as she picked up the phone. 'Bernie, my love, how are you? Yes, I'm fine. We must get together soon. I'll give you a call so you and Doreen can come over for a meal and a gossip. Listen, I have a very important client with me who needs legal advice. When can you fit her in? No, that's no good. How about today? Let me check.' She covered the mouthpiece and turned to me. 'He can see you in about an hour. Is that all right? It's only up the road.'

'That's fine,' I said, stunned at how quickly things were falling into place.

'Hi, Bernie, she'll be with you shortly. Her name's Gina Kingston. Great. How about Friday? 7.30? Perfect. See you then. Love to Doreen. Bye.'

With that she hung up and gave me a card with his details. A few minutes later I was out the door with her business card in my pocket and the mortgage as good as arranged. I walked up the road and shortly found myself outside the solicitor's office. Realising I would be early, I decided to stop for a coffee at the café in the park opposite, which had an outside seating area. Despite my large breakfast, I couldn't resist the Danish pastries and settled down with Woof at my feet to pass the time. Although I still needed my jacket it was a beautiful Spring-like day, with the sun shining brightly. There were signs everywhere of the flowers breaking off their winter mantle and showing summer was not far away. That reminded me of my plans for the swimming pool, so I phoned Terry to see when he could give me a quote. He answered immediately and I gave him a brief update of the further discovery in the sub cellar.

'Good Lord, that's a turn-up. Are you all right? I know the police sergeant, so I can give him a bell to see when we'll be allowed access. As soon as he gives the go-ahead, I'll come over to discuss what you want done with the pool, and also about securing the sub-basement. Speak to you soon. Take care, my pet.'

No sooner had I finished the call when my mobile rang again. My face broke into a smile as I realised it was Steve. 'I don't want to rush you but I've been in touch with the professional wine valuer and we can come tomorrow if it's convenient.'

I was pleased to hear him say "we" and told him that would be perfect.

'Looking forward to seeing you, about eleven, then.'

Realising time was getting on, I paid my bill and headed towards the solicitor's office. I was told it would be fine to bring Woof in with me, and after only a few minutes Bernard come out to greet me. He was a big, round, jovial man with a bushy white beard and I couldn't help thinking he would make a perfect Father Christmas. Although he was smiling and jolly, I soon realised he was very astute.

As I told him the outlines of our financial situation, he asked several questions that made it obvious he understood where I was coming from. He complimented me on having the good sense to put things on a legal basis rather than relying on our previous affection for each other, particularly where third parties were involved. Noticing my querying look he added 'I happen to know the young lady involved. Let's just say, "What Gloria wants, Gloria usually gets," but you never heard that from me. Now, about the wine. A professional valuation is a very wise move.'

Jenny had already told me he had an interest in wine, but I was surprised when he asked if he could be in on the meeting the following day as my representative. After I had given my permission, he outlined what he intended to put in the legal agreement between Paul and myself.

'I should have a draft ready for your approval by Tuesday. Here's a print-out of my expected costs and fees. If you'll sign here, giving your agreement to the Ts and Cs we'll be all set.'

As I walked back with Woof, my mind was buzzing at how quickly things had moved. It was astonishing to realise it was less than twenty-four hours since Paul had first admitted he was seeing someone else. As soon as we reached home I dug out the necessary documentation to prove my ID, then scanned and e-mailed them over to Jenny immediately.

Shortly afterwards the police arrived and I stayed in the lounge while they sorted out the removal of the skeletons. As I was waiting for them to complete their grisly task the phone rang. It was Terry.

'Hello my love. I've had a chat with the sergeant, and he's given me the all-clear. He should be with you soon, if he's not there already. I can come over tomorrow afternoon if that suits you.'

The next day was going to be a very busy one. Within an hour the policemen had finished and the sergeant came into the lounge to update me. He mentioned he had already spoken to Terry, and because the crime was so long ago they had done everything necessary. There was no reason why he shouldn't proceed with any work I wanted done. Once the others left I offered him a cup of tea, then asked for more information on the man they had apprehended in the sub cellar.

'I believe you're acquainted with Miss Gloria Anderton,' was his opening remark.

'Yes, I know her,' I replied, 'but what has she got to do with this?'

'The man we have arrested is her brother. He's given us a full explanation of his reasons for being in the house, and implicated Miss Anderton. It seems that she had, er, developed an attraction for your fiancé and intended to have both him and the house for herself. Her ancestors at one time lived here and she knew of the sub cellar and the secret entrances from their family history. The idea was her brother would break in and scare you into wanting to move. I think he was more frightened than you when instead of running away screaming in terror, you and your dog gave chase and locked him in,' the sergeant explained, trying hard to hide the smile on his face.

'I also think he got more than he bargained for when he came face to face with the other skeletons down there. He was quite relieved when we rescued him. Well, I'd better get moving now, Gina. Thank you for the tea. Good luck for tomorrow; I hope you manage to finish all your renovations and finally enjoy your home in peace.'

After I had seen him out I phoned Paul and told him what I had decided. His first concern was to apologise for Gloria's behaviour.

'The police have been to see her already, and we've both been subjected to a grilling. I assure you I knew nothing about her plans and I'm going abroad on

Thursday. Until then I'm staying at the inn in the village, as I've already moved out of Gloria's house.'

I told him about the further discovery of more bones and that the police had just left. He was full of concern and even offered to come over if I wanted support. Rather sharply I cut him off, saying, 'Woof and I are fine. I'm putting the financial side of things on a legal footing. I've arranged a mortgage and seen a solicitor.'

He was quiet for a moment then said, 'You were never one to let the grass grown under your feet, Gina. I wish you all the luck in the world and you can rest assured I'll co-operate in any way I can. I hope we can still be friends after all that's happened.'

It seemed an appropriate time to bring up the value of the wine in the cellar, and I explained about the assessment arranged for the following day. Again he paused.

'Would it be convenient for me to call in tomorrow morning before they come? Don't worry if it's not, but it would be nice to have one or two bottles as a memento. I'm happy to sign over the rest to you. You can do what you like with them. The other reason is I would like to see you again before I leave the country. Just for old-time's sake.'

I was surprised at his sentimentality but agreed to see him and suggested he come about ten. With mixed emotions as the call ended, I took Woof for a final walk to clear my brain of all the thoughts battling for supremacy. It had been quite a day.

After making notes as reminders of the information I had gathered, I settled down for an hour in front of the TV to unwind before having an early night. Without conscious thought I dug out my most attractive outfit for the day for the following day. I wasn't sure whether it was to let Paul know what he was missing or to impress Steve. Either way, looking good gave me the poise to feel confident in facing the various professionals who would be soon be arriving. Not wanting to muck up my clothes I let Woof out for a run round the grounds, promising him we'd have a proper walk when everyone was gone, then berated myself for talking to the dog as if he was a human being.

Chapter 25. Goodbye and Good Luck.

Shortly before ten the doorbell rang and I opened it to find Paul on the doorstep.

'You're looking great, Gina,' he said as he gave me a kiss on the cheek.

I had prepared coffee and led him into the lounge so we could sit and talk business. Although he looked as handsome as ever, I was surprised how unemotional I felt. Considering I had been engaged to this man and we had been lovers, I now regarded him as if he was an attractive but out-of-bounds colleague, or someone I used to know. He was full of apologies and I detected a tinge of regret as he realised I had accepted our split and was ready to move on. Not wanting to cheat him, I tried to make it clear exactly how much the bottles in the cellar were potentially worth. In answer he handed me a signed document which effectively relinquished all his rights to the contents of the house, including the wine.

We descended into the cellar so he could make his selection, and he finally chose two.

'Only two?' I queried. 'I thought you'd want a lot more than that.'

'There were a couple of others I liked,' Paul replied, 'but although I'm not an expert, these two must be worth at least several hundred pounds. You know, Gina, I never really belonged in this house. You found it, you arranged all the renovations, you put up with the mess and hassles while the building works were going on. It was your ideas and drive that transformed it from a rundown wreck to what is a beautiful home. But it's your home, not mine. I wasn't even here for the wine sale; you organised all that on your own. Whatever profit you might make is purely down to your hard work. I had no part in it.

'I'm more than happy with our agreement, with the two bottles of wine as my dividend. You've been very fair considering the way I let you down. You deserve every penny you make and if I was more of a decent human being, I wouldn't take the wine. Thank you for that. I really appreciate it.'

Reminded of the lovely man he used to be before it all went wrong, I was moved.

'Thanks for being so reasonable,' I replied. 'Out of interest, which were the other bottles you liked?'

'I was trying to decide between a couple,' Paul said as he pointed out the ones he had considered, 'but these I picked are perfect, if you're sure about letting me have them.'

'No problem,' I said as I mentally noted the other wines he had indicated.

As we went back upstairs, with Paul clutching his precious bottles, the doorbell rang and I opened it to see Bernard, the solicitor, standing on the doorstep. I introduced him to Paul then left them alone in the lounge while I made more coffee. When I returned, Bernard was going through a wad of legal looking papers which Paul was examining carefully.

'Is everything okay?' I asked as I put the coffee pot and fresh cups on the table.

'It's fine,' Paul answered before Bernard could speak. 'As far as I can see there's nothing in here that we haven't already agreed.'

'This is only a draft,' Bernard answered me. 'Paul has explained that he's leaving the country shortly, but as there don't seem to be any disputes I can have the final documents completed and e-mail you a copy later today. Paul is calling into the office tomorrow to sign them. Once the mortgage has been finalised, we can transfer his monies to his bank account and everything will be completed.'

Turning to Paul he said, 'Subject to unnecessary gremlins you should have your cash by the end of the month.'

He had only just finished speaking when the doorbell rang again and I opened the door to find Steve, Geoff and a stranger, who Steve introduced as Herbert Cunningham, and they all shook hands. I noticed Paul glance at me and raise his eyebrows when he was introduced to Steve.

'Sorry to cut and run,' he said. 'I'll see you tomorrow, Bernard. Nice to meet you gentlemen. Gina, I'll be in touch. Goodbye, everyone.'

'I'll find you something to put the bottles in, Paul' I said. 'Give me five minutes then meet me in the kitchen.' Diving back down to the cellar I picked up the other four bottles in which he had showed an interest. As I put them in a carrier, he came in. I added the first two then we looked at each other for a moment.

'Are you sure, Gina? It's not too late to change your mind,' Paul said into the charged atmosphere and I knew he wasn't talking about the wine.

'I'm sure,' I replied before he pulled me into a bear hug for our final goodbyes.

'Thanks for everything,' he whispered. 'Have a good life and stay in touch. You'll always have a big piece of my heart.' He picked up the wine carrier and went out to his car without looking back. I could see I wasn't the only one with tears in my eyes as I watched him drive away.

The end of an era.

Chapter 26. First new steps.

I took a few moments to compose myself before going back upstairs to join the others. As I went into the lounge, I saw Steve's concerned glance and gave him a shaky smile.

'Well, gentlemen,' I said, 'shall we get this show on the road?'

We all trooped down to the cellar and I showed Herbert how the racks were arranged. Steve and Geoff were of course already familiar with them, and Bernard too seemed fascinated. Herbert examined every bottle methodically and made copious notes in an old-fashioned lined exercise book. It would have been a lot quicker if he had a laptop, but he seemed to be of the old school, and my knowledge of what was in the cellar was nothing more than bottles, wine and cobwebs.

After about an hour Bernard suggested we leave them to it and go upstairs for a quick chat. He showed me the draft he had been going through with Paul and explained a few of the more technical details.

'I must admit to being pleasantly surprised how cooperative Paul has been,' he remarked. 'Obviously, everything needs to be above board, but I think you will be amazed at the final value of the wine stock. At the end of the day my first duty is to you, my client, but once everything is settled, if you wanted to send Paul a "friendship gift" then everyone should be content in both the factual and actual spirit of the law.'

I was surprised at his comment, which made me wonder exactly what sort of figure the expert would come up with. It was already gone two when the three men emerged from the cellar, rather grubby and dusty but with beaming smiles. I had prepared snacks for lunch, and after washing their hands they all tucked into the food with gusto. As I handed Steve a plate he winked at me and, turning in embarrassment, I noticed a grin on Geoff's face, which I thought had nothing to do with the business at hand. Herbert consulted his notebook and gave me a summary of what he had found. Some of what he said went over my head when he was talking about vintages and good and bad years, although Steve and Geoff seemed to be able to follow it without a problem. Even Bernard nodded in agreement at certain remarks and comments.

'I'll send you my formal valuation shortly,' Herbert said, 'but meanwhile may I congratulate you on a superb collection. I think my friends here have already suggested that rather than flooding the market you should drip feed every few months. Here's my card and my bill. Please contact me when you are ready to proceed. I'll be more than happy to assist in the disposal of these excellent vintages.'

Bernard gave him his own details and asked if he could be sent a copy of the report. 'Would you have a spare card, Herbert? In my own small way, I'm somewhat of a wine buff and would like to keep in touch, if you're agreeable.'

'Of course, my dear chap. Gina, once again my congratulations on your contribution to vintner's history,' Herbert smiled. 'It's not often we discover unexpected treasures such as you have here. Do you want a lift, Geoffrey?'

'Yes, thank you. That would be appreciated,' Geoff replied. Turning to me he gave me a hug and a wish to see me again soon.

Bernard took his leave saying he would be in touch and with that they were all gone, leaving Steve and me alone. Feeling suddenly shy, I opened the envelope containing Herbert's bill and was taken aback to find it was not much short of £500, including VAT. Seeing my shocked face Steve smiled.

'He might not be cheap, but he is the best. Whatever his bill might be, in the long run you have a gold mine down there, and it will be worth every penny not to get ripped off on its true value.'

Before I could reply there was another ring at the bell. I wasn't sure if I was pleased or disappointed to see Terry standing on the doorstep with Danny, one of his workmen. With everything going on, I had forgotten they were coming. After introducing them to Steve I told him to make himself comfortable while I showed them the sub cellar.

'Perhaps I should go, if you're busy?' he suggested.

'No, we won't be long,' I called as I led the workmen downstairs.

There were no lights, but with a torch and the glow from the ordinary cellar above, there was enough for them to see round. It was in the same state as the original vault had been before the renovations and, being almost empty looked even larger. The damp, fusty odour of a long-neglected property pervaded the stale air. I followed Terry and Danny down the rope ladder, and as I wandered around, couldn't help noticing the shackles on the wall. That must be where the other poor girls had been chained and it sent a shiver up my spine.

'What did you intend to do with this area?' Terry asked. 'Obviously we'll need electricity installed, and a proper staircase. Apart from that I need to know your plans so we can start designing the layout.'

'I haven't really given it any thought,' I replied. 'Until forty-eight hours ago I didn't even know it existed. To be honest, I can't see me wanting to spend a lot of time down here, but apart from that I don't have a clue.'

'If I could make a suggestion?' Terry said. 'I know you haven't made any decision yet about restarting the vineyard but you still have a lot of bottles upstairs. We could make this into a modern storage with proper racking, and if you went ahead with the vineyard there would still be enough space for all the equipment. That would leave the main cellar free if you felt more comfortable there. In the long run you might even consider having it as a shop area, for tasting, or even as a reception for wine tours. It'd be more practical that way.'

'That's a brilliant idea, Terry,' I replied. 'Let's see what Steve thinks. First though, shall we have a look at the swimming pool area before it gets dark? I'd like to get that organised for when the better weather comes, and a lot of the rest will depend on the finances, so I want to make that a priority.'

'Of course.' He and Danny followed me up the ladder, then through the main cellar to the outhouses leading to the pool. They walked around the area, examining the flagstones and broken tiles, and measuring up. There was not a lot I could do, so I left them to it and went to put the kettle on. It gave me an opportunity to chat to Steve alone. He was sitting on the settee working on his laptop when I went into the lounge. He looked up and smiled as I apologised for deserting him for so long.

'Don't worry, I've been fine,' he replied. 'I've used the time to do my own investigation. Have you given any more thought to revitalising the actual vineyard?'

'Funnily enough, that was what I've been discussing with Terry downstairs. He thought it would be a good idea to move the existing wine to the lower cellar, and free the space in the upper one. He wanted to know if I intended to restore the vineyard but to be honest, it would be a giant step. It's one thing to have experts helping me sell the existing stock, but I wouldn't know where to start in running a vineyard. I assume it would take years to get it productive, and apart from needing the right people, there's also the question of finances.'

'You're right,' Steve replied. 'I apologise for interfering; after all it's none of my business. Perhaps I'd better be making a move.'

'No, don't go yet. I haven't ruled out the idea completely. I was going to ask if you'd have a chat with Terry and let him know if it would be viable to move the wine to the lower level. He should be in soon. Oh, sorry! I should have realised you have work to do and I'm keeping you here wasting time.'

'It's never a waste of time being here, Gina,' he smiled. I felt a blush cross my face then berated myself for thinking like a giggly schoolgirl. Obviously he meant the wine and the business opportunities, not my company. Embarrassed, I mumbled something about putting the kettle on and escaped to the kitchen. A few minutes later I heard Terry and Danny come in, and then the men's voices discussing Terry's suggestions.

'We won't be long,' Steve called as he poked his head round the kitchen door. 'I'm going with Terry to have a quick look at the sub-basement.'

Chapter 27. More history.

That left me playing hostess with Danny, who I hardly knew and who seemed rather shy. To make conversation I talked about the property and he soon relaxed and became full of enthusiasm. It seemed his great grandfather had worked on the estate and he had heard all the tales through his family. I wondered if there was anyone in the village who wasn't in some way connected with the estate, or whose ancestors hadn't worked there. As if reading my thoughts, he told me the village had developed around the old manor. All the families worked for the squire and all the cottages and surrounding land were owned by him. If they didn't work in the vineyard they were employed in the house, or in other trades such as blacksmiths or millers. Either way, their livelihoods depended on the squire, and anyone who upset him would be cast out. The whole family would be penniless, homeless and with no chance of obtaining work elsewhere, as he would spread the word to the neighbouring landowners. We were deep in conversation when Steve and Terry came into the lounge chatting nineteen to the dozen.

'It would be perfect,' Steve said as he sat down. 'The temperature down there is even better than in the main cellar, and the layout is superior. With a lick of paint and new racking it would be ideal. Not only that, it would look more professional and in keeping with the superb stock when you hold another auction.' He gave me a sheepish grin and said, 'Sorry. We're getting carried away and it has to be what you decide. Let's start again. In my professional judgement it would be a good idea.'

'And in my professional judgement,' Terry chipped in, 'it shouldn't be very expensive and I would be happy to undertake the work at your convenience.'

Woof suddenly looked up and barked as if he was agreeing with the others. We laughed as I jokingly replied, 'Even the dog's ganging up against me. What chance has a poor female on her own with you males all sticking together? Okay, Terry, do your quote, but I still want to know what the pool renovations will cost before giving the go-ahead.'

'I'll have it with you tomorrow,' Terry replied. 'I'll give you individual quotes for the two jobs but actually it would be cheaper to do them together, so I'll let you have a combined price as well. That way we can be getting on with the sub-basement while the cement outside is setting, rather than wasting time. You fit, Danny? We'd better be off or my wife will be putting my dinner in the bin.'

'It was nice to talk to you, Danny,' I said as I showed them out. 'Thanks, Terry, I'll wait to hear from you.'

As I returned to the lounge Steve stood up and said, 'I'd better be making a move too.'

Before I could engage my brain, I heard myself saying, 'Or your wife will be putting your dinner in the bin too?' I couldn't have been less subtle if I'd tried, but he merely smiled.

'There's no one to put my dinner in the bin except me. I was going to pick up a take-away on the way home. Unless…'

'Unless?' I asked, holding my breath.

'Unless you'd care to join me for dinner?'

'I have a better idea,' I said. 'How about if I cook something here? I've got plenty of supplies in and

I won't be offended if you put it in the bin if you don't enjoy it.'

'I'd love to,' Steve replied immediately. 'If you like, I can pop out and buy a bottle of wine.'

'With a whole cellar-full downstairs?' I laughed. 'How about if you select something to go with say, Chicken chasseur?'

'Perfect. Woof, do you want to help me choose?'

As if he understood, the dog shook himself and padded after Steve to the basement. I went into the kitchen to start preparing the sauce and decide what I would serve with the chicken. About ten minutes later Steve came back clutching two bottles of wine.

'I didn't take the expensive ones,' he said as he put them in the fridge to chill, 'but I think you'll enjoy these. Can I help, or would you rather I got out from under your feet? I could take Woof for a quick run, if you like.'

'That would be great,' I replied, slightly embarrassed about having a strange man watching me cook. I was used to it with Paul, but I had only met Steve a couple of times, and it was different being alone in the house with a virtual stranger, and no close neighbours.

As dinner simmered, I put candles on the table and dimmed the lights. Although they looked beautiful, I decided it might give the wrong impression as it looked very romantic. Before I had a chance to remove them the front door opened and Steve and Woof returned, looking like two drowned rats. Standing in the doorway, Steve called to ask if he could borrow a towel before he dripped all over the carpet.

'You're soaked,' I said, stating the obvious. 'You'd better get out of those wet clothes before you catch your death.' Even as the words left my mouth I felt my face redden. To hide my embarrassment, I dashed upstairs and grabbed a couple of towels, then found an old pair of jeans and a T-shirt Paul had left. I thrust them at Steve who was busy mopping off Woof with paper towels from the kitchen. 'Why don't you take a hot shower while I finish drying him?'

Steve smiled his thanks then disappeared. I dug out an old towel, dried Woof, then gave him his dinner. He slumped in the lounge for a snooze while I finished preparing the meal and setting the table. As I put some music on, Steve returned. I did a double-take seeing him in Paul's clothes, and looking drop-dead gorgeous. Although they were a similar height and build Steve was slightly chunkier. Of their own accord, my eyes drifted downwards, and I couldn't help noticing the tight fit of the jeans.

Praying Steve hadn't noticed my glance, I dived into the kitchen to start serving the meal. I nearly jumped out of my skin when I turned to find him right behind me, asking if he should take in the wine. 'Yes, fine,' I replied, making sure I kept my gaze on the dishes I was carrying. It was a relief when we were both seated at the table, as it meant I could only see his top half. Pouring the wine, Steve raised his glass in salute.

'Thank you for taking pity on a poor, starving bachelor and giving him a proper meal. This looks delicious. Here's wishing you every happiness in your beautiful home and every success in your business. Any advice or help you need you only have to whistle and I'll come running. Cheers.'

'Cheers. And thanks for all your help today.'

For a few minutes we ate in silence with the music as background, then Steve asked how I felt about starting the vineyard up again. I admitted I didn't have a clue where to begin and after that the conversation flowed easily. I realised how much expertise he had in the field, and also how knowledgeable he was about the original vineyard on the estate which had surrounded the house. For a moment I felt spooked as I thought of Paul, and how I had discovered he was related to the original owners of the manor. It gave me a chill to think it was probably his ancestors who were responsible for the horrors endured by the young girls whose bodies had been found in the basement.

It felt like déjà vu. Could I be repeating my previous mistake by becoming involved with a man whose history was tied in with the house? Steve noticed my change of mood and seemed to sense my unease.

'Look, if you're uncomfortable, perhaps it'd be better if I left now,' he said. 'I don't want to, but it'd give me an excuse to get out of clearing up the dirty dishes.'

His understanding and thoughtfulness made me realise I was being silly and I was able to respond in the same light-hearted manner.

'No way, Mister. You don't get off that easily. Whoever heard of the chef having to clean their own pots?'

After that the conversation turned to our favourite music, films, books we had read and the hundred and one other things people learn about each other when they first meet. After making coffee, on an impulse I dug out a bottle of brandy left over from Christmas. As I put down the bottle and glasses it seemed natural to take the seat next to him on the settee, rather than in one of the matching armchairs. When we relaxed, I could feel his arm leaning along the back of the couch and coming to rest lightly on my shoulder. I felt mellow and happy, and realised that the two empty wine bottles put out for recycling probably had something to do with it. It had also been good for my ego to know that Steve was attracted to me after finding out Paul had been two-timing.

I had liked Steve from the off and even though we had become better acquainted, I had too much respect to take him on the rebound. I didn't want to treat him as a salve to my wounded ego. He seemed tuned into my aura, and stretching as he glanced at the clock, pointed out it was already gone one and this time he really must go. I couldn't believe how the time had flown.

'If it's all right with you,' he said, 'I'll leave my car here, grab a cab home and walk back tomorrow to pick it up.'

'I feel guilty now for keeping you, and causing you so many problems,' I mumbled.

'You'll never be a problem to me,' he said softly as he took out his mobile and dialled a number. Unsure how I felt, I took the glasses and the now-empty brandy bottle into the kitchen. When I returned it somehow felt wrong to sit where I had been almost snuggled in his arms. I hovered for a moment until Steve stood up and formally shaking my hand, thanked me for a delightful evening and a superb meal.

'I meant it when I said about offering any help you need to get the wine business off the ground,' he reiterated. 'I don't want to push you into anything, but I think we could make good business partners. The village would be delighted to see the estate winery re-established so I hope you'll give it serious consideration.'

Although I appreciated his words I felt let down. Perhaps his interest was after all purely business, and I had misread the signs. As if to prove me wrong he pulled me close and whispered in my ear, 'Of course I also have an ulterior motive. It would give me chance to see more of you.'

As our lips met I melted into his embrace, feeling the bulge in his borrowed jeans pressing against me. At that moment the doorbell rang and with a wry smile he said, 'Saved by the bell. Thanks for everything.'

With a quick kiss he went out to the waiting cab and was gone.

Chapter 28. Finances and developments.

What a day. So much had happened in such a short space of time it seemed unbelievable to think it was only this morning, or rather yesterday morning, that I had opened the door to Paul. Since then we had formalised our split, I had made new plans for the cellar and sub-cellar, arranged a valuation of the wine, sorted the refurbishment of the swimming pool, decided to commit to starting a business, and spent an evening with a new man.

'Quite an achievement for one day, Woof,' I said. 'But now it's time for you to make a quick visit outside then off to bed. What do you think?'

'Woof' he said in agreement as I opened the door. He was back quickly and I locked up before we both went to bed to sleep and dream sweet dreams. Despite my late night I woke at a reasonable hour to find the sun again streaming through the window. When I opened the door to let Woof out, I noticed there was still a chill to the breeze to remind me that summer had not yet arrived. I wandered down to the cellar and looked around at the rack upon rack of wines stored there. Even if they were only worth a few pounds each there were so many, Paul must have realised what they were worth, and would surely want more than a couple of bottles of the best ones.

Returning upstairs, I opened my laptop to find the promised valuation from Herbert. I looked at the figure, looked again, then decided he must have made a typing error, as there were so many noughts on the end. He also requested payment for his fee as soon as possible, and had given his bank details so I could make a direct transfer. The sum he had charged was a pittance, if the figure he had given me was correct.

I went onto my online bank account and sent off the payment, then replied with a brief e-mail thanking him for his services. I noticed that he had also copied in Bernard the solicitor and remembered that Paul was visiting him this morning to sign the various papers. I wasn't sure whether I was pleased or not. It was great the wine was worth so much, but it might also mean the simplistic settlement with Paul could be dragged out and perhaps turn awkward.

There was nothing I could do about it now, and some fresh air would help clear my mind. The sun continued to shine although all the rain the previous night had made everywhere muddy. When I kicked off my boots, the sodden edges of my trousers encouraged me to make some washing the order of the day. With my mucky clothes in the machine, I had just put on a dressing gown when the phone rang.

'Good Morning, my dear,' Bernard's jovial voice boomed through the speaker. 'Congratulations on a splendid result.' It took me a minute to realise he meant the wine valuation, and I was at a loss how best to explain my concerns. Before I had a chance to answer he told me, 'I've already seen Paul and everything has been finalised. Although I didn't give him the exact figures, I indicated there were substantial assets in the value of the bottles. However, I'm happy to confirm Paul has signed the legal papers relinquishing all rights, and confirmed in writing that his only financial settlement would be the return of his original investment for his share of the purchase price for the house.

'I've also heard from Jenny that, subject to a valuation and your signature on the legal mortgage documents, the funds should be available by the end of the month. If it's convenient, the valuer could call this afternoon, and I've pencilled in an appointment for you to sign the papers on the 29th March at 11 a.m.'

'That was quick. Thanks Bernard. Any idea what time the valuer will be here?' I asked.

'Probably around three. One final thing. With your agreement I would like to send part of the mortgage funds direct to Paul's bank account as settlement of his interest, but we can discuss that further when I see you on the 29th. Goodbye for now, my dear.'

My mind was in turmoil at how quickly things had moved, but I decided to phone Paul personally to make sure he was happy with the arrangements. He answered on the second ring and seemed delighted to hear my voice. When I tried to tell him more about the value of the wine he cut me off.

'Gina,' he said, 'I'm not going back on my word a second time. I'm really sorry for the way things turned out between us, but I meant it when I said everything connected with the house belongs to you. I saw your solicitor this morning and signed all the papers so it's now all legally yours. I feel bad about asking for my half of the house purchase money but as I told you, I need it to buy my own place. Otherwise I wouldn't have put you through the pressure of arranging a mortgage. Your solicitor said I might get the money within a couple of weeks. It would be great if that was possible, but if it causes any problems I don't really need it until the end of June. Anyway, let's not talk about all that. My flight doesn't leave until ten tomorrow night. Is there any chance I could see you tomorrow, just to say goodbye? I know I don't deserve it but I would like us to part as friends.'

'I feel the same way, Paul. Thanks for being so reasonable about everything. How about we meet for lunch in the pub in the village? I could see you there about twelve thirty.'

'It's a date. See you then, Gina. Look forward to it. Bye for now.'

As he put down the phone I could have sworn I heard him say, "Love you" but maybe it was my imagination. I made myself lunch then went back to Herbert's e-mail and opened up the attachment. It was a comprehensive spread sheet listing each individual bottle in the cellar, complete with a short history of its vintage, the particular attributes and a guide price. I was astounded he had been able to provide such a thorough guide when his only equipment during his visit to the cellar had been a pencil and a notebook. Obviously his expertise had shown him what to look for, but I was delighted with the information he had provided. Not only did it confirm his overall valuation but it also allowed me to become more knowledgeable about my legacy.

I realised time had flown. It was already two-thirty and I was still sitting in my dressing gown when the front door bell sounded.

Oh, Hell, I thought, *don't tell me the valuer's early.*

I couldn't leave him standing on the doorstep so I went to open it, rehearsing a speech in my mind that I had just got out of the bath. It wasn't the valuer, it was Steve. I stood there with my mouth open as he said, 'I came to return the clothes you lent me and pick up my car. I hope it's not an inconvenient time. Perhaps I should have phoned first?'

'Come in. Sorry about the attire, I've just got out of the bath.'

'Don't apologise on my account. You look fantastic in anything.'

'Do you want a coffee?' I asked.

'Love one, if it's not too much trouble.'

As I took the tray into the living room I decided to tell the truth. 'Actually, I haven't just got out of the bath. I was muddy from the fields earlier and have been slobbing around like this ever since.'

'I know,' came the surprising response. 'I called earlier when you came back, but being a gentleman, I beat a retreat when I saw you stripping off your muddy clothes. It would have been easier on my libido if I'd been a cad, or you had closed the curtains.'

I blushed bright red but had to laugh at the stricken look on his face as he said, 'I'm so sorry for embarrassing you. I should never have mentioned it; however pleasant it was at the time. By the way, have you heard from Herbert yet?'

'I received his valuation a short while ago. The final sum he came up with was astounding.'

'I'm not surprised,' he said. 'I had a pretty good idea about the rarity of some of the bottles I saw. It's such an extensive collection even the lower value bottles should fetch a reasonable price purely from the association. Have you thought any more about holding another auction or even starting the vineyard again?'

'Well, I definitely intend to have another sale, maybe Mid-June. Would you and Geoffrey be able to help me out again?'

'Of course. Let us know the date you have in mind. I'm sure Geoffrey will be delighted to come.'

'That's great,' I said, 'only this time I insist on paying you properly. After all, without your help for the first one I would have had no idea of its true value.'

'We can settle that up later,' Steve replied as he sipped his drink. 'I'm pleased it all went so well and you took our advice about spacing out the sales. An auction every six months or so would be perfect timing to promote interest and get the best price possible. You'll also have a steady income to cover the initial expenses for starting up the vineyard if you did decide to go that route.'

I remembered the time and noticed it was nearly three. I was still in my dressing gown, with the valuer due any minute. Explaining about the mortgage valuation I asked Steve to hold the fort while I dashed upstairs to get changed. Sure enough, I was only half dressed when I heard the front door bell ring. I caught the sound of the front door being opened and then two male voices as Steve let him in. Throwing on the rest of my clothes, I dashed downstairs to find the lounge empty. It was such a large house it took me several minutes to catch up with them. It seemed Steve had started showing the valuer round, beginning in the grounds and pool area, then leading him through the spa room, downstairs kitchen and cellar, and up to the main kitchen, which was where I eventually found them.

'Hello, I'm Gina Kingston,' I said, holding out my hand to the valuer. 'I apologise for not being ready when you arrived.'

'My name's Blake. Not a problem, Mrs Kingston. Your husband has been very informative and helpful.'

Both Steve and I started explaining at the same time, but Mr Blake suggested we move on to the rest of the house as he had another appointment. Steve said he'd catch me later, and before I had time to protest, he winked then blew me a kiss as he reached his car. I continued the guided tour, showing Mr Blake the main downstairs reception rooms followed by the bedrooms and bathrooms upstairs. When we finished, I offered him coffee but he insisted he should get off.

'Well, Mrs…er…Kingston,' he said, glancing at his papers, 'I must admit this is one of the most beautiful houses it has been my pleasure to value. You must both be very proud of having such a delightful home. Needless to say, it is more than adequate to cover the small mortgage you requested. I understand you have spent a considerable amount on the renovations, and I must compliment you on the sympathetic way they have been done. Being a local boy myself I knew this estate of old. I can tell you I shared the apprehension of the villagers that it might be converted into a modern monstrosity. Instead you have brought it up to date without losing any of its original charm.

'My thanks and congratulations, my dear. You should receive a copy of my report within a few days, but rest assured, there won't be any problem with your mortgage application. Providing you don't forget me when it comes to giving out your invitations to the house-warming,' he added, smiling to show he was not serious.

His parting comment reminded me I had discussed with Paul the idea of holding a reception for all the villagers. Even though he wouldn't be around, there was no reason I shouldn't go ahead. I began by making a list of who I should invite and what needed to be done. If it was held mid-May, it would hopefully give me time to complete the swimming pool area, and by then the weather should be reasonable for a barbeque. That would leave four weeks to prepare the next auction for mid-June, with perhaps a follow-up before Christmas. All these plans in place confirmed I had accepted this was now my home, and no way would I be selling up or planning to move. It had been a very full couple of days so I decided to catch up with some sleep while I had the opportunity, and by ten I was in bed.

I woke in the early hours disturbed by a strange noise. Throwing on my dressing gown, I went downstairs. As I descended the cellar stairs, I found myself looking at the back of a tall man wearing a style of clothes from a hundred years ago. There were no lights on but the whole of the cellar seemed to be bathed in an eerie red glow, and the figure gave a maniacal laugh before turning to face me.

'Welcome my dear,' he smirked and I found myself looking into Paul's face, except this man was about twenty-five years older than Paul, and part of his face had been burnt away. He was carrying a shackle and moved towards me with a horrible leer.

'First a kiss, my sweet,' he said, 'and then we can have some fun.'

I screamed at the top of my voice as I felt his tongue touch my cheek, and then woke to find Woof licking my face. I was still safe in bed. It had only been a nightmare but had felt so real. Why had I imagined Paul's face on the madman when Paul himself had been so reasonable? Why had he appeared in old fashioned dress and looked so much older than his actual years?

Perhaps I had been hearing too many of the stories about the old Lord of the estate and it had all become mixed up in my dream after the stress of finding the intruder. As usual, Woof seemed attuned to my worries and had come to gently wake me up, right at the crucial moment. Eventually I slept again, but woke the next morning feeling lethargic. Knowing that the dog needed to go out I went downstairs to open the door for him. As he came back, I heard a man's voice talking to him, followed by a knock on the half-open kitchen door.

'Morning,' said Terry as he came in. 'Hope I didn't disturb you too early, but I saw this young man running around so guessed you must be up.'

'Morning, Terry,' I said. 'Do you fancy a tea or coffee? I was just making some.'

'Have you ever known me to refuse a cup of tea?' he smiled as I put the kettle on. 'I thought you might be eager to start the other works, so I brought your estimates. As I said, we could do the foundations for the pool renovations at the same time as we work on the lower cellar.'

With that he handed me his quotes which I glanced through. They seemed very reasonable and, as he had promised, the combined total for both jobs showed a discount from the two individually.

'I'm not trying to push you,' he said, 'but a big job I was meant to be doing this week has been put back, and I could start straight away, if you like.'

'Well, as you know, I do want both jobs doing, but I'm in the middle of sorting out the finances. It should be finalised in a couple of weeks, but at the moment I can't afford to pay for the pool as well as the sub cellar. The cash I'd put aside for the pool will have to go on the cellar. I need to know it's safe, and have the lights and so on finished first.'

'That's not a problem, my lovely,' Terry replied. 'If you can come up with a third of the total say, by Easter, that will give me enough to get all the supplies in and pay the boys. Then the rest we can spread out over a couple of months. You've been very fair with us and I know I can trust you not to let me down.'

'That's brilliant, Terry,' I said. 'It shouldn't take that long but I appreciate your offer. I'll settle up as soon as I can.'

'That's sorted then. I'll give the chippy a ring and we can start this morning if you want.'

'You don't hang around, do you?' I laughed. 'I need to go out lunchtime but you know where the kettle is, so I'll leave you to it.'

I put some washing in the machine then went upstairs to clear up my bedroom and decide what I was going to wear to meet Paul. Shortly afterwards I heard the front door bell ring, but before I could go down to answer it I heard Terry call out, 'I'll get it, Gina. It's only my boys.'

'Okay, Terry. Thanks,' I called then turned back to perusing my wardrobe.

I wanted something alluring, but as I would be walking across the fields to the pub, girlie shoes were out. In the end I settled for my favourite tailored black trousers, black boots, a blue V-necked top which showed a bit of cleavage and my black leather jacket. Adding hooped gypsy earrings and a dab of perfume I decided I looked smart, yet casual enough for a lunch time meeting. The overall effect was slightly spoilt as I had to take a large shopping bag to carry the six bottles of wine I had decided to give Paul as a farewell present. When I went downstairs shortly before twelve the boys were emerging from the cellar to put the kettle on. I felt my face go red as Terry let out a prolonged wolf whistle.

'If only I was twenty years younger,' he said which made me smile at the compliment. 'He's a lucky fella, whoever he is. Have a good time and don't worry about us. If you're not back when we leave, I'll make sure to lock up. By the way, Woof will be fine if you want to leave him. We can let him out for a run before we go.'

'Thanks, Terry,' I said. 'I was wondering whether to take him or not. I won't be all that long so I'll probably be back before you go, but if not, I'll see you tomorrow.'

After saying goodbye to Woof, I set off for my assignation, not sure whether I was sad or relieved it would soon be all over. It might possibly be the last time I would see Paul, and I was in two minds how I felt. I arrived at the pub early and saw Gloria hovering by the door, as if she had been waiting for me. She glanced at the bag I was carrying and with a sneer on her face said, 'That's not enough to bribe him, if that's what you're thinking. The estate belongs to him. It's his inheritance from his forefathers, and once you realise that, he and I can share it together the way it was always meant to be.'

Rather than rise to her taunting I took a deep breath and pushed past her.

'Yeah, whatever, Gloria. You're welcome to my cast-offs. I've finished with him. Help yourself.'

I felt a little ashamed of myself, even if she deserved it with her snide remarks. I hadn't noticed Anna the barmaid, who must have come out of the ladies and overheard every word, until I registered a quiet clapping.

'That's my girl,' she said with a smile, then chatted about the weather as we went into the pub lounge. Paul was already there, sitting in a corner alcove waiting for me.

'Hello,' he said. 'I'm so pleased you came. I've got a drink for you but haven't ordered anything to eat yet. What would you like?'

I spent a few minutes glancing through the menu although I already knew it more or less by heart. As I started telling Paul what I had decided, I noticed Gloria heading towards our table, obviously intent on causing trouble. Following my gaze, Paul saw her and his face became thunderous.

'I'll go and place our order,' he said, taking the menu, even though I hadn't told him what I wanted. He grabbed Gloria's arm as he passed her, and more or less dragged her with him. It was too far away to hear what he was saying, but his body language and the expression on his face told the story. He looked angrier than I have ever seen him and although she tried to argue, in the end she turned on her heels and slammed out the door. For a moment he stood there, as if trying to compose himself. Then he approached the bar where Anna was waiting to serve him. For a moment he looked confused, then came back to our table with two more drinks, even though I had scarcely touched the first one. Anna appeared behind him and winked at me.

'Men, they'd forget their heads if they weren't on top of their necks. What was it you wanted, Gina, love?'

After she had taken our order Paul and I sat in silence for a while until he said, 'I'm really sorry about that. Anyway, how are you? How are things going with the house? Have they started on the pool yet?'

I realised he didn't mean not asking what I wanted to eat and intended to change the subject. As he didn't mention Gloria I decided I wouldn't either. After all, this could be the last time I saw him. I thought of telling him about discovering the sub cellar and the intruder when I realised he probably already knew all about it from Gloria.

'Terry's there now, looking at what needs to be done. I'm hoping to have everything ready by May for a barbeque,' I said instead. 'Oh, by the way,' I added, handing him the bag, 'I thought you might like these. Oh, hell. I never thought. Will you be able to take them on the flight?'

'Don't worry about that,' he replied. 'I'm having the rest of my belongings shipped over. I think I'll take one bottle with me though, to think of you and celebrate when my house purchase goes through. Thanks so much, Gina. I really appreciate this.'

With that he leaned over and gave me a kiss. Not the sort of lover's kiss we used to share but one more intense than you would give a friend or relative. I felt very emotional, not because we were parting, but from my memories of all the good times we had shared together.

'How are things going with your own property purchase?' I asked, before I became tearful. Soon we were discussing his new life, his work and all the things we used to talk about when we were together. By the time we had started on the second bottle of wine with our meal I had even plucked up courage to ask him about the lady he had mentioned.

'I think you'd like her,' he said, 'and I know she would admire you. She's not a great one for party life and doesn't possess your drive to be successful. In a way, she's quite old-fashioned, but is looking forward to being a housewife and mother.' At the last bit, he glanced at me, but when I smiled he visibly relaxed.

'It's funny, we never made serious plans about having children, did we?' I replied. 'We talked about buying somewhere to live, where we would have the wedding reception and the honeymoon, but we never really went any further than that. It's as if we both knew how things would turn out. I think you will make a wonderful father and I wish you all the luck in the world.'

'You've been brilliant, Gina. I didn't really deserve someone as good as you. If ever you come to my new home, you know you'll be more than welcome as my oldest and closest friend, even if you have a boyfriend or husband in tow. I hope you'll be happy and keep in touch. Maybe we can Skype sometimes so you can let me know how things are going?'

He gave me a card with his overseas mobile number, address and other details, then gave me a wry smile when he noticed me looking at my watch.

'It's gone six. I'd better get a move on or I'll miss my plane. Be happy.' With another kiss he was gone.

I realised it was finally over with Paul. I was a free woman again, on my own with no-one to tell me what I should or shouldn't do. That was the good part. The bad part was there was no one to share my triumphs or cheer me up when I was feeling down. Except Woof. With a start I realised I had left him alone for far too long. Jumping up as Anna came over to the table to ask if everything was okay, I told her I was fine and offered to pay the bill but Paul had already settled it. Calling goodbye, I ran all the way home. Even though it was so late, I saw lights on and realised Terry had been waiting for me.

'I'm sorry I was so long,' I puffed. 'Thanks so much for waiting. Has Woof been behaving?'

'Good as gold,' Terry replied. 'Danny took him for a quick walk this afternoon but we haven't fed him yet. We were going to give it another ten minutes and then pack up. We'll be back in the morning, about nine if that's okay?'

'That's fine. How did you get on today?'

'It's probably better if I show you in the morning. The surround for the pool looks a bit of a builder's site at the moment, but actually it's gone very well. We've dug up the foundations and taken out the old broken tiling. The base should set overnight so we can get on tomorrow. I thought you might be worried about security with the sub cellar. We've made that safe. All the holes have been blocked up and we've made a start on the plastering. The sparks will be in tomorrow to wire it up, then the chippy can start on the new storage racks.'

When they'd gone, I venturing down to the cellar with Woof at my heels and even plucked up enough courage to shine a torch into the sub cellar.

Although it was still gloomy, it showed where Terry and his crew had started making it habitable. I didn't trust myself to examine it more closely. That could wait until the following day, so I returned upstairs and opened my laptop to catch up with my messages. There were several from friends and family who I had been neglecting of late, but then I saw a text from Paul, sent a few minutes previously.

'I'm at the airport, but wanted to say how good it was to see you and be able to part on good terms. Thanks again for the generous gift. Love, from your friend, always and ever in my heart.' This was followed by a long line of kisses.

To take my mind off things I worked for a while on my usual lists. I made plans for the barbeque party, the organisation of further wine sales and produced cash flow, income and likely expenditure figures for the coming months.

Chapter 29. Looking to the future.

Despite unpleasant dreams I had a sense of well-being, as if I had regained control, even if Monday would mean work, and eating on the run. When Terry arrived with his crew, I accompanied them to the sub-basement to see the progress, and confirm what needed to be done. Once I was there, it didn't feel as spooky as I had expected. The workmen had removed all signs of the chains and shackles from the walls and started plastering. It looked like a basement in course of renovation. Terry referred to the notes he had made from his discussions with Steve and listened to my ideas about colour schemes and racking designs. Knowing his long experience in the trade, I was happy to take his advice.

He always treated me with respect and never ridiculed my ideas but took time to explain why he thought something would work better a different way, or suggest an alternative layout. After an hour or so we had everything agreed, and I left them to it while I went to make the ubiquitous cups of tea. They worked on steadily until Terry popped his head round the door.

'We're off for a quick lunch break. Shall we meet up by the pool in about fifteen minutes to talk about what you want done there?'

I made myself a sandwich then, with Woof at my heels, wandered into the grounds to meet up with Terry. We walked around the area discussing the options as we had in the sub cellar.

'I was wondering, Terry. It would be nice to make a "secret garden" of the pool area with hedges all round to provide privacy. What do you think?'

'Good idea, but you'd need advice about which plants to use. I could recommend someone who runs a garden centre a few miles outside the village.'

'That would be great. I'm back to work next week, but I could go tomorrow. Are they open on Saturdays?'

'Sure. I'll give him a ring and tell him to expect you.'

As usual, Terry was proving invaluable, both with his experience and his contacts. The sun had gone behind the clouds, and as we walked back to the house, the heavens opened. We sprinted for the outhouses and made it without getting totally drenched.

'Right, I'd better get back to work or I'll have the boss lady on my case,' Terry teased.

As we had gone in the back way, I took the opportunity to look at the work in the sub cellar and although it was far from complete, I received an impression of what the end result would look like. *This is going to be great,* I thought as I went back upstairs. What was not so great was spending the rest of the afternoon cleaning, hoovering and getting the washing and ironing up to date before work on Monday. Around six Terry came to find me.

'We'll be packing up shortly, Gina, but we'll be back for a few hours in the morning. I thought you might find this useful when you go to the garden centre.'

He handed me a plan of the area surrounding the pool, complete with measurements. He was definitely worth every penny I was paying him and I resolved to settle his bill as quickly as humanly possible once I had the mortgage money.

As I put the fresh laundry in the airing cupboard, I realised it included Steve's clothes from when he had got soaked a few days previously. With the confusion of the valuer's visit yesterday, he had forgotten to take them. As if handling his garments had sent a silent message the phone rang.

'Hello. Mr Kingston here,' a cheerful voice joked.

'Sorry about that misunderstanding, Steve,' I said. 'Actually, I was just thinking about you.'

His voice dropped a level as he replied, 'Were you really? I've been thinking a lot about you too.'

I felt my cheeks colour as I explained about his clothes. 'When would you like to collect them?'

'I'm busy tonight,' he replied. 'What if I pop round about eleven tomorrow morning?'

I started to explain about the garden centre and before I knew it, had asked him if he wanted to come too.

'I'd love to. Pick you up about ten thirty?'

I spent the rest of the evening in a tizz, and tried unsuccessfully to concentrate on a film, before giving up and having an early night. My dreams that night were restless and confused. I imagined jumping into the pool and discovering I was fully dressed and wearing men's clothes. The whole area was surrounded not by hedges, but by row upon row of wine bottles. I woke with a start as the sun was coming up but drifted off to sleep again. The next thing I knew it was gone nine.

Terry and his gang arrived shortly afterwards, but dispersed straight to the cellar and the garden. Whether through excitement or hunger, my stomach was churning, so I settled for toast and coffee before picking up my bag and the pool area plan Terry had given me. It was gone ten when I glanced in the mirror and realised I looked a wreck. I dashed upstairs, changed into new jeans, put on make-up and added a dash of perfume.

I heard Woof barking and Steve's cheerful voice calling out to him, as I ran down to open the door. Woof greeted Steve enthusiastically and I felt embarrassed as he jumped all over him. Ruffling his fur and laughing, he gently pushed him away as I stuttered out an apology.

'Wow. How can you look so gorgeous so early in the morning?' he said as he came in.

'Let's just say, "With a little help from my friends,"' I replied. 'No, Woof, not this time. You be a good boy. We won't be long.'

'We could take him,' Steve said. 'There's plenty of room in the Landrover if he's okay in a car. What do you think, Woof? Do you want to come and give us your expert opinion on the best trees?'

Woof barked once then stood by his lead, as usual giving the impression he understood every word.

'Okay,' I said. 'What chance do I have against two domineering males?'

With Woof at my heels, even though I was laughing, I was concerned if the dog would behave in the car, as I had never taken him in one. I needn't have worried. As soon as Steve opened the door he jumped in the back and settled on the seat as if it was his usual mode of transport. Even though still quite chilly it was a beautiful day, and I relaxed as Steve drove us through the countryside. He didn't need the SatNav, as he was apparently a regular visitor at the garden centre. He told me about his family and their connection with the original estate. It seemed everyone who lived in the area had an association in one way or another. The more he spoke about his ancestors the clearer the picture became in my mind of them being on the opposite side of the fence to Paul's relations. For some reason I had begun to associate Paul as a descendent of the cruel despot, and Steve as being from the local country folk who had lived under the tyrant.

In some ways it was a relief when we arrived, and my mind turned to less fanciful matters. Steve was obviously well known to the receptionist, who gave me the once over while she flirted with him. Despite her obvious interest in my companion, when I mentioned my name she welcomed me warmly, and disappeared round the back to call the owner. True to his word, Terry had given him a breakdown of what I needed and I was treated like a valued customer. I wasn't totally surprised when Gordon, the owner, also greeted Steve as an old friend. This was networking at its best, and I felt grateful to have been accepted into such a loyal community.

Gordon studied the plans and dimensions Terry had provided as he took us on a guided tour, with particular emphasis on suitable fast-growing shrubs for the area surrounding the pool. Woof was accepted as part of our design committee, and even though I kept him on his lead, I had the feeling there would be no problem if I allowed him to wander freely. He behaved perfectly, sniffing with approval at some of the offerings and turning his nose up in disdain at others. It was amazing that having listened to Gordon's expert advice and considering Woof's, Steve's and my own preferences, the final choice suited us all. We sorted the logistics of numbers required and arranged delivery for the following Saturday.

'I have an appointment to sign some documents at eleven, but it shouldn't take too long,' I told him.

'No problem,' Gordon replied. 'About four?'

'Perfect. Thanks.'

'I can come over and help with the unloading,' Steve added.

I readily agreed as it seemed an ideal opportunity to see him again without making my interest too obvious. Once priorities were settled, I couldn't resist a further browse and ended up adding a range of cacti, rose bushes and other potted plants to complete my dreams of transforming the garden. On our way out, we passed the herb section. I had always loved the idea of having fresh herbs for cooking and had to go back to add some for the small garden I intended to plant next to the conservatory. Despite my indulgence, the total bill came to less than I had expected. The miserly side of me was worried about the extravagance, but this was money well spent, and my happy mood was contagious.

Smiling at my delighted face, Steve remarked 'If all it takes is a few plants to make you so happy, I'd better buy a garden centre.' Woof chose that moment to let out a bark of agreement. Laughing, he added 'Okay, I'll buy a pet food shop too.'

Woof gave another short bark then settled back on the seat as if he was satisfied his needs would also be considered. As we neared home Steve must have read my mind as, glancing at his watch, he suggested, 'Lunchtime. Why don't we pull into the pub for a bite to eat?'

With my stomach rumbling, and knowing Woof would be welcome I readily agreed. As Steve parked the car Woof disappeared into the bushes, then without waiting for us made his way into the pub to find his friend, Anna. She greeted him warmly and waved at me. Noticing Steve, she cast him an appraising look, then gave me a huge wink before coming over to take our order. I felt obliged to introduce them, explaining that Steve was the wine expert who was giving me advice about resurrecting the vineyard.

'Pleased to meet you, Steve,' she said as she shook his hand. 'I've seen you around but we haven't been formally introduced. I hope you're taking good care of this lovely lady.'

I felt myself flush but Steve responded lightly, 'I'd better, or Woof will have my guts for garters!'

After organising our drinks, we perused the menu before Steve went to place our food order. I saw Anna chatting to him and glancing in my direction, although they were too far away for me to hear what they were saying. When he came back he asked me if I had thought any more about the vineyard. I had the feeling he was deliberately leading me away from commenting on what he had been discussing with Anna. Knowing there would be no point in pushing, I told him I was interested in pursuing the idea but had no clue where to start.

Chapter 30. Nothing ventured.

Before I knew it, we were deep in discussion about the logistics of setting up such a venture. Even when our food arrived we carried on talking about the initial financial outlay, staffing requirements and all the other factors necessary to make it a going concern. Steve was so enthusiastic he made it seem like a foregone conclusion. Although I knew it would involve a lot of work and hassle, I did want to give it a try once my finances were organised. He thought there could well be grants available to assist with initial set-up costs, and promised to investigate.

'It would be worth looking at setting up a charitable trust,' he suggested. 'The ancient heritage aspect of the estate could well make it viable.'

'That reminds me,' I responded. 'I've got an appointment with Bernard my solicitor next Saturday. I could sound him out.'

It turned out Steve knew Bernard well. He suggested that with my permission he would make an appointment for his advice on the legal aspects.

'It's daft to make two appointments. How do you feel about joining me once I've finished signing the mortgage documents, then we could all discuss it together?'

We had become so carried away with the project I hadn't thought how much influence Steve was having in my life. He pulled me back to reality by reminding me it was my decision, and although he was happy to help in any way possible, we were in fact almost strangers. It made me stop and think. After all, what did I actually know about this guy? So far, he had played more than fair over the wine valuation, but the initial introduction had indirectly come via Paul. I had always been one to trust my instincts and the very fact he had brought it up helped to reassure me. I told him I was happy to have a three-way conference, and he promised to contact Bernard to make sure an extended meeting would not disrupt his schedule. With that out of the way we returned to discussing practicalities.

'It'd be a good idea to put thoughts on paper in the form of a draft business plan,' Steve said. As that would entail us spending time together to work things out, with a great effort, I managed to keep the huge grin off my face, and we arranged for him to come over on Wednesday after I finished work to start things off.

When Woof nudged me, I realised it was gone five and I really should be heading home.

'Of course, I don't want to delay you,' Steve said as he signalled to Anna for the bill.

'You are one lucky lady,' Anna teased as she patted Woof. 'Not only have you got this gorgeous beast, but the other one isn't bad either.' I had to laugh as Woof gave her a lick goodbye, but as I turned to look at Steve I realised she was right.

'Thanks for the meal and looking after us,' I said, then gave her a wink.

When Steve dropped me home I invited him in for a coffee but he refused, so I wandered round to the pool to see what progress Terry and his gang had made. There was obviously still a lot to do, but I could see the beginnings of what would be a beautiful area, and felt a sense of satisfaction, knowing the plants would complement it perfectly. I even ventured into the cellar, not intending to go any further, but I noticed the new light switch at the top of the stairs by the sub cellar and turned it on and peered downwards. With the benefit of electric light, it looked a lot less spooky and more like part of the house. Although I didn't go all the way down, I could see the outline for the new wine cellar was already taking shape. All in all, it had been a satisfying day, and things were progressing nicely.

I still couldn't make up my mind about Steve. One minute he seemed like a suitor, the next a business colleague. Only time would tell. Returning to the kitchen, I fed Woof, who despite his big lunch of leftovers was still looking at me expectantly. Sunday morning I put on some comfortable old clothes with the intention of doing some housework, but before getting stuck in, opened my laptop and spent a few minutes jotting down some notions for the vineyard. I didn't have much idea about the actual business, but wanted to have suggestions ready to combine with Steve's business plan on Wednesday. It seemed a long time to wait and I pondered on the vagaries of time. How was it that the hours were flying past and yet somehow the days were crawling? As if to prove my point, I glanced at the clock and saw it was already nearly eleven.

Stopping for a break from spring cleaning, I made lunch then took Woof for an extended run, before indulging in a long, pampering bath and putting on a dressing gown, ready to work on my laptop while half watching an old weepy film. Monday loomed and I needed to get my mind back into working mode to cope with the week ahead.

The following morning the postman handed me a large bulky envelope which I thrust into my bag to read on the train to work. As expected it was the valuer's report on the house. I was astounded to see the final figure valuation which was already half as much again as what I had originally paid for the property. His covering letter advised me both the mortgage company and my solicitor had been sent a copy, and that I needed to sign the final papers on the following Saturday. I must have looked odd to the other travellers as I had a big smile on my face, despite it being a typical Monday morning, with a light drizzle and the usual problems of commuting.

Work was the normal hassle and I was late leaving; it was gone seven when I arrived home. Terry had left me a note saying things had gone well, and he had even fed Woof before he left. What a diamond. I was tempted to see what they had managed that day, but it was dark, and I was tired, hungry and didn't have the energy. I put a ready meal in the oven then settled down with a coffee to work on my business plan. After I had eaten, I returned to my laptop but felt brain-dead and couldn't concentrate. Eventually I gave up trying to think, locked up and took myself off to bed to read, but the effects of the hectic day kicked in and I was soon fast asleep. I found myself wide awake at three, and wondered what had disturbed me, but all was silent, and the next thing I knew was the ringing of the alarm clock telling me it was time to get up to face another day at work.

Tuesday was a repeat of Monday and again it was gone seven before I arrived home. I felt guilty when I found another note from Terry confirming he had fed Woof. It was dark and raining so I postponed my idea of visiting the cellar and pool area but determined to be home early the following day. I tried to convince myself it was so I could catch Terry and thank him personally, but the fact Steve was coming round was also a consideration. Finding myself smiling reminded me of the practicalities of his visit. He'd said he would be round about seven, but would he have already eaten or be expecting me to cook? As if he had read my mind an e-mail popped up on my computer.

'Hi. Are we still on for tomorrow? Is seven OK? Do you like Thai food? Shall I bring a take-away so we can eat while we work? Steve. x.'

I replied immediately, my stomach fluttering, but trying to convince myself it was because I was hungry. Once I'd eaten, I knuckled down to work on my ideas for the vineyard. All went well at work the next day and I couldn't wait to get home, to see how much Terry had achieved, and then to have the pleasure of Steve's company for the evening. Sod's law. At five to five I was surreptitiously packing up when my direct line rang. My boss was attending an important conference in Germany, and urgently needed some figures for his meeting. I tried to explain I had an important meeting myself and was just leaving, but he was in full work mode and not listening.

'It shouldn't take long,' he said airily. 'The last three years will do, oh, and a projection for this year would be helpful. I'll need the individual figures for the three companies and a combined summary. Set up a spreadsheet and e-mail it to me. Thanks. I'll let you know how it goes. Bye.'

Why had I answered the phone? I was committed now. I started putting the figures together then found the current files only went back two years. That meant digging out the archives. Then the scanner went on go-slow and the printer ran out of paper. Someone had used the last packet of the reserve supply and not bothered to replace it. Tearing to the stationery cupboard, I grabbed a couple of reams, loaded the paper, then had to count to one hundred when the damn machine decided it needed new cartridges before it would print. It was already six by the time I sent the information, closed down and dashed like a lunatic to catch the next train, only to watch it pull out as I charged onto the platform. That meant a twenty minute wait, kicking my heels until the next one. Diving through my bag, I found Steve's mobile number to tell him I had been delayed, only to discover my battery was dead.

My blood pressure at an all-time high, I decided there was nothing I could do except relax and think rationally. I was on my way to a telephone box to make a phone call the old-fashioned way, when I heard an announcement over the tannoy. The train I had seen depart was the five-fifty which had been delayed, and the train now pulling into platform three was my intended train; except it was leaving from platform twelve. Another sprint worthy of a gold-medal winning athlete and I threw myself onto the train before it could pull out. At least I managed to get a seat but I was hot, tired and a total wreck. Not exactly the cool femme fatale I had intended to be when I greeted Steve.

As I opened my front door, I could hear Woof barking as if reprimanding me for being late.

'Okay, okay, I'm coming,' I yelled then jumped as I entered the front room and a shape emerged from the settee.

'Sorry,' Steve said, 'I didn't mean to startle you. I arrived about ten minutes ago as Terry was leaving, and he thought you wouldn't mind if he let me in to wait for you.'

'No, that's fine. I'm sorry I'm so late. It's been one of those days. Let me feed Woof and let him out then I'll be right with you.'

'I have a better idea. How about if you show me where everything is, and I sort him out while you freshen up? You look all in.'

I wasn't sure whether to be grateful or insulted but showed him where I kept the dog food and, calling to him to help himself to a drink, dashed up for a quick shower and change of clothes. The warm water helped me relax and I luxuriated under the spray which washed away some of the stress of the day. When I had finished I threw on some comfortable but smart harem trousers and a favourite top. Gypsy earrings, a dab of perfume and light make-up, and I felt ready to face the world again. Guilty at taking over thirty minutes and neglecting my guest, I went down to discover Steve in the kitchen, wiping the worktop. Woof looked up from where he was finishing his dinner as if to say, *See, who needs you?* I could feel the heat from the oven and the tantalising smell made me realise I was hungry.

'Dinner is served, Modom,' Steve said with a smile, 'and may I say how beautiful you look tonight?'

'Why thank you, Jeeves,' I joked to hide my embarrassment as I went into the living room to sort out the table. It was already laid, complete with cutlery, napkins, corkscrew and wine bucket. Steve followed me, carrying two plates of delicious-looking food, with a bottle tucked under his arm.

'This is not up to the standard of your cellar,' he explained as he expertly opened the bottle, 'but I think you might like it.'

He sat down opposite me and I tucked into the food while he topped up my glass. It was delicious and we soon settled into a comfortable companionship while we ate. Soft music provided a perfect background. I felt more human by the time I was fed and watered, and totally relaxed. However, we had work to do, so after clearing up we sat together on the couch to go through our ideas for the vineyard. There was silence for a while as we each read through the other's presentations. It was obvious Steve must have put a great deal of time and effort into his plan. It was very comprehensive and made my scribbled notes look amateurish.

His was set out under various headings with projected costs and difficulties to be overcome. At the end he had even listed a prospective time scale, cashflow forecast, organisational chart and list of things needing further investigation. When we had finished reading, I looked up at him and complimented him on what he had done.

'It makes my efforts look childish,' I said.

'Not at all. Mine was strictly factual. Yours shows all the passion and enthusiasm for the project. You've made some good points I hadn't considered. With a combination of the two we'll have an excellent plan.'

I reddened at his praise but it broke the ice for an open discussion. We argued, agreed, discussed and compromised until eventually we came up with a document with which we were both totally happy. I sat back and glanced at the clock. Surely it couldn't be one o'clock?

He followed my gaze and said with a smile, 'I've outstayed my welcome. Sorry to be so selfish. You have work in the morning. I'll e-mail you a copy tomorrow so we'll be on the same wavelength for

Saturday. By the way, I forgot to mention, Bernard said it would only take twenty minutes or so to go through the mortgage documents, so he suggested I get to his offices around eleven-thirty for our discussion. Okay?'

I had been so wrapped up in the plans for the vineyard I had almost forgotten I was due to see Bernard to sign the legal papers, which would provide the funds to finally cut my ties with Paul.

'Sure,' I said. 'I'll meet you there. Would you like a nightcap before you go?' I bit my tongue as I realised it sounded as if I couldn't wait to be rid of him, which was not my intention at all.

'Another time. I'd better leave you to get your beauty sleep. See you Saturday.' With a quick kiss on the cheek, he left.

Despite the late hour I couldn't sleep, my mind buzzing with the project which had at first felt like a dream but was now becoming a reality. The vineyard was intertwined with thoughts of Steve and whether he saw me as a business partner or something more. Amazing to think only a few short weeks ago Paul was the love of my life, but now he was gone forever, or at least he would be after Saturday.

After a restful night, I dashed off to catch my train, knowing Terry would be arriving shortly to carry on with the final works to the sub-basement which was to be the foundation of my enterprise. It was as if I was living two lives; the humdrum nine to five and the fantasy dream of the country estate vineyard.

True to his word, Steve e-mailed me a copy of the revised business plan. I read it through that evening, then started researching some of the matters we had queried, including the average wages paid for workers in the industry, and Health & Safety and employment laws. Friday finally arrived; a reasonable day at work, then home to relax and prepare for the weekend. It was to be a busy one, almost a turning point in my life. That was quite a frightening concept, so a toast seemed in order. Summoning up my courage, I called Woof for moral support and descended to the cellar to select a bottle of wine. I hadn't been down there since Terry and the boys had started working on the sub-basement.

I felt comfortable in the cellar and spent time browsing through the racks, and for the first time realised what an extensive collection it was. Making sure I picked up two of the less expensive bottles, I left them at the bottom of the stairs ready to carry up, then, taking a deep breath, descended the next set of steps into the new sub-basement. I wasn't as confident down there, but the electric lights, the renovations and the nearly-completed racks made it seem almost homely. It would work well for storage, leaving the upper basement free. It occurred to me if we were serious about restarting the vineyard, we would need somewhere for the equipment, and a production area. Collecting my bottles of wine, I returned upstairs and began investigating what would be necessary, to try and get an idea of the costs involved.

Although I had thought about the need for bottling equipment and barrels or casks, there were a myriad of other things I had never even considered. Generators, trailers, ramps, pallets, jacks, cleaners, bungs, dipsticks and measuring instruments needed to be added to the list. There was also the practicality of how we would get the finished product up to ground level. I needed to speak to Terry to see what could be done about installing a hoist or lift mechanism, annoyed I hadn't thought of it before he'd finished redecorating. There again, it was only now I was seriously considering the idea of making my own vineyard an eventuality.

I polished off half of one of the bottles of wine while I was eating, cleared up and decided on a reasonably early night. The next day would be a long one.

Chapter 31. Progress.

Despite having so much on my mind I woke early, feeling refreshed. To my surprise Terry and his boys turned up shortly before nine although I hadn't been expecting them.

'I hope it's not inconvenient,' Terry said 'but I wanted a chance to show you how things are going.'

'That's fine,' I said. 'I've actually got an appointment later this morning but I've things to discuss with you too.' As I accompanied him downstairs, I told him briefly about going to the sub-cellar, my decision to try to set up the vineyard, and the need for a hoist mechanism.

He had a smile on his face as he showed me round, pointing out how much they had achieved, saying, 'By next weekend we should have everything completed.'

As they were so close to finishing, I felt bad when I reminded him about the extra work, and asked him when he could give me an idea of what it would cost.

'I can do better than that my beauty,' he replied, 'I can tell you now.' I felt a bit bemused as he led me round to the rear of the sub cellar then, with a big grin, informed me the price would be, 'A packet of biscuits to go with our tea.'

Apologising for teasing me, he opened a new, wide full-length door to reveal, hidden behind it, an enormous dumb waiter. 'We discovered this when we were removing the old woodwork,' he said. 'I'm sure the sub-basement must have been the original production area for the old vineyard. This would have been how they transported the finished product up to the ground floor for the dray horses to collect. All it needed was a bit of cleaning up and a spot of greasing and it works as good as new.'

I was flabbergasted. What I had imagined as a major problem was already sorted. The new vineyard was destined to be. Brimming with excitement, I threw my arms around this angel of a workman and gave him a resounding smacker and a big hug.

'Well,' he said, turning slightly pink, 'with that sort of thank you I'll even forget about the biscuits.'

'Terry,' I said, 'you have no idea how much I appreciate everything you've done for me. I really can't thank you enough. You and your boys have not only done a brilliant job but so much more. You've taken care of Woof while I've been at work. There's not a single thing you've done that I've not been more than satisfied with, but most of all you've been a true friend.

'As a woman on my own with no experience of this type of work it would have been so easy for you to take advantage. Instead you've done everything and more than I could have ever asked of anyone. There's no way I can make up for what you've achieved.'

I could feel myself becoming emotional and Terry also seemed overcome.

'Gina, my dear,' he said giving me a hug back, 'if I might be so bold. You've always played more than fair with me and the boys; you've trusted me, let us get on with things without interfering, and I've come to look on you as a daughter. I think you might be surprised by how many people in the village are on your side.'

He stopped for a minute as if unsure whether to say any more.

'We don't take kindly to interlopers, but you've fitted in as if you were born here. Modernising a place like this could have alienated someone who came in as a "know it all" or looked down on the old-fashioned village ways. The fact you use the local shops, employ our tradesmen and even visit the pub regularly hasn't gone unnoticed. Everyone is behind your idea of resurrecting the vineyard. They know you'll be looking to the locals for their expertise, and they appreciate the fact you're trying to keep the old traditions going.'

He turned away and seemed lost in thought before continuing.

'Well, before I get too carried away, I'd better show you how the swimming pool area is coming on. I know Gordon is delivering from the garden centre this afternoon, and I can't have him saying my workmanship doesn't match up to his plants.'

I followed Terry upstairs and over his shoulder, he said, as if it was not something he felt confident in saying to my face, 'By the way, lass, we were all sorry to hear about that Paul taking off, but for what it's worth you've got a good-un in young Steve.'

My delight was obvious as we neared the pool space, and for the first time I saw the nearly completed project. The overgrown, disused area had been transformed into a welcoming and modern spa, but still retained the old-world charm. The once murky water was now clean and inviting, the surround decked and tiled, leading to the changing area, shower and hot-tub room. It suddenly struck me how much had been achieved in such a short space of time. Could it really have been only three short months ago that I had moved into a decrepit wreck of a house, waiting for

Paul to spend time with me for our first Christmas together in what was to be our new home?

Time was moving on and I had to prepare for my appointment with the solicitors. Thanking Terry again, I went to change. 'I should be back about one,' I told him, 'so I'll probably catch you before you finish.'

I drove into the village instead of walking and as I parked outside, couldn't help comparing the process to London, where it often took longer to find a parking space than to actually drive somewhere. This was where I belonged.

Chapter 32. Sorting the paperwork.

As I looked up and down the village high street, I realised how quickly this place had become my home. Not wanting to be late, I hurried in to be greeted by a smiling receptionist. I told her my name and she buzzed through to let Bernie know I had arrived, before offering me a coffee. No sooner had she gone off to make it, than Bernard appeared and genially ushered me into his office, a large but somehow homely room. The big, comfortable leather armchairs were more in keeping with a gentleman's club. Rather than sitting behind his enormous, carved antique desk, he took another armchair facing me.

'Lovely to see you again, my dear,' he said jovially and again I thought what a perfect Santa Claus he would make. Despite his appearance he was excellent at his job and explained every detail of the paperwork he had ready to sign. Although it was a big decision, I felt confident it was the right one. This loan would give me the funds to complete the break with Paul, as well as allowing breathing space before making the initial investment in the vineyard. I signed on the dotted line and also gave him authorisation to remit part of the monies directly to Paul's bank. The rest Bernard told me should be in my bank account on Monday, or Tuesday at the latest.

Once the legal part was over, Bernard asked about my plans for the vineyard. We had only been talking for a few minutes when there was a knock on the door and the receptionist showed Steve in. The two men shook hands and Steve surprised me by giving me a kiss on the cheek before settling down in the chair closest to me. Then he became all business. Although I was happy to listen while the experts talked, both of them took pains to make sure I wasn't left out of the conversation. Either Steve had already primed him or Bernard had done his homework, as he had a wealth of information available about grants and trusts. It was well over an hour later that Steve and I left with our minds full of hopes, dreams, information and ideas to follow up.

Steve and I? All of a sudden I realised it had become a joint venture, but strangely I didn't mind. When Paul and I had discussed plans I always felt that either he had not been interested or he was humouring the "little woman." With Steve, however much we might disagree, I felt we were a partnership with the same ultimate aim.

'How about if I pop into the bakers to get some fresh rolls then follow you home,' he suggested as I went to my car. 'We could carry on our discussions over lunch and I'll be there when they deliver the plants this afternoon.'

'Sounds good to me. See you in a bit.'

When I arrived home, Terry was just leaving. Thankful I had caught him, I wrote out a cheque towards what I owed him. Knowing the banks wouldn't be open until Monday I was confident that by the time he had paid in my cheque, the mortgage funds should be in my account. Bernard had also arranged to make the final transfer to Paul as soon as it was confirmed the funds were available. Although it was a great deal of cash, I was pleased things were going well and my financial obligations would soon be cleared.

I was making coffee when Steve arrived, and the wonderful aroma of fresh baking wafted in as I opened the door. Rolls, pasties and a couple of fresh fruit tarts for dessert were devoured in a very short time until all that was left were a few crumbs. We spent a couple of hours going through the information we had collected, in particular, the implications of setting up a trust. Bernard had explained it in some detail and had agreed to be my fellow trustee, and suggested it would be a good idea to have a third person on the board. Although my decision would be the one that counted, he felt an extra person would be useful in providing a broader range of ideas. To my mind the obvious person would be Steve, although I hadn't said anything to him, still conscious that I hardly knew him. After the way things had turned out with Paul, I was reticent about making a quick decision which could affect my life.

We were still deep in discussion when I heard a van pull up and realised with a start it was the delivery from the garden centre. Steve followed me out, and once I had directed the driver round to the pool area, helped him unload. Ten minutes later Gordon himself appeared and started preparing the ground ready to take the various plants. Steve pitched in with the hard work while I fetched and carried and gave directions. Terry's electrician had installed lighting in the grounds, which I switched on as dusk fell. It was only when I heard my stomach rumbling, I realised how late it was.

'Only a few more minutes and we should be finished,' Gordon said when I mentioned the time. 'One thing, Gina, would it be okay if I took some photos to show the final effect? They would be great publicity for the shop to show what can be done.'

'Of course, Gordon. It looks marvellous.'

Fifteen minutes later he had his shots and I had pressed him into taking payment for his time. At first he refused, saying it was for the good of the village, but eventually we compromised, although the amount he accepted was nowhere near its true worth. Luckily Woof had spent the afternoon wandering around the grounds so I didn't feel the need to take him out. Steve suggested ordering a take-away rather than me cooking, particularly as he was feeling rather grubby after all his hard work.

I persuaded him to have a dip in the hot tub while I phoned through our order and dug out some of Paul's clothes for him. Although it was only the end of March it was a fine and mild night. Terry had come up trumps with a gazebo, complete with heating, on the edge of the pool area. With the greenery in place and the twinkle of the stars competing with the man-made lighting, the thought of dining al fresco was irresistible. The vicinity of the downstairs kitchen also made it easy to set two places outside, and to try out the so-far unused glasses and crockery stored there.

I popped down to the cellar and picked up a couple of bottles of wine to chill in the pristine fridge. As an afterthought, I added a bottle of Champagne and set out candles in an antique candelabrum. When I heard the ring of the front door bell, I again blessed Terry for his forethought in connecting it up so it could be heard in the garden. I paid off the delivery man, then set the meal on the plates, just as Steve re-appeared, looking adorable with his hair still wet.

'Perfect timing,' I said as he joined me at the table. He poured the wine and we ate in silence for a while as we were both ravenous. It was not an uncomfortable silence and once most of the meal had disappeared we sat back and grinned at each other.

'I do love a woman who enjoys her food,' he said as I mopped up the last dregs on my plate.

'Are you accusing me of being a pig?' I retorted. 'I notice you didn't leave a lot for poor Woof either.'

'I love pigs,' was his unexpected reply. 'My father used to keep them, as well as chickens and ducks and a few cows, when I was a kid.'

'Have you lived here all your life?' I asked. 'I know you live locally and seem to know everyone in the village.'

'I was brought up here,' he replied. 'All my family came from hereabouts and my ancestors date back to working for the local lord of the manor, who originally owned this house. My grandfather used to tell me stories of the history of the area which fascinated me, even as a child. He was the one who first got me interested in wine, although sadly he's been gone for many years now. I learnt a lot from him and realised it was what I wanted as my career. After doing courses I joined a company as a very junior junior but gradually worked my way up.'

'Did you always work in the same place?'

'Once I'd gained more experience I travelled and lived all over the world. In this game you never stop learning, and although the company I originally worked for are no more, I'm still in contact with my old mentor. He's in his nineties and house-bound now, but I rely upon his opinion when I come across something new. I hope you don't mind, but I contacted him for advice when we were first talking about resurrecting the vineyard. Having been brought up locally, he was able to give me some invaluable information about the original workings of the estate, and he was delighted to hear you might be thinking of starting it up again.'

This was the most Steve had ever opened up about himself, and I let my mind drift on how lucky I had been, as an inexperienced novice, to come across such expertise. Everyone seemed to be on my side and wanted to help in whatever way they could to make my venture a success. Even though it was not yet Spring, there was something about sitting in the grounds of the estate, with my dog close by, and the house and surroundings restored to their former beauty, that made me feel as if I was experiencing how it would have been in the more peaceful days of the past. I didn't want to think about the horrors that had been uncovered, destroying the idyllic existence of those far off days, but they were as much a part of the history of the house as the bricks and mortar of its structure.

'From a practical point of view, Steve,' I said, 'do you really believe we can make the vineyard a reality? After all, I have no experience whatsoever, and although I appreciate what you've done, I can't rely on you for everything.'

'It's not only me, honey,' Steve replied, 'the whole village is behind you, and there are a lot of old-timers still around who would be only too happy to give you their advice. I think your biggest problem might be stopping them taking over.'

'Thanks for your support, Steve,' I said. 'There's something else I wanted to discuss with you too. Feel free to say no, but would you consider being the third trustee?'

Steve grinned. 'I'd be honoured, Gina.'

I shivered suddenly, more from the look Steve gave me than the cold, but he suggested we move back

239

indoors. Clearing up after our meal broke the strained atmosphere, and by the time we were settled in the lounge with coffee and brandies we were back to discussing business. I couldn't believe it when I noticed it was already two in the morning. Steve gave a wry grin.

'This is becoming a habit,' he smiled. 'Maybe I should leave a change of clothes here, but then I wouldn't have an excuse to call back tomorrow to return them. Unless, of course, you're busy tomorrow?'

'No, I've nothing on,' I said, blushing.

'I'll leave you to your beauty sleep then,' he replied. 'Not that you need it. How do you feel about meeting in the pub for lunch tomorrow, maybe about one?'

'Yes, that would be nice,' I replied, not sure whether I was disappointed at his leaving, or pleased I would be seeing him again in less than twelve hours. I showed him to the door and for a moment we stared at each other. Then he gave me a quick kiss and hurried off. I was confused; was he being a gentleman or was it merely business?

Chapter 33. New arrival.

Yawning, I locked up and went to bed. It had been such a long, life-changing day, but I found it difficult to sleep. Eventually I dozed off but woke, realising less than an hour had passed since Steve had left. I listened to the silence and strained to catch the sounds at the limits of my hearing. For a moment I thought I heard screaming, then the sound of a wolf howling. Only half awake I jumped out of bed, worried that something might be wrong with Woof. Flinging open my bedroom door, my heart leaped when a dark shape brushed past my leg. It was only my dog. I hugged him, but what had disturbed him?

His ears were back and his tail down as if he too could hear something. I had tried to convince myself the screaming was only the sound of foxes mating, but I knew dogs had more sensitive hearing than humans. To my surprise, Woof went to the cellar door and started whimpering. I was tempted to investigate, but realised that would be a stupid thing to do with only the dog for protection. As I stood there dithering and trying to pull Woof back, I heard a ping on my mobile. It was Steve saying thanks for a lovely evening and he was looking forward to seeing me the next day. Realising he must still be awake, I dialled his number and he answered on the first ring.

'I'm so sorry Gina,' were his first words, 'I hope I didn't wake you.'

'It's not that, Steve,' I babbled. 'I heard screaming. Woof wants to go down to the basement. I think there might be someone down there.'

'Don't touch the door. I'll be with you in ten minutes,' then the line went dead.

A few moments later I heard a screech of brakes, and recognised Steve's car. As soon as I opened the door he pulled me into his arms and asked if I was okay. By then I felt stupid for dragging him out so late at night and acting like an hysterical child. Even so, I was pleased he was there, especially as Woof wouldn't settle, but kept scratching at the basement door. Steve had brought in a heavy iron bar, which he had put on a table as he cuddled me.

Noticing me looking at it, he said 'It might be a bit OTT but better safe than sorry. I've got a torch but I want you to stand at the top of the stairs with another torch and your mobile in your hand. If you hear me shout, 'Go', slam and lock the door and phone the police. Okay? Can you do that? Woof, come with me.'

As usual Woof seemed to understand every word and trotted obediently next to him to the cellar door. I collected the large torch and my mobile and waited behind Steve as he switched on all the lights. As he descended the stairs Woof shot past him and ran off barking into the depths of the cellar. Steve followed him and disappeared behind the racking while I stood uncertainly waiting at the top. After a few minutes I could stand the suspense no longer and called out, 'Steve? Are you okay?'

For what seemed a lifetime there was no response, and I was about to investigate when I heard his reply. 'We're fine. Stay where you are. We'll be up in a minute.'

That minute felt like an hour until I saw Steve at the bottom of the stairs, with Woof hot on his heels. I felt myself shaking as he reached the top and then quietly closed and locked the door behind him. Woof nuzzled me for a cuddle, and as I obliged I could see he was much more relaxed. It was only then I noticed Steve was holding something: a small fawn, looking scared and lost but snuggling into Steve as if he was her father.

'What on earth…' I began, then fell into silence as the tiny animal looked at me with her big brown eyes.

'It seems we have another intruder for the menagerie,' Steve smiled. 'I don't know how she got in but I found her cowering near to where you said you first discovered Woof. She seems fine, just scared. I'm at a loss as to what to do with her now. She seems too young to let her loose. I'm worried she'll find her way to the road and be run over.'

'Bring her in here while I find some blankets for her to sleep on. I wonder how she found her way in there?'

Steve looked as if he was going to say something then changed his mind as he answered, 'Maybe she slipped past me when I was in the tub and I never noticed her come in.'

'I'll see if I can find her something to eat and drink,' I said, rather than ask him what he had originally intended to say.

In the kitchen I found some fruit and vegetables and put milk into a bowl. She looked skittish when Steve released her so we watched through a crack in the door, and left her to get acclimatised. After a few minutes she approached the food and drink. Although she still kept glancing round, from our vantage point we could see her tucking in.

'I'm so sorry to have dragged you out again, Steve. I really believed there was someone down there. I must be getting neurotic to be spooked by a deer. I should have gone down and found her myself without disturbing you.'

'NO,' Steve almost shouted although, up to then, we had been whispering so as not to disturb the fawn. 'I mean, you did the right thing. Call me anytime, night or day if you're even the slightest bit worried about anything. Promise me.'

'Okay, I promise, and thanks.'

His reaction reminded me of his explanation about how the fawn had managed to find its way in. I was convinced there was no way it could have got past him and into the cellar without him noticing. Something else was bothering him. Maybe it was more than the animal he had found down there. Before I could ask him about it, he gently tapped my arm and pushed the living room door open wider. Glancing over his shoulder, I nearly laughed out loud at the sight that met my eyes. Woof had returned to his bed, and the fawn had snuggled up next to him with his big body protecting her. He opened one eye as we went for a closer look as if to say, *She's all right, go to bed now.* Smiling, we left them to it as we crept out of the room and ended up by the front door.

'Look,' Steve said. 'I don't want to leave you alone after the upset you've had tonight. Would it be too much trouble to find me a blanket or something and I'll bed down on your settee for a few hours?'

'There's no need for that when I have a perfectly good bed upstairs,' I replied. What I had actually meant was there were plenty of spare bedrooms, but the sizzling look he gave me stopped me from explaining.

Chapter 34. Taking the plunge.

Taking my hand, he led me upstairs and excused himself for the bathroom once he had seen which room was mine. I dithered in my ensuite as I washed my hands, wondering what to do next. Then I heard him come back into the room, and taking a deep breath went to face him. He was getting into my bed wearing only his underpants, and I couldn't help but notice he was all male before he pulled the duvet up.

'Which side do you usually sleep?' he asked.

'Um, it doesn't matter,' I said nervously. As I climbed into bed next to him, he pulled me into his arms and held me without speaking. Gradually I relaxed, especially when he gently stroked my hair. Surprisingly I felt my eyelids drooping and despite the circumstances of having a new bed mate, I fell fast asleep.

I opened my eyes to hear a soft voice saying soothingly, 'It's okay, honey, it was only a dream. You're safe. I'm here; nothing's going to hurt you.'

As my brain caught up, I remembered what had disturbed me. I had been in the cellar with the evil hooded man trying to stop me escaping from the horrors of his dungeon.

'Sorry,' I said. 'I'm not usually such a wimp, but these dreams are getting more and more vivid. Maybe I should give up and sell this property. I have the feeling the original inhabitants don't approve of my plans, and are trying to drive me out.'

It sounded so weird, speaking out loud about my fears and nightmares, and I was embarrassed but to my amazement Steve responded seriously.

'A lot of people scoff at things they don't understand,' he said. 'Don't forget this is a very old estate and so much has happened here it's not surprising some of the evil from that time is still making itself felt. If you really want to give up and move, no one can stop you, it's got to be your decision. Remember though, there are a lot of genuine people in the village who are on your side, both physically and mentally.'

I stayed quiet, thinking over what Steve had said and deciding on my future. That morning everything had seemed to be going to plan. There was even the thought of a possible romance between Steve and myself developing slowly but surely. Now I was in turmoil. Was I being a fool to take on a project when I knew absolutely nothing about producing wine? Even with all the help and assistance on offer, ultimately, I would still be responsible, both legally and morally for the employees and the success of the venture.

I turned to Steve to express my concerns, but his eyes were closed and he was snoring softly. Perhaps it was the bad dream that had unsettled me and everything would be clearer in the cold light of day. Having decided worrying about it would not solve anything, I snuggled up into his arms and prepared to sleep again. Maybe the movement disturbed him but the next minute he was awake and kissing me gently. As I responded, his caresses became more intense, and before I knew it, we were making passionate love.

After Paul had let me down so badly, I had decided to keep men at a distance but somehow I knew Steve was of a different ilk. I felt safe and comfortable with him. Nevertheless, when we were both satiated and exhausted I felt embarrassed at having given myself so completely to a man who was still a relative stranger.

'Wow!' was his only comment as he smiled at me tenderly. 'If it's that good when we're exhausted, imagine what it will be like when we've both had a good night's sleep.'

Without any awkwardness he got out of bed naked and padded to the bathroom. My eyes followed his taunt muscles as he headed for the door. I decided to follow his example, and made use of the ensuite to freshen up while he used the guest bathroom. As I returned to bed, he came back and took me in his arms, this time to sleep. At least it was Sunday and there was no need to get up early. Even as this thought crossed my mind, I realised I had no idea what plans Steve had for the day or even where he lived. For all I knew he could be married with six kids and be a total con artist. Despite these disturbing thoughts I believed he could be trusted, and contentedly drifted off again for some well-deserved sleep.

The sun shining through the window woke me and for a moment I lay luxuriating in a feeling of well-being. In my half-awake state I put it down to sorting out the legalities of the previous day, until I remembered Steve sharing my bed for the night. Although the pillows showed evidence of his having been there, his clothes were gone and there was no sign of him. I wondered if he had already left, perhaps not wanting to see me again, or thinking of it as a one night stand. No sooner had the thought crossed my mind than he came into the bedroom carrying a laden breakfast tray.

'I wasn't sure what you wanted but knowing you enjoy your food I've done a bit of everything,' he said as he placed the tray on the bedside table before giving me a quick kiss. 'By the way, you look gorgeous all ruffled and sleepy.' I couldn't help the huge grin that spread across my face as I regarded the tray, before noticing he was fully dressed and looking fresh as a daisy. 'Sorry to cut and run, honey,' he said, 'but there are things I need to sort out today.'

He must have noticed my smile fading as he explained, 'I've fed Woof and let him out for a run. Bambi was fine but a bit restless after being cooped up indoors, so I've given her some warm milk and raided your fruit bowl. I let her loose in the garden and she headed straight for the wooded area at the back. I think she'll be safe enough there, but we can check on her later.'

Seeing me looking at him open-mouthed, he suddenly turned sheepish. 'Whoops, I've taken over, haven't I? Sorry about that, but I didn't want to disturb you as you were sleeping so soundly. Is it still okay if I come back this afternoon? Maybe about four?'

'Of course it is,' I replied. 'Thanks for everything. I should have got up and seen to the animals myself instead of lazing in bed. Do you really think Bambi will be all right?'

'I'm sure she will. She seemed happy enough in the woods but I want to check later to make sure there are no holes in the fence where she can get onto the road. See you soon.' With that he blew me a kiss and was gone.

I finished off my breakfast, had a shower then took the tray down. Steve had left the kitchen immaculate. Woof had gone back to his bed but got up to greet me warmly when I entered the lounge.

'Hello, my friend,' I said, 'it seems we both had a new bed companion last night. Thank you for looking after her. Did you sleep well?'

A sloppy kiss was my answer so I decided he deserved a good walk. I grabbed his lead and a jacket, and I let my mind wander as he hunted and sniffed, enjoying the beautiful spring sunshine. It was nearly one by the time we returned home and despite my big breakfast I was feeling ravenous after all the exercise. Before we went inside, I decided to have a quick look at the wooded area in the estate to see if Bambi was safe. Woof followed me as I tramped through the trees without catching sight of her. I had decided to give up when Woof suddenly took off through a particularly dense thicket. I struggled to follow him and by the time I caught up it was to see an amazing sight: Bambi snuggling up to him, while he gave her a good wash with his tongue. She nearly skittered away when she sensed me but Woof put a paw around her as if to say, *Don't worry, you're safe with me.*

If only I had a camera with me, but I remembered my mobile phone and edged further away before taking a picture of the heart-touching scene. Woof gave her a final lick then hastily followed me. It seemed for all his caring nature, food was his priority. I scoured the Internet for information on how to feed Bambi and improve her habitat. Then I was distracted with a wealth of e-mails and messages which had been neglected while I sorted out my life. Despite being Sunday, there was a communication from Bernard, confirming he had remitted the necessary funds to Paul, who no longer had any interest in Alderslay. A ring on the old-fashioned bell made me jump, and opening the door I found Steve standing there, looking gorgeous as usual, with an enormous bunch of flowers clutched in his arms.

'Hi,' he said, 'hope I'm not too early. These are for you as a small thank you. Have you had a good day?'

'Come in,' I replied, sniffing the wonderful scent of the flowers. 'You wouldn't believe what I saw when I went to check on Bambi.'

As I made coffee and put the flowers in water I regaled Steve with all the happenings of the day, including the wonderful sight of Woof protecting Bambi in the woods. I had raided the cupboards for some old bowls, filling one with a mixture of milk and water and the other with the remains of my fruit and vegetable store. Before it became too dark, we took them into the woods to try to find her and ensure she was settled for the night.

Woof came bounding along with us and again it was his nose that smelled out her hiding place. There was an old wooden shack in the grounds, and Steve gathered some branches and grass to make her a comfortable bed inside. I put the bowls down and we retreated behind some trees to watch what she would do. For a while she stayed where she was, until Woof nudged her towards her new home. She seemed to trust him completely, and before too long she entered the shelter and enjoyed her evening meal. By the time we finished watching it was nearly dark, and hand in hand we returned to the house, with Woof following shortly afterwards.

'That was amazing,' Steve said as we settled on the settee with a coffee. 'She obviously trusts Woof and I think before long she might accept us too. There's plenty of food and shelter for her in the woods so she should be happy enough, even if she gets lonely. Talking of food, do you have any plans for dinner? I know you're working tomorrow so we won't make it too late. There's a nice little Italian recently opened in the village if you fancy an early supper.'

'That sounds great. Are you sure it will be open? It is Sunday, after all.'

'Damn, I'd forgotten that. I'm a dab hand in the kitchen though, if you've got anything in. How about I cook you a meal if you supply the wine?'

'You're on! I'll leave you to it while I have a quick bath if that's okay. I feel grubby after all that tramping through the woods.'

'You look perfect to me,' Steve smiled, 'but you go and have a good soak and I'll call you when it's ready.'

Half an hour later I felt cleaner and more desirable. I was undecided what to put on for the evening; should I go for the femme fatale look or something more comfortable? In the end I compromised with a loose-fitting day dress that, with its lacy look and short skirt, seemed to fit the bill. But it might give Steve the wrong impression, that I had set out to entice him but as I decided to change, he called up the stairs to say dinner was ready. As I hurried down he was coming out of the kitchen, carrying two glasses and a bottle of chilled wine. He looked up and the appreciation on his face was matched by the single word *Wow!*

Taking me into his arms he whispered in my ear, 'You look good enough to eat. I'm tempted to turn the oven off, but knowing how hungry you must be, I'd better play the gentleman and get back to my chef duties.'

With that he kissed me soundly before pouring me a glass of wine and retreating to the kitchen. I was shaking, and pleased to have a few minutes to compose myself before he reappeared carrying a dish that smelled delicious. The salad to accompany the baked pasta was already on the table, and we settled down to eat in silence while we savoured the food. Later we chatted about the vineyard and how we could actually make it a reality. I was impressed by how much he had already achieved. He had sent out feelers for prospective employees, even going so far as to compile a short list of people who had expressed interest in working for us.

'Time for bed,' Steve said eventually, and I couldn't resist the shiver that went down my spine, only to be crushed by the words that followed. 'We both have work tomorrow so I'd better leave you to get your beauty sleep. Sweet dreams, Princess.'

The kiss he gave me as I showed him to the door had me quivering again, but to no avail. Once I was alone, the stress of the weekend hit me, and I yawned. When I let Woof out for his final run I couldn't help glancing towards the forest. I thought I saw a flash through the trees and imagined it was Bambi enjoying the freedom of the night. Locking the door, I settled Woof and went to bed. I was soon asleep but spent a restless night, waking again in the early hours from disturbing dreams.

Chapter 35. Planning for the future.

The strident ring of the alarm reminded me it was Monday, and I forced myself to face the hassles of the working week. Terry would be in later to let Woof out to roam the grounds, so I locked the door behind me with an easy conscience and headed for the train. Once I'd found a seat my thoughts wandered as I gazed out the window and saw the first signs of spring. Within a week, all the renovations would be finished and it was time to consider the long overdue house-warming party. So much had happened over the weekend I felt as if months had passed, rather than days.

I needed time to think and regroup. It even crossed my mind about giving up my job to concentrate fully on developing the vineyard, but I had a mortgage to consider. It seemed unbelievable that only three months ago I was planning to spend my life with Paul. Now he was gone and already I had a new man in my life, or at least in my bed. I knew nothing about Steve except that he was charming, funny and a brilliant lover. Was I on the rebound, clutching at any man who would rebuild my self-esteem?

Before I knew it, the train was pulling into the station and I made my way to the office to start another working week. It was a typical Monday, stressful, manic and everything that could go wrong did exactly that. It was gone six before I finally left and had a chance to think about anything other than work. Even then I was so tired all I had in mind was food and sleep. By the time I eventually arrived home Terry had fed Woof and left. I owed him a lot, and not just cash;

things could have been a lot different without his help and support.

Settling down with my laptop to catch up with e-mails, I read one from Jenny, the building society consultant. She confirmed everything had gone through smoothly and all the mortgage funds had been credited to my account. As I finished reading, a message from Paul arrived. For some reason I felt apprehensive about opening it but decided I couldn't put it off forever. He was effusive in his thanks that I had sorted out the repayment for his share of the house so quickly, and confirmed he had received the full settlement in his bank account that morning. There was even a photo of the property on which he had put a deposit, and he said I would be welcome to visit at any time.

His comment that he was sorry if he had hurt me sounded condescending, especially as I was pleased he was now actually out of my life. He finished by wishing me happiness for the future and signed off with love and a row of kisses, which I thought were rather inappropriate in the circumstances. I dashed off a quick reply telling him I was pleased everything went through satisfactorily, and wished him good luck with his property purchase. I signed off with only my name, then pressed the send button before I had second thoughts about adding more.

There was also a message from Geoff, Steve's friend, who had valued the wine. He congratulated me on the success of the last sale and confirmed if I intended to hold another one, he would be pleased to offer his services. Thinking about Steve seemed to summon him up as another message appeared. It was a friendly note saying he hoped I'd had a good day, thanking me for a brilliant weekend and promising to

255

phone the following evening. I wondered what he was doing, and whether he thought of me as a one-night stand or a longer-term relationship. I knew so little about him, not even where he lived, although it must be fairly close by. He might be married with a couple of kids, although how he would explain to his wife about staying out all night I couldn't imagine. Perhaps with a job that took him away a lot she wouldn't have found it particularly unusual.

With my mind working overtime, I decided to tackle the rest of the e-mails, several with names I did not recognise. Most were from wine connoisseurs asking for details of the next prospective sale or requesting prices for particular vintages. I replied to Geoff, suggesting another sale at the end of June, and confirming I would contact him once a date was finalised. Meanwhile I took advantage of his expertise and asked his advice on the queries I had received. Feeling guilty I hadn't consulted Steve first, I convinced myself a second opinion was always useful. In the mood for making arrangements, I decided to have the house-warming party in the middle of May. That would give me about six weeks to sort things out and by then the weather should be reasonably fine, and it would leave another six weeks to prepare for the second wine sale.

My life seemed to have spiralled out of control lately, so it felt good to get back to my normal routine of list-making. I felt much happier once things were organised and I could concentrate on replying to Steve. Everything had happened so quickly between us I was still unsure whether it was a knee-jerk reaction after losing Paul. It felt comfortable to outline plans and keep things on a more formal footing.

'Hi, Steve. Yes, great weekend, I enjoyed it too. I've been thinking about planning another wine sale, and having a house-warming, probably in May. Perhaps I can pick your brains when you phone tomorrow.'

Reading it back before pressing the send button, I initially felt it struck the right balance between business, being friendly and hinting at something more, without becoming too clingy. Then it seemed cold, considering we had spent the night together and had been lovers. As a compromise I added a few kisses at the bottom.

I decided that was enough for one day and opened the door to let Woof out. As he returned, I caught a glimpse of Bambi wandering through the trees. It was as if she was waiting for him to say goodnight, but she darted off as soon as she caught me watching her. Woof gave a gentle bark then came in and settled down in his bed. With thoughts of Steve running through my mind I went to my own.

Chapter 36. April Fool.

The first day of April and so-called Spring. It was bucketing down with rain and freezing cold. I got soaked on the way to the station and then the train was delayed. When I eventually dripped my way into the office it was to find all the computers had crashed and the I.T. guy had called in sick. We killed time gossiping at the coffee machine, in between doing odd bits of manual work. Usually we were too busy to do more than nod at people from other departments but a guy I knew only by sight approached me and started chatting.

'You're Gina, aren't you? I recognised your name from one of the publications I follow. Patrick. Nice to meet you. That last sale did really well, I hear. Are you doing another one?'

He wanted to know more about the estate and the treasures discovered in my cellar. He even knew Steve by reputation and mentioned he had seen him at several wine auctions over the previous few years.

'He really knows his stuff,' Patrick volunteered, 'and as for his wife, wow, what a cracker.' I opened my mouth to grill him for further details as one of the secretaries ran in to inform us all the processors were now up and running, and staff should return to their usual workstations. Patrick had a reputation as the office gossip, so perhaps he had got it wrong.

'Thought it was too good to last,' he grimaced as he headed back to his own office. 'It's been great talking to you, Gina. Let me know about the next auction. On my salary I can't afford the good vintages but I would love one of the cheaper bottles.'

The rest of the day turned into a total nightmare, trying to catch up with the lost hours. Although abroad on business, my boss had been informed about the problems and he phoned every five minutes asking if this, that and the other had been done. He didn't seem to appreciate that, apart from his needs, we were behind with all the daily routines which were normally handled first thing in the morning. By five o'clock I was at screaming pitch with only half of the urgent tasks completed. With no way of reaching home at a reasonable hour, I took a quick break to send a text to Terry.

'Sorry. Meant to see you to pay the rest of the money I owe but won't be home until 8.30 or 9 tonight. Nightmare day.'

Almost immediately I received a reply. *'No problem, Gina. Few final bits to finish. See you Friday night. If not, Saturday morning, to make sure everything ok. I'll see to Woof. Safe journey home.'*

Bless the man. Steve had arranged to see me that evening, so before getting stuck into work again I sent off a quick e-mail telling him I wouldn't be home until very late, and would be in touch when I was free. Still reeling from learning I might have slept with a married man, I had the added problem that he was also my business partner. Where did I go from here? My thoughts were interrupted by another phone call from my boss, and once I had finished with him, I resumed the pile of unfinished work before I left. It was almost seven when I received a reply from Steve.

'Work comes first. Sorry about tonight. Away now for a few days on business myself. Be in touch when I get back.'

He signed off with a work emoticon and his name. No kisses, no 'love Steve', no regret at not being able to get together. It was as if he realised I had discovered his guilty secret and he was responding as a business associate. Half of me was relieved I'd have time to think about my approach without becoming over emotional, the other half felt anger at letting myself be duped a second time. Maybe it was for the best, and I should let what had happened stay in the past. By eight o'clock I'd had enough and most of the backlog was under control. Yawning, I shut down my computer and headed for the station. At least the train was on time and I even managed to find a seat.

As I unlocked the front door Woof came bounding out to meet me, then disappeared into the grounds and was lost from sight. Usually when he went out for his late night visit, he stayed near the house and came back after a few minutes. Tonight he seemed to have decided to play up and a quarter of an hour later he had still not returned. Great! All I needed after the day I'd had, when all I wanted was to eat, unwind and sleep. Sighing, I put some shoes back on, grabbed a flashlight and throwing my keys into my jacket pocket, set out to look for him.

He was not near the pool or the conservatory and despite me calling, he did not appear. Eventually I made my way down to the forested area at the end of the property. It was dark and creepy and for a minute I was tempted to turn back and leave Woof to his own devices. But I wouldn't be able to sleep, so I carried on deeper into the woods. Suddenly I heard him bark and a minute later he came bounding towards me. I let my annoyance show as I turned towards the house expecting him to follow me, but instead he went back to where he had been hidden in the trees.

'Either you come now or you stay out,' I yelled, feeling tired and irritable. He came to my side and then turned back to the trees. Woof was always so obedient, it occurred to me he must be trying to tell me something. I followed him and he barked softly then led me deeper into the forest.

'What is it, boy? What's wrong?' I asked quietly, sweeping the flashlight around the area. I jumped when it picked up the outline of something a few yards away. Then I heard a mournful yelp, and summoning up my courage moved closer. It was Bambi, caught in a hole in the fence surrounding the estate. The more she struggled to free herself the more she became entwined and she looked totally exhausted. Maybe she was too tired to resist or perhaps she knew I was trying to help, but as I approached she stopped struggling and let me stroke her.

She flinched when I touched her leg, and I saw it was covered in dried blood with wire digging into it. She squealed as I tried to pull her out, and I realised I couldn't free her by using only my bare hands. Woof looked up at me as I made my way back to the house.

'It's okay, boy. You stay here and keep her company. I'll be right back.'

As if he understood, Woof settled close to her, using his body to keep her warm. Once I cleared the outskirts of the wooded area I ran to the house, grabbed an old blanket, and rooted around in my tool box for something to cut the wire. It contained an old carpet knife which looked a bit rusty but still had a sharp blade, a small hand saw, a pair of shears and a hammer. Trying not to panic, I took a deep breath to think clearly. From the kitchen I grabbed a couple of chef's knives and a meat cleaver, then bundled everything into a bag along with a spare torch and another battery for the large flashlight.

I had my mobile phone but no idea who I could call for help at this late hour. My first thought was Steve, but I remembered he was away. It was down to me, but at least I had Woof for company. A few old bandages completed my haul then I hurried back to Bambi. Until then I hadn't realised how extensive the woods were, and I hunted around for a few minutes trying to find the exact spot where I had last seen her. This was ridiculous, getting lost on your own property. Then my brain cleared and common sense kicked in.

'Woof, Woof, where are you?' I called. Silence. I moved to another spot and called again. This time I heard an answering bark. 'Woof, come here, I need you.'

I heard a rustling in the bushes off to my right and Woof appeared out of the darkness. 'Good boy,' I said, ruffling his head. 'Now lead me back to Bambi. Where is she?'

He turned and took off back through the trees with me rushing to keep up with him. At one point I thought I had lost him, but he seemed to realise and waited for me to catch up. I followed the boundary fence until I found her. She let out a plaintive cry and I noticed fresh blood on her leg. Poor thing. She must have thought we had both deserted her and tried again to free herself. Taking the blanket out of the bag, I threw it over her as she was shivering with shock.

Propping the flash light on its stand I used the torch to see the best way to free her. After several unsuccessful attempts to cut through the wire with the scissors I realised they were not strong enough. I had more success with the carpet knife but it was a long, slow process and Bambi was getting weaker. Woof had been watching me but he started scrabbling at the base of the fence. I tried to push him off as he was in my way, but he insisted. Then I realised what he was doing. By freeing up the base of the post I would be able to pull it right out which would make it a lot easier to loosen the wire.

That dog was so intelligent it was almost uncanny. We worked together, him digging and me cutting, and in a few minutes the post was loose. Carefully I lifted Bambi free and was then faced with the dilemma of what to do with her. I couldn't see how wounded she was by torchlight, and if I left her out on her own she might not survive. Decision made, I collected the tools, threw the bag over my shoulder and started carrying her to take her indoors. With my arms full it was impossible to hold the flashlight and before I had gone more than a few yards I dropped it. Luckily it was encased in rubber so it didn't break. Before I could decide what else to do Woof picked it up in his mouth and with him leading the way, we made it safely to the house.

Once inside, I examined Bambi's leg properly. As I cleaned off the blood I was relieved to see the cuts were only superficial, and after some warm milk and something to eat, she seemed a lot happier. The question of where she was going to sleep was soon settled as she curled up next to Woof in his basket. Before I went to bed I peeped in and found them both sleeping peacefully. I hoped to enjoy the same luxury, and turning off the lights decided everything could wait until the morning. Despite thinking I wouldn't sleep I woke suddenly, shortly before three and got up to check on Bambi. She was awake and although a nocturnal animal, it seemed she was loathe to disturb Woof who still snuggled up next to her. He opened one eye, wagged his tail once then went back to sleep.

The next thing I knew, a weak sun was trying to shine through the bedroom curtains. Woof would take care of her but I was worried Bambi would go back to the woods and perhaps become caught in the fence again. Even worse, she might force her way through the gap and end up on the road, but I couldn't take the day off work. I was considering phoning in sick when I heard a knock at the door. Terry, my guardian angel.

'Sorry to call so early, Gina, but I was hoping to catch you before you left. I only need an hour or so to finish up, but the lady of the house has talked me into taking her away for a few days to visit the grandchildren. I won't be around if there's anything you aren't satisfied with.'

'No, everything's fine. I'll get my cheque book.'

'Don't worry now. That wasn't the reason I called. I didn't want you thinking I'd left without telling you. What's the matter, lass? There's something on your mind.'

I was reluctant to burden him, but gradually he dragged the story out of me.

'You leave it to me and go off to work. We don't go until the morning so I've plenty of time today to go round the fence and make it secure. I'll give Danny a call. He can give me a hand. By the way, Danny's father's a vet. Do you want me to ask him to give the fawn the once-over?'

'Terry, you're a life-saver. I really don't know what I'd do without you. Yes, if you could ask him to take a look at her I'd feel a lot happier. Now, how much do I owe you? Let me pay you up to date, and then I can give you the rest on Saturday, if that's all right with you?'

'You go and catch your train, my pet. Leave things to me. Do you want me to feed Woof before I leave? I'll probably be here until about five.'

'That'd be brilliant, Terry. Thanks so much for everything. Have a lovely holiday and I'll see you Saturday.' With that I dashed out of the house and just managed to catch my usual train. Although I had little sleep the previous night and was still worried about Bambi, I knew she was in safe hands and was able to concentrate on work. Things went fairly smoothly and with the computers working I was able to catch up the rest of the backlog. Around three I received a message from Terry.

'Bambi is fine. Vet has been. She's a bit stiff on her bad leg but no major damage. Soon be right as rain. Examined the entire perimeter fence and found most of it is rotten, so I've replaced it all. Sorry if I've taken too much on myself but thought you'd rather it was done than risk Bambi getting into trouble again. Thought it'd be better security for the estate too.'

I sent him a quick reply saying how much I appreciated his thoughtfulness and would make it up to him on Saturday with double biscuits. With my mind at rest, I was able to concentrate on work and even managed to catch the early train home. It wasn't quite six when I opened the front door, and as Woof was still polishing off his dinner I assumed Terry had not long left.

I picked up a torch and made my way in the half-light to the end of the grounds where I had found Bambi the previous night, and discovered what had kept Terry so late. The new fence looked fantastic, and as the paint was still tacky, had not long been completed. With an antique finish it suited the surroundings perfectly. I jumped as something touched me but relaxed when I saw it was only Woof. He followed me as I trailed the boundary, then took off into the trees, where I tracked him before drawing back into the shade of the trees to watch him. He was standing face to face with Bambi and it seemed they were kissing as they nuzzled each other.

He dropped his head to examine her leg, looking exactly like a doctor studying his patient. Bambi stood quietly under his scrutiny until, seemingly satisfied, he gave it a quick lick before trotting back to me. As we headed towards the house we passed the outhouse I had envisaged as Bambi's shelter. A saucer was filled with clean water and there was a fresh supply of vegetables and fruit. Inside, hay covered with an old blanket formed a soft bed. I assumed this was the vet's doing, which reminded me about settling his bill. As we walked away I sensed a presence behind me, and turning, was in time to see Bambi enter the barn as if she was returning home for her evening meal. With a big smile on my face I opened my own front door, and although I knew fawns were nocturnal, at least I had the peace of mind of knowing she was safe.

Checking my laptop for messages, I saw one from a name I didn't recognise but realised it was from Danny's father, Peter Blake.

'Have put bedding for Bambi in the barn. Woof led me to her and I've given her a thorough

266

examination. The wound was not infected and should be completely healed in a few days. I have attached a check list of "How to care for deer as pets." Do contact me if you have any questions.'

'*Thanks so much for all your help and advice, Peter,*' I replied. '*I've seen Bambi tonight and she looks well and settled in her new home; no sign of last night's trauma. I'll await your invoice but really grateful to you for attending to her so quickly.*'

A few minutes later I received a reply. '*This one is on the house, but as a wine lover an invite to the next sale wouldn't be refused. Hint, hint. Best Wishes. Peter.*'

It seemed everyone in the village was a wine buff and the number of invitees for the house warming was growing larger by the day. Even so, I felt grateful to the number of people in the village who had not only accepted me but were supporting me in so many different ways. I decided to give Terry a quick call before it became too late, and although his wife Maggie answered, she seemed to know who I was even before I gave her my name.

'He should be back shortly,' she said. 'Was it about the fence? He wasn't sure about going ahead without talking to you first but I convinced him. If it was the wrong thing to do, you'd better blame me.'

'I'm delighted with it, Maggie. Can you thank Terry and tell him I'll see him Saturday to sort out paying him?'

'Fine, but more importantly, how's Bambi?'

'She's doing well and with the new fence installed it's much safer. Thanks so much for persuading Terry to do it. I'm sorry for taking up even more of his time.'

After wishing her a nice holiday I hung up feeling a lot happier than I had the previous day. A nudge from Woof reminded me of his presence so I gave him a doggie treat as a thank-you for his doctoring of Bambi, and indulged in a large glass of wine before heading for bed and an early night. I read the leaflet the vet had left me then turned off the light and slept soundly.

Chapter 37. Weird coincidences.

When I let Woof out he headed straight for the woods, so I followed him to check on Bambi before setting off for work. She was heading towards the barn with Woof by her side, and as I watched she entered, ate some food from the bowl and then settled into her bed. With a final glance back, Woof joined me and together we returned to the house for breakfast. I arrived early for work, and after opening my computer headed for the kitchen to make myself a coffee, where I bumped into Patrick again.

'Morning, Gina. How's things? Any more wine sales being arranged?'

'The next one will probably be at the end of June,' I replied, over the noise of the kettle boiling.

'I assume Steve will be there,' he said, and I rather reluctantly confirmed that he would be. 'Great,' he replied. 'I hope he's bringing his gorgeous wife. That reminds me, I found some photos of a sale I attended in France last year. You might find them interesting. I'll send them to your office e-mail. Catch you later. Don't work too hard.'

If Steve had introduced Patrick to his wife, the faint hope Patrick had jumped to conclusions seemed unlikely. My mind was in turmoil, and my earlier good mood evaporated. Rather than think about it, I decided to work off my apprehension by concentrating on the urgent tasks in front of me. I replied to e-mails, made phone calls and completed various projects. Pleased with the progress I had made, I was hoping for an early finish when an e-mail popped up from Patrick. He had attached an album of photos and I was interested in seeing how other wine sellers set up their sales. Most of the pictures showed a very extensive estate with dozens of helpers officiating. The vineyard itself was beautiful and bathed in sunshine. I wondered if I had been naïve to think I could compete with only my few acres and the typical English weather.

In one photo my attention was caught by a group in the background, holding wine glasses and obviously in deep discussion. Increasing the zoom, I saw him - Steve. Gazing into his eyes was a beautiful brunette. Trying to convince myself she could be another delegate I quickly scanned the remaining photographs. There were several of Steve and the woman I now assumed must be his wife. In most of them she was holding his hand or he had his arm around her waist. What was it about me and men? The two important males in my life had both been involved with other women when they were supposed to be with me: my fiancé and my business partner. Both had deceived me. Paul was history but what should I do about Steve? Realising I should be working, I forwarded the e-mail to my personal one and sent a quick thanks to Patrick before deleting it from my office computer. Determined to forget about the photos, I dedicated myself to work for the rest of the day.

At least when I got home I found one male I could rely on; Woof leapt out to greet me and I hugged him, grateful for his loyalty. Collecting fresh food, we set off down the garden to check on Bambi. Woof bounded away to find her, and I caught a glimpse of her behind the trees, looking as if her leg wasn't causing her too much discomfort. I put down fresh food and plumped up her bed to make sure she would be comfortable, and as I did so noticed an old-fashioned tap in one corner of the building, almost hidden behind piles of junk. Pushing the rubbish aside, I turned it without much hope, but to my surprise water gurgled out. At first it was slow and brackish but soon it was running strong and clear. As I filled Bambi's saucer, I realised how convenient it would be to have fresh water to hand without having to lug it from the house. A trough or bowl would be easier for Bambi but as I hunted around for something suitable, I uncovered a black metal object and realised it was a large, antique deed box.

It was locked, but I could hear something rattling inside. I found a bowl to hold Bambi's water, and realising it would be easier to examine the box indoors, I picked it up and called to Woof. As we left Bambi sneaked into her home, and I was pleased to see she was walking well and seemed to have recovered from her ordeal. With one of the animals fed, I sorted out the dog then started preparing my own meal. Once everything was bubbling away I opened my laptop, and looked again at the photos of Steve I had browsed through earlier. There was no denying the closeness between him and the lady I assumed was his wife. Even if Patrick was wrong and she was only his girlfriend, the fact she had travelled with him to France told me all I needed to know.

The smell from the kitchen reminded me how long I had been perusing them, so I shut down my computer and dished up my meal. While I ate I came to some conclusions; first I would meet Steve and tell him I knew his secret. Without becoming emotional I would inform him all romantic contact between us was over. Secondly, I would ask if he wanted to remain my business partner. If he agreed, I would make it clear

271

that from now on it would be on a professional basis only.

With that thought straight in my mind, I remembered the old black box and clearing a space on the table, set to work to open it. Even if I had a key, the lock was so rusted it was doubtful it would open so I tried a piece of bent wire. When that didn't work, I jabbed away with a knife to try to lift the lid. One bent knife later I found some lubricating oil to clear away the corrosion. That helped but still the top stayed firm. Realising there was movement at the back hinges I set to work again with the oil and a chisel on the weaker point. Success; the hinges gave way and I was able to bend the top back. Half expecting to be disappointed, I examined the contents and found a treasure trove of history. Carefully, I took out the papers and set them on the table.

The parchment was fragile and obviously very old, borne out by the dates on some of the documents. These appeared to be original deeds relating to the legal transfers of the property, death certificates and sale contracts, including legal restrictions imposed on the purchasers of the estate over the years. Laying these to one side to examine in more detail later, I discovered what appeared to be a series of journals written in an old fashioned, hard to read script. Before I had a chance to scrutinise them, my attention was caught by a bundle of faded photographs. Several showed what was presumably the squire, resplendent in hunting attire and surrounded by magnificent horses and a pack of hounds, formal family photos with the lord, ladies in long ball gowns and coiffured hair styles, and women who from their dress were servant girls.

One looked familiar, and using a magnifying glass I examined it in more detail. Apart from the clothes I could have been looking in a mirror; the face looking back at me was my own. I stared in amazement. What an eerie feeling. Then I remembered the weird dream I had all those months ago and the conversation with Betty the old lady from the village. Perhaps the photograph I was looking at was my own great grandmother, Georgina, which would explain the resemblance. At her side was a large wolf-like creature who was the spitting image of Woof. In the background I could see the side of the estate with what appeared to be a fawn peeping through the trees.

Laying them to one side I browsed through the other photos. There were several of the manor and grounds which, apart from the vineyard, looked little different from the way they did now. I examined them closely and was surprised to see how far the grape vines extended. In those days it was obviously a very important part of the estate. They covered all the area down to the woods where Bambi lived, and up as far as what was now the swimming pool and my hot-tub and kitchen buildings. It was apparent these outhouses had been where the wine was processed before being stored in the cellars.

Another surprise was the fencing surrounding the rear of the grounds. It was exactly the same as the one Terry had installed. Without realising it, I was replicating the estate as it had been in my great grandmother's day. It was as if fate had brought me back to this place for a reason. One way and another it had been an emotional day and by eleven I was yawning and ready for bed. With so much going through my mind I was unable to sleep straight away despite feeling so tired.

There had been so many discoveries; the way I had accidentally found the house, the grisly history of the bodies in the cellar, Paul leaving me when I thought our future together was set, Steve deceiving me about being married, finding the photos of my ancestors, the odd coincidences of the fence around the estate and even the quirk of Woof and Bambi's predecessors being the companions of my great grandmother. Then there was my idea of developing a vineyard even before I knew this was the original purpose of the estate.

Finally, I dropped off to sleep only to have a recurrence of my haunted dream. Although it was still set in the cellars, this time it seemed I was in charge and my prisoners were men begging for mercy, while I sneered at their discomfort from being chained to the walls.

I woke the next morning in a cold sweat, horrified at how I had imagined such a vision. Perhaps it was my subconscious wanting to get back at the men who had hurt me. I had always thought of myself as a decent person who would forgive, forget and move on without animosity. The shock of thinking I could be capable of such cruelty, even in a dream, made me shudder.

The alarm brought me back to reality and I got up and opened the back door to let Woof out for his morning run. He greeted me with his usual love and affection and I realised how much the dream of the night before had affected me. I followed him and was pleased Bambi accepted me and came within touching distance while I refreshed her water and food supplies.

Returning to the house to prepare breakfast, I felt peace returning. The normal routine of catching the train, work and the familiarity of a typical day restored my equilibrium. Even when I bumped into Patrick again, I was able to keep the discussion focused on vineyards and wine sales without mentioning Steve or his wife.

When I opened my front door to the usual excited greeting from Woof, I realised he had missed having Terry around to keep him company during the day. That reminded me both Terry and Steve should be back the following day; one I was looking forward to seeing, the other not so much. I sent a message to Terry saying I hoped he had enjoyed his holiday and I would be at home on Saturday if he had a chance to call round. As far as Steve was concerned I decided to leave it to him to make the first contact, then I would play it by ear as to how to broach the subject of his wife and our future professional relationship.

Chapter 38. Plans and confessions.

Despite only being early April, the weather was perfect. After dinner I walked down to the end of the estate and enjoyed the barmy evening heralding the promise of spring. The following weekend would be Easter and I hoped the weather would hold so I could get to grips with all the things I wanted to do in the garden. For my housewarming party I had decided on the May bank holiday as a suitable date. Planning and organising helped me to concentrate on pleasant things instead of worrying about the meeting with Steve and the dreams of the previous night.

I ventured to the cellar to collect a bottle of something to wash down my evening meal and celebrate the start of the weekend. For some reason it no longer frightened me, although I was happy to have Woof's company as I descended the stairs. I did a quick inventory of the wine stock for the June sale and selected some for the housewarming. My next priority was the usual list-making to ensure everything was organised for my hospitality day. The names of people to invite grew and I realised how many new friends had been made since I moved here.

Others included Bert and Mary, my old landlord and landlady from the London flat, as well as the two boys who had lived there and helped me when I moved. Obviously, Terry and his wife should be invited, as well as his crew and their partners. Then there were Peter the vet, Anna from the pub, Betty, Gordon from the garden centre, Jackie and various other shop keepers from the village, as well as the local police sergeant and his constable. Added to the list were all the people who had been involved in helping me purchase the house, Bernard the solicitor, Mr Blake the valuer, Jenny from the building society. The list seemed endless.

Obviously, Steve should be invited, but should it be extended to include his wife? That would have to be a decision for after I had seen him and discussed our business partnership, which reminded me to add Geoff as he had helped with the valuation. Next would be to include some of the people who might become employees once the vineyard was up and running. Knowing them on a social basis before actually offering them a job would make life easier. Living in such a secluded space, I realised how nearly all the villagers were involved one way or another and finally decided it would be politic to extend an open invitation. With an estimated one hundred guests I needed to contact Penny about the catering sooner rather than later.

I sent off an e-mail giving her the date, an estimate of how many were likely to attend, and asked her to confirm she would be available. With the numbers involved, it might be easier to have a barbeque in the grounds, with the refuge of the downstairs kitchen should it turn cold or start raining. Hiring a marquee would be helpful as the kitchen would be cramped if everyone turned up and we had typical bank holiday weather. From a small thank-you for a few friends, my house warming had snow-balled into a major event, and I needed to consider some form of entertainment. While I was pondering the options, I received a reply from Penny confirming she would be happy to organise the food, and suggesting we have a chat to sort the logistics. No time like the present, so I phoned her straight away.

'Hi, Penny. Thanks for getting back to me so quickly. What I want is to issue an open invitation to the entire village. Do you think they would want to come?'

'Hi, Gina. It's a wonderful idea. I'd assumed the guests would be your personal work colleagues and friends but it'll be a great way for the village to welcome you to the community. Everyone's behind you. I know some of the village ladies will be happy to help with the catering. No charge, obviously.'

With the basics in place, I fed Woof, had something to eat, checked on Bambi and settled down to finish my drink and watch a film on TV. I had no bad dreams and woke refreshed and ready to face the world. After a healthy breakfast I wandered down to check on Bambi and top up her food and water bowls. With Woof showing me the way, I entered her house to find her settling down to sleep after her night on the tiles. She accepted my presence and didn't take flight when I went near her. Woof gave her a quick lick and we left her to wander around the end of the estate. As I checked the fence and compared it with the photos I had found, a voice me made me jump. Woof had given no warning but turning I saw Terry, who was immediately given a sloppy welcome by Woof. Laughing, Terry pushed the dog away then asked if I was happy with the new fence.

'It's perfect. I hope it didn't delay your holiday at all.'

'No problem, my pet. We couldn't have Bambi getting into trouble. How is she anyway?'

'Come and see for yourself,' I said as I led him back to her shelter. She was sleeping peacefully and only opened one eye as she felt us watching her before we crept away. I remembered the photos I had found in her den, and told Terry about the strange coincidence of having exactly the same fence as the one in the original estate.

'That was odd,' Terry replied thoughtfully. 'When I went to get the wood I had ordered, there had been a delay in the delivery and they didn't have any in stock. I knew you wanted the job finished so I accepted the alternative the woodyard offered. It wasn't one of their standard timbers and they only had it due to a wrong delivery the day before. They were going to return it but it seems it was fated to end up round the estate as it was in the old days. If you're not happy I can change it and replace it with a modern oak or plywood.'

'No, Terry, it's fine and it suits the surroundings. Let's leave it as it is. Come back to the house and we'll sort out what I owe you. I might even find some chocolate biscuits to go with a cup of tea.'

'You're a wicked woman tempting an old man like that,' Terry joked as we headed indoors. Once I had settled the rest of his bill, I explained about my plans for the house warming. Like Penny, he was sure the open invitation would be well received by the villagers and expressed his appreciation at my hospitality.

'By the way, did you know the village has its own brass band? And some folk and pop groups who I'm sure would love the opportunity of doing their thing.'

'Sounds great. Any idea what they might charge?'

'Well, I'd be surprised if they wanted anything. If it's for the good of the village I think they'd be pleased to offer their services.'

I seemed to be on a roll, with support coming from all sides. The community spirit of my adopted home solved problems almost before they arose. As I was getting carried away with enthusiasm for the project, a ring at the door startled me. Opening it, I came face to face with Steve, looking tanned and strikingly attractive. I wasn't sure if I was pleased our first meeting after my discovery was in company, or if it would have been better if we had the opportunity to speak privately. As he leaned forward to kiss me, I turned away and led him into the living room where Terry was sitting. Steve looked surprised at my reaction but perhaps he thought I was embarrassed as there were other people around.

As I updated Steve about my plans for the house warming, I casually dropped in the prospect of whether he would be able to make it. We all chatted generally until Terry said he would take his leave before his wife thought he had run off with me. Smiling, I let him out and thanked him again for all his hard work.

'I'll be in touch once I've spoken to the various band and group members but feel free to contact me any time if there's anything you need.'

I stood for a minute at the door waving goodbye before turning to face the problem with Steve.

'How have you been?' he asked. 'I tried to contact you several times but had no reply. I wondered if you'd gone away for a few days.'

'No, I'm fine. I've been busy, that's all.'
Almost for the sake of something to say I briefly told
him about Bambi, having the fence repaired and
discovering the old photos.

'I've decided to invite all the villagers to the
open day so I can get to know some of the possible
employees for when the vineyard opens. I'm going to
hold another sale at the end of June. Would you be
available to help with the auction again?'

'Of course. Now, can you tell me what's
wrong? Have you had second thoughts about making
me a trustee? If so, I understand. I can still be around to
help you but without the legal involvement, or is there
something else worrying you?'

Without looking at him I tentatively tried to
explain. 'I've never thought it's a good idea to be
involved with someone both personally and
professionally,' I began. 'I'd like you to continue as
trustee. To be honest, I don't think I'd be able to
continue without your expertise. Your knowledge is
invaluable but we need to have a proper written
contract so we both know where we stand. Also, I think
in future we should stick to being business partners.'

Steve let me finish without interrupting
although his eyes looked sad. 'You know I'm here for
you however you want me. I'd hoped our personal
relationship would have a chance to develop but if
that's how you feel then so be it, as long as it doesn't
stop us being friends.'

'Of course we're still friends, Steve. Thanks for
understanding.'

After that it was easier to slip into work mode
and we discussed the necessities for getting the
vineyard up and running. Even though he had been

away working, I realised he had put a lot of time and effort into the plans to make it a reality. We discussed the information - who we would need, what sort of wages we should pay and how we could organise the production. He told me about an old guy in the village who had worked on the estate before and knew all there was to know about vineyards. He had already spoken to Arthur who had expressed his interest in helping to start up. I suggested he invite him over at the weekend so I could meet him, and we could see how things went from there. Glancing at the clock, I saw it was already seven o'clock. Following my look, Steve told me he had to leave but would be in touch when he had finalised arrangements with Arthur.

'All being well we can come over around eleven Saturday morning? In the meantime, I'll let you know of any other progress.'

As I showed him out, I felt hurt he had taken my rejection so easily but decided it was probably the best way if we were to continue our professional relationship. Nevertheless, I couldn't resist calling out as he was driving off, 'By the way, I look forward to meeting your wife at the house warming.'

He stopped the car and I thought he was coming back to talk to me. Instead, his arm waved from the window before he drove off again. So it must be true. I wasn't sure if I was disappointed or relieved now I knew for certain. With a heavy heart I went indoors, fed Woof and prepared dinner. Then I settled down with my laptop to work on my plans for the future. Although I had friends to help, I was once again a woman alone. As if to prove me wrong Woof nudged my leg. Instinctively, he seemed to have sensed my mood and gave me his support. Hugging him, I felt motivated to proceed with the arrangements.

Easter was late that year, but I needed to start organising if I wanted everything to be ready in time. I designed and printed out a house-warming poster and decided I would call at the pub the following day to ask if they would display it. Feeling I had done enough for one day, I went out with Woof to check on Bambi while he had his evening run round the grounds. At first I couldn't find her, but then noticed her running off through the bushes and trees, closely followed by Woof. A few minutes later he came back with his tail wagging as if to say, '*Yes, she's fine. I've said goodnight.*'

Laughing, I locked up, read my long-neglected book and then turned off the light and settled down to sleep. The next morning I knew I had been dreaming but could not remember anything. I went out into the grounds to decide how I could set things up for my open day. The weather was bright but chilly; a covered shelter was a must. Browsing through the weekly village newspaper, I found a local firm specialising in marquees. They were even open on Sundays and their address was close to the pub.

In the cellar I had flashbacks of my dream from the night before but my memories were fuzzy and incomplete, so I decided to put it to the back of my mind. I collected Woof's lead and set off for the pub where Anna was opening up as we arrived. She gave us her usual friendly welcome and put down a bowl of water for Woof. As it was quiet in the bar, I was able to tell her my ideas about the house warming at Alderslay, and asked if she would let me put up a poster to inform all the villagers. She thought it was a wonderful idea which would be appreciated by all the locals. I also mentioned I was looking for people to help if and when I got the vineyard operative.

'Arthur's your man,' she replied immediately. 'Are you in a rush? He always comes in for a pint on Sundays while his wife's doing the roast. He should be here in about an hour or so if you want to talk to him.'

Steve had arranged to bring him over the following weekend but it would be good to meet him before then.

'How is the lovely Steve?' she asked. Noticing my face, she diplomatically changed the subject and asked about the poster.

'I have something ready if you could put one up here.'

'Even better, make extra copies and I'll put them up in the Post Office, the Village hall and the church to make sure everyone sees them.'

'Thanks, Anna. I was thinking about a marquee. I saw in the local paper there's a supplier in the village. Do you know if they're any good?'

'That'd be Phil. I definitely recommend him.'

'I thought about visiting him this morning. Is it far?'

'Come, I'll show you,' she said as she came to the door with me to point out his premises. I went to call Woof who had disappeared behind the bar, but Anna insisted it would be fine to leave him with her. Several customers came in so telling her I wouldn't be long, I set off to find the shop. It turned out to be more of a warehouse with a small reception area at the front. I was greeted by a smiling middle-aged lady sitting in a wheelchair behind the low counter.

'Good Morning, Gina,' she called as I approached. 'It's nice to meet you at last.' Then she laughed as she explained, 'Sorry to be so informal but I don't know your last name. Village gossip hasn't got that far. By the way, I'm Liz, Phil's wife. Is this a business visit or were you only passing?'

I explained about needing a marquee for the house warming, and after putting the kettle on she found a notebook and took details. Like the others, she thought it a brilliant idea when I explained about making it an open day for the villagers. A tall, smiling man poked his head round the door and grinned at me as he said to Liz, 'Do I smell coffee?'

'You and your coffee,' she smiled back. 'I'm sure that big nose of yours can smell it from a hundred yards away. In case you hadn't guessed, Gina, this reprobate is my husband, Phil, who thinks he's the boss of our little business.'

'Hello, my lovely,' he replied. 'That'll be the day, when she lets me be in charge. Any cake going?' Despite his jovial manner, once we had finished our elevenses he showed his expertise as he took me round the warehouse so I could decide exactly what I wanted. The range and variation of the shelters and tents available was amazing. I appreciated his advice as he explained why some would not be suitable, and the pros and cons of other types. It didn't come as a surprise when he told me he knew the estate well from his childhood, as both his grandfather and father used to work there.

'How about if I call round on Good Friday?' he suggested. 'I know you've carried out some changes so it'll be good to see the new layout, and I can work out

285

logistics, where the marquee should go and that sort of thing.'

'Good idea. That's fine with me.'

Returning to the reception area, he told Liz and she made another note in her book. As he handed me a brochure with all the terms and conditions of hire, Liz told me to ignore the price list. 'As it's going to be a celebration for all the village, we can forgo the profit as long as we cover our costs. It'll probably be around half the rate listed there.'

With new friends and another item ticked off the list, I went back to the pub full of confidence. Anna waved as I sat at a table and Woof came dashing out to say hello before disappearing behind the bar again. As I placed my order a distinguished military-type gentleman came to my table. Doffing his hat, he asked, 'May I join you?'

'Of course,' I smiled. 'I'm Gina. Nice to meet you.'

'The pleasure is all mine. Arthur Pembleton at your service, Miss Kingston.'

So this was Arthur the vineyard expert everyone had recommended. Anna must have told him I wanted to meet him. Once we had broken the ice, I found him easy to talk to and realised how little I knew about running a vineyard. The rest of the week passed in a blur. I tried to juggle work, research how to run the business, prepare for the open day and not think about Steve. Thankfully it was a short week as by Friday I felt exhausted as I donned wellies and raincoat to deliver the posters to the pub for Anna to distribute. In the village I dropped the menu off to Penny. She confirmed she would be able to provide an industrial size barbeque and sufficient staff to serve all the guests.

With the use of the lower kitchen she could supply a range of both hot and cold food, salads, party nibbles and desserts. We agreed she would offer a range of soft drinks while I would supply the wines from the cellar stock. Anna had agreed to lend me the necessary glasses so at least all the catering side was in hand.

I'd printed personal invitations for special guests to be delivered individually, the rest I put in the post. In the pub I met the leader of the brass band and a couple of members of the pop group as well as the folk duo. All confirmed they would be happy to provide a couple of hours of entertainment free of charge. Anna had suggested a DJ to play music in between the live bands and had given him my number. That only left me to sort out some kind of time-table and the entertainment would be in place. Phil had said he would call about three, so after finishing my pub lunch I collected Woof and headed home. After a short while working on my laptop there was a ring at the bell and I opened it to greet Phil, accompanied by Liz in her wheelchair.

'Hope you don't mind, my dear,' he said, 'but the trouble and strife insisted on coming so she could make sure about access for the less-abled. Some of the old girls from the village are not as steady on their feet as they used to be.'

'Not so much of the old girls,' Liz admonished him. 'A lot of your cronies wouldn't be able to get to the pub without help from their walking sticks.'

'Actually, that's something I hadn't thought of,' I said. 'It would be a good idea to have seating around the gardens and in the marquee, especially for when people are eating.'

287

'No problem, my love,' Phil replied. 'We can sort that for you. About a hundred you said? We can set up chairs and tables in the marquee and a few bench tables outside in case the sun decides to shine. Right, shall we start the guided tour, to make sure we know where everything's going?'

Liz led the way as I took them into the grounds and to the area between the conservatory and the swimming pool. Most of the way was easy for the wheelchair but there was one part where we had to cross the grass which proved bumpy and difficult.

'We can lay some decking as a base for the tables inside the marquee,' Phil suggested, 'and if we extend it, we can make a path to link with the concrete ones.'

'Won't that be a lot of work?' I asked.

'Not at all. We use grooved planks that slot together so it'll take less than an hour, then another half hour or so to put the marquee up and we'll be ready to roll. Have you thought about where the bands and food and drink are going to be set out?'

'It depends on the weather, I suppose. If we cram everything into the marquee it's going to be rather crowded.'

'How about if we set up a gazebo for the band? With open sides it wouldn't restrict anyone's view but would still give them protection from the elements.'

'That's a good idea,' I said thoughtfully, 'then I could use that area of the main marquee for the food and set out the drinks in the conservatory.'

'Right, that's all settled then,' Liz said. 'What time are your guests arriving?'

'I thought about twelve thirty, and having the barbeque going for when people arrive. The brass band's doing the early shift and could play until maybe two-ish. Then the folk group would do a set in the afternoon with the DJ following them while we serve tea and cakes. Maybe I can say a few words to thank everyone for coming and tell them about the plans for reopening the vineyard. Arthur will be on hand to take details of anyone interested in working for me.'

'Were does Steve fit into all this?' Liz asked, although Phil tried to shush her.

It seemed as if everyone knew my business, although I wasn't sure whether they meant on a professional level or if they realised our personal involvement.

'I'm not sure of his commitments at the moment,' I said quietly. 'Hopefully he'll be able to make it so he can help Arthur, but if not we can manage without him.'

They exchanged a look then Phil asked, 'What time do you expect this shindig to finish?'

'Well, the pop group said they could do a couple of hours from about five or so. I thought we could finish with a final set from the DJ and then wind down about eight.'

'With a firework display for a finale,' Liz volunteered.

'That's a brilliant idea. Do you know anyone who can supply them?'

'Funny you should say that,' Phil grinned. 'Leave it to us. About ten minutes should be enough, I think. You'll probably be tired after such a long day, so if you don't mind, we'll leave it to the following morning to clear away. I'll be in touch beforehand to confirm the final details, but we'll be there on the morning about nine to set everything up.'

'And I'll drop you a breakdown of the costs,' Liz said. 'You'll get a proper invoice once it's completed, but I expect you'd like to know the total in advance.'

'Thanks, that would be good. It seems to have snowballed from my original idea of a few people, with nibbles and wine.'

'You're doing the right thing,' Phil said. 'It might seem a big expense but it'll be repaid ten times over by the goodwill you'll generate in the village.'

As I waved them goodbye, I wondered what I had got myself into. Ever since I had moved to Alderslay the place seemed to have taken over my common sense and pushed me into more and more fantastic ideas.

'Too late to worry now,' I said out loud, to which Woof barked his agreement. I decided to check on Bambi before it became too dark, and with Woof at my heels we walked to the bottom of the estate where I replenished her food and water and checked her bedding. 'One down, one to go,' I thought as we returned to the house and I fed him. As it was still early, I spent time on my laptop updating my lists of arrangements. There was a reply from Geoff confirming he would be delighted to attend the open day and looked forward to seeing me so we could discuss the proposed wine sale in June. Nothing from Steve.

As I dropped off to sleep, I remembered Steve had promised to introduce me to Arthur on Easter Saturday. He wouldn't know I had already met him, so I presumed he would still turn up. There again he might not come at all. I wasn't sure whether that thought brought me comfort or anguish.

Chapter 39. Preparations.

True to her promise, Liz had sent a message confirming the details and giving me the combined total. Even with all the extras the price was still reasonable and I knew they must be doing it at cost price. I dug out the black box and looked through the contents again, but in more detail. As I opened another packet of photographs I hadn't seen before, there was a ring at the bell. I invited Arthur in, but glancing behind him, was surprised to see he was alone.

'Hello again, Miss Kingston,' he said. 'Thank you for inviting me to your home.'

'The pleasure's all mine, Mr Pembleton,' I replied, 'and please call me Gina. Can I offer you a coffee or something?'

'That would be lovely but would it be possible to have a look round first? It's some years since I've been on the estate and I'm intrigued to see how much it's changed. I hope I'm not imposing. By the way, please call me Arthur.'

'No problem, Arthur. What would you like to see first?'

We started off at the end of the grounds where Bambi lived and he recognised the outhouse straight away. He told me that sometimes the workers slept there, and during the summer months they would hold small parties, out of sight and sound of the main house. I told him about finding the box and promised to show it to him. He surprised me by stopping to examine the fence.

'It looks new but is exactly how I remember it,' he explained. 'I recall the original one being taken down and how the squire was so proud of his new fence. He boasted how the wood was exclusive and specially imported at great cost. How strange you managed to obtain its duplicate.'

As we strolled through the grounds, he told me more about the estate in the old days. His father and grandfather had discussed the disappearance of local village girls, and although he was too young to understand fully, he knew their opinion of the Lord of the manor. Both his ancestors had worked on the estate at the time of the fire, and as he matured, he appreciated why hatred had developed between the owner and the villagers. He firmly believed the fire had been started deliberately to destroy the evil and as an act of revenge. Before the developer bought the estate, he and the other boys from the village used the grounds as their private play area. In his teens he had worked there as a casual labourer before the developer went bust. He even remembered the original swimming pool being installed. He complimented me on the way I had improved the property with the conservatory and new pool, but had still managed to keep the original character of the place.

'I'd love to take all the credit but although most of the ideas were mine, the tribute belongs to Terry and his boys.'

'Yes, I know Terry. A good workman and a gentleman. An excellent choice.'

By now we had returned to the house and I took him via the lower kitchen and hot tub room into the cellar. He remembered those buildings and asked if the dumb waiter was still there. I confirmed it was, and explained how we intended to use the lower cellar and told him more about my plans for the vineyard.

Suddenly he shivered but when I asked if he was cold, he merely remarked that the coffee I had offered would be very welcome. I had the feeling he knew more than he was saying, but as he seemed loathe to explain we went back up to the lounge.

Before I had chance to make coffee I heard someone at the front door. 'Don't worry, I'll get it,' Arthur called and I heard Steve's voice greeting him. I fetched another cup and saucer and carried the drinks in as nonchalantly as I could.

'Hi,' Steve said. 'Sorry I was a bit late but it seems you and Arthur have been managing fine without me.'

'He's been telling me his memories of the estate,' I replied. 'It's been fascinating but we haven't actually discussed the house warming or anything about setting up the vineyard yet. By the way, Steve, will you be able to make it?'

'Yes, of course I'll be here. What time are you starting?'

I was sure he put an emphasis on "I'll" but I didn't say anything. Having not seen or heard from him recently, he knew nothing of my plans. I ran through briefly what I had organised, the timetables for the day and who would be helping.

'Wow, you've been busy. You seem to have everything under control. What about starting up the vineyard? What's your thoughts on that?'

'Well, I've decided to go ahead with it but beyond that I haven't a clue. I've no idea how it would work or what would be needed.'

'There's plenty of experience in the village, Miss…er…Gina,' said Arthur. 'I'd be happy to oversee the start-up and run things until you're on your feet.

I'm not a young man any more but I do know what I'm doing, and I wouldn't be looking for wages or anything like that.'

'I'd be relying on you, Arthur,' I replied. 'I wouldn't be able to provide a large salary but obviously I would pay you. How many employees do you think we'd need initially, and what sort of wages would they expect?'

Once we'd overcome the initial embarrassment it became easier to discuss facts and figures, and I was satisfied with the progress we made. Arthur pointed out that primarily the workforce would be labourers, clearing the ground, preparing the soil and planting the vines. It was only once we started production we would need the experience of blenders, tasters and winemakers. Initially he would oversee the planting, supervise the vine growth and make the necessary decisions on fertilizing, pruning and harvesting. He explained that it could be up to two years depending on weather conditions and other factors before we had a finished product ready for sale. There would also need to be a big investment in the machinery and other equipment required. It gave me a lot to think about.

'Some of the larger items wouldn't need to be new. Second hand would work perfectly well,' Arthur suggested.

'I'll have a word with Geoff,' Steve offered. 'With his contacts I'm sure he'll be able to source what we need.'

'That's a good idea. Can I leave it to you to get in touch with him and see what he can come up with?' I said.

With most things sorted Arthur thanked me for my hospitality and took his leave. After I'd seen him out I went back to face Steve. 'Do you need anything?' I asked, 'Tea, coffee, a sandwich maybe?'

'I'll tell you what I do need. I need you to explain what's wrong. I'm sorry I've had to leave everything to you over the last few days but I really had no option. Is there something you want to talk about?'

'Well, yes, actually there is,' I replied and then, before I could stop the words coming out of my mouth, I blurted out, 'Our partnership. We need to have a proper contract drawn up, sort out all the financial aspects, salaries, share of profits, what happens if we want to pull out, etc. We also need to decide about payments for staff we take on, look into the legal aspects of employment and all that kind of thing.'

He gave me a funny look then merely replied, 'Fine. Do you want to set up the meeting with Bernard or shall I?'

'Can I leave that to you? I'm not sure if he does evenings or perhaps could make it next Saturday. I might be able to arrange to leave work early one day but I'd need notice.'

'Okay. I'll get it organised and let you know. Was there anything else we needed to discuss?'

'No, I think that's everything.'

'I hate to disagree with you, Gina,' Steve said quietly 'but something's wrong, and I'm not talking about the business. I mean us. Do your regret the fact we were lovers? I've been thinking about it a lot since you said you wanted to keep our relationship on a professional level. I thought at first I understood your reasoning, but the more I went over your words in my mind, the more I believe there's something behind your decision. Is there someone else? Is that the reason?'

Anger and frustration burst out of me before I could compose a proper reply. 'It's not me who has someone else, it's you! Like the wife you conveniently forgot to mention.'

Steve stared at me and I had a hard time keeping tears in check.

'You mentioned my "wife" before, when you asked me about the house warming. What gave you the idea I was married?'

'You forget the wine industry is a closed shop. It's not surprising we have mutual acquaintances; people have seen you together even if it was abroad.'

'What on earth are you talking about?' He did genuinely look puzzled. Turning to my laptop, I brought up the photos and scrolled through until I found the ones I wanted.

'That wife, the one hanging onto your arm and gazing into your eyes. Incidentally, if she ever gets fed up with you, Patrick at work thinks she's drop dead gorgeous and I must admit I agree with him.'

Steve leaned in to look more closely, then to my surprise burst out laughing. Without saying another word, he pulled out his mobile phone and dialled a number.

'Hello, darling, how are you?' I heard him say. 'Do me a favour, take a selfie and send it to my phone now.' He listened for a moment then laughed and replied, 'You always look wonderful. I'll explain later, just humour me. I'll call you back in a minute.'

A few seconds later a picture appeared on his phone of the lady in the photos. I recognised her immediately, despite the dark glasses she was wearing even though she was indoors.

'Now press redial,' Steve said as he handed me his phone. When a female voice answered I tried to hand his mobile back but he said, 'Talk to the lady.'

Confused, I could only mumble a hello.

'Hello to you too,' came the reply. 'Oh, now I get it. You must be Gina. What's that reprobate brother of mine up to? Trust him to not even bother to introduce us properly. It's nice to talk to you anyway. Hopefully by the time you have your house warming I should be able to see properly, and we can have a proper girlie gossip. I'm looking forward to it.'

'Me too,' I said as Steve took back his phone.

'Take care of yourself, sis. I'll speak to you soon. By the way, you've got an admirer. Yeah, I'll explain another time. Bye.' Steve pressed end and took a breath before explaining. 'Sandy has been partially blind in one eye for years. When we went to France she'd recently had major surgery, which was why she was hanging onto my arm because she couldn't see clearly. Thankfully the operation was a success. It's been a long recuperation but they reckon she should have 20/20 vision very soon. Anyway, I took the liberty of inviting her to your open day so you'll be able to see for yourself. She's looking forward to meeting you. So, is there anything else I need to explain? What made you assume I was hiding away a secret wife?'

'Yes. There is one other thing I want to know,' I said and then felt sorry when his face dropped. 'Why haven't you kissed me yet?'

'I humbly apologise,' he replied with a big smile on his face as he took me in his arms and rectified his error. It was several hours later and nearly dark by the time we finished talking. Not only had we discussed our business partnership but also our

297

personal one and our plans for the future. By the time we had cleared up after our meal it was nearly midnight, so for the second time Steve slept in my bed.

It became a regular thing that if he wasn't working he would spend the weekend with me. We made the appointment with Bernard the solicitor, signed the formal papers with the three of us as trustees and sorted out the financial aspects. Geoff came to see us with details of machinery he had found and we measured up the cellar and worked out where everything would go. We agreed we would proceed with the vineyard and intended starting things straight after the house warming. Our long-term plans were for the wines to produce an income within three years, and we would examine the overall feasibility after five years. We had several meetings with Arthur and it began to feel like a reality.

Surprisingly both Arthur and Geoff agreed we should commence growing as soon as the ground was prepared, even though normally vines were planted in early spring. They both had high expectations we would have our first crop within a year, although I had read it usually took two to three years before full production. The days and weeks sped by and soon it was the morning of the open day. I was very nervous but felt I had done as much as I could. The rest was in the hands of fate.

Chapter 40. Open day May Bank Holiday.

At first the weather looked grey and overcast. Phil and his team turned up promptly, closely followed by Geoff, Arthur and Penny. The sun came out and with all the team involved in their various tasks, I felt superfluous. Steve had a business meeting but had promised to be with me by the time I opened the gates to welcome my guests. Feeling as if I was in the way, I decided to take Woof for a run to give him some exercise and help calm my nerves. When I returned an hour later, I did a quick check to find everything under control and nearly all the preparations completed.

After showering I changed into my glad-rags, less worried but still with butterflies in my stomach. The estate looked wonderful and I decided to take some photos before everyone arrived. I was taking snaps of the marquees when I felt someone behind me, and turned to find myself facing Steve.

'It looks fantastic,' he said as he gave me a kiss. 'Let me take some of the lady of the manor with all this in the background.' In keeping with the history of the place I had decided my outfit should reflect a bygone era and even I had to admit the photos looked perfect. A stranger came up to me and introduced himself as a reporter from the local paper. He had a professional photographer with him and they took more pictures and conducted a brief interview about my achievements. Afterwards, I left them to wander around while I greeted the members of the brass band who were already set up and tuning their instruments. The barbeque wafted out delicious smells and the sun blazed down from a clear blue sky.

I joined the welcoming staff by the front gate and then at 12.30 precisely opened the gates only to find - no one. Not a soul in sight! The one thing I hadn't allowed for was that nobody would turn up. I only stopped tears welling up when I turned to find the photographer wanting to take photos of me greeting my guests. About to tell him he was wasting his time, we were interrupted by the beeping of horns and turned to see two coaches pulling up, closely followed by cars and people carriers disgorging what appeared to be every single inhabitant of the village. For the next hour or so I didn't have a second to myself as everyone introduced themselves and thanked me for my hospitality.

I was grateful for the help of Penny's assistants who guided people towards the barbeque and refreshments, and the entertainment which was now in full swing. Eventually I left two of them to greet any late-comers while I mingled with my guests. The folk group took over from the band and I made sure the musicians were given something to eat and drink as I thanked them for starting things off so well. Taking the leader to one side I again offered to pay for their services.

'No, honestly, it's fine,' he declined. 'It's been good publicity for us and we've already had one or two enquiries from people wanting to hire us for their own parties.'

Steve found me and insisted I take a break and have something to eat. It was a good excuse to check on the catering, and I went into the old kitchen to find them replenishing empty dishes before the next rush. 'How's it going?' I asked.

'We've been rushed off our feet,' Penny replied, 'but we've had nothing but compliments and I've picked up a couple of bookings for a wedding and a twenty-first party next month. At this rate I'll end up owing you commission.'

Over the tannoy I heard the folk group announce the end of their set to rapturous applause, and then the sound of the DJ playing modern music. I thanked the folk group who told me they had really enjoyed themselves but had to rush off as they were doing a gig later that evening. When I mentioned payment they refused, saying it was for the good of the village, but left me some business cards in case I heard of anyone who was looking for similar entertainment. I walked around greeting my guests, humbled by the warmth and thanks of the villagers, and the way they were all behind me in everything I had done. I'd heard that newcomers to any village took years to be accepted, but it seemed they had all taken me to their hearts.

Making my way over to the DJ's stand I felt overwhelmed at the way my house warming had gone and so thankful that I had invited them all, despite the hassles and cost. This was reinforced when the DJ gave an announcement over the loudspeaker that the hostess wished to say a few words, and everyone congregated to listen. My prepared formal speech went out of the window as I spoke from my heart about the overwhelming emotion at being accepted into the community.

'As a novice I thought it was a pipe dream to even imagine resurrecting the vineyard, but I have received so much support I intend to give it my best shot to make it a reality.' The cheers greeting this announcement left me dumbstruck at the enthusiasm for my declaration. 'Heartfelt thanks to all the various people who have assisted me today. Without them I would never have had the courage to open the doors to my friends and neighbours.'

Another resounding cheer was followed by applause which went on for several minutes. I was quite tearful as I finished by saying, 'Arthur's available to take the details of anyone who might be interested in helping to resurrect the vineyard. There are no promises as to its success but I'll do everything in my power to make my neighbours proud. Thank you all for the welcome and hospitality you've shown me. I promise to respect the ancient traditions of the beautiful estate that, although legally is in my name, I actually think of as belonging to the whole village.'

As I handed back the microphone to the DJ I was overcome with emotion, grateful when I found Steve next to me. He smiled as he whispered in my ear, 'I think that went down rather well.'

When the DJ asked for three cheers for the hostess the noise was deafening, and then I was surrounded by people shaking my hand and thanking me for inviting them. I told them it was my pleasure, how pleased I was to meet them all and reminded them the refreshment kitchen was open for anyone who fancied afternoon tea. Realising I hadn't spoken to Arthur since I started the open day, I went to see how he was. It took me a while to reach him as I was stopped every few yards by someone wanting to congratulate me on a wonderful afternoon. Eventually I found him sitting at a table near the main marquee in deep discussion with a couple of young lads.

He looked up and smiled as he said, 'Gentlemen, may I introduce you to your possible future employer Miss Gina Kingston? Obviously the final decision will be hers, but I'll be in touch as soon as possible to let you know one way or the other.'

Both the boys nodded at me and smiled shyly before saying, 'Pleasure to meet you, Miss Kingston.'

'Nice to meet you too,' I said. 'Please make sure you have something to eat and drink and enjoy the rest of the afternoon. I look forward to seeing you again once I've had a chance to discuss things with Arthur.'

As they went off I said to Arthur, 'I'm so sorry to have deserted you. How's it been going?'

Glancing down at the pad in front of him he replied, 'As I said, Gina, the final decision is yours but I think I've got a good short list of possible employees to start the ball rolling. Perhaps I could call on you one day in the week so we can finalise the names and get the formalities completed? The sooner we start, the sooner we can repay your outlay.'

Steve came up and stood listening to the conversation.

'Are you available on Wednesday evening?' I asked him.

'That's fine with me. It'd be as well if Bernard was there too. I'll find him.'

He returned with our solicitor and fellow trustee in tow. Bernard confirmed he was free on Wednesday and we arranged to meet at the house about 7.30. The rest of the afternoon sped past, with the younger crowd dancing as the pop group began their set. All in all, it had been a perfect day. Although a few of the older

303

people left after thanking me for a wonderful time, the grounds were still packed when the DJ made his final announcement. The fireworks were stupendous and I cheered as they lit up the night sky, providing a perfect ending to the day. By nine o'clock Penny and her crew had cleared the kitchen and the barbeque, a crowd of helpers had collected all the rubbish, and apart from the marquees and the furniture, the grounds were restored to their normal condition.

I let Woof out for his final run, checked on Bambi and was pleased when Steve suggested he stay the night, even though he would have to leave early the next morning. I had taken the following day off from work, and although I was shattered, I wanted him around after all the excitement of the day. As if he understood my mood, he didn't suggest making love and I fell asleep cuddled in his arms. The morning sun streaming through the window woke me and I turned to find Steve awake and gazing at me with a look of love on his face. Fully refreshed, we made love and I began to believe my future lay with this man. He was the perfect lover, perfect business partner, perfect friend and soul-mate, understanding when I needed comfort and when I was ready for love.

He even made me breakfast in bed before he left so I could luxuriate in a few extra hours sleep. I hadn't long been dressed when Phil and his team arrived to dismantle the marquees and decking. Once they had finished, I checked on Bambi then on impulse took my first dip of the year in the swimming pool. Although the sun was shining the water was chilly, but I felt invigorated as I used the showers in the hot tub area to warm up. With the day before me I set to work on my laptop. I needed to plan for the next wine sale and the prospect of opening the vineyard. It seemed as if my life had been taken over and I was on a roller-coaster ride from recent events. I downloaded the photos from my camera and was pleased with the pictures of the open day, which all showed smiling faces and reassured me how successful it had been.

It made me think of the parties that must have been held on the estate in the olden days. Opening the black box, I perused the reminders of days gone by and discovered a sealed envelope I hadn't noticed before. It seemed a shame to break the red wax seal only to discover it contained another set of pictures from that bygone age. I browsed the snaps of the serving staff in their old-fashioned uniforms, and admired the ladies in their Sunday best, who appeared to be attending an exclusive house party. One of the photos made me stop dead. I was looking at a picture of guests at a summer party on the estate, and for a moment I thought I had mixed up the old and new pictures. The marquee and gazebo were exactly the same as I had ordered for my open day. The lady posing in front of the pergola looked exactly like me. Her dress, her face, her smile were like gazing in a mirror. The photos were identical, even though they were a century apart. I was spooked.

Chapter 41. History

Then I burst out laughing at my own stupidity. I remembered Betty telling me my great grandmother and her mother had been friends and both had worked on the estate. The photo I was looking at was probably my great-grandmother. Not surprising then that I looked like her. Still, I was intrigued as to the capacity in which she had been employed. As it was only early afternoon I decided to walk to the old church and see if they had any records. I called Woof and we set off and entered the grounds through the rusty gate surrounding the ancient churchyard. An elderly lady came out of the small building attached to the church and called out a greeting. 'Good afternoon, my dear,' she said. 'I was wondering when you'd find the time to pay us a visit. Do come in and have a cup of tea.'

'Thank you, but I've got my dog with me.'

'Oh, he's not a problem, are you, my lovely lad? I'm sure we can find a bowl of water and a few biscuits for you too.'

We sat and chatted and I discovered she was the housekeeper to the vicar. As I had already realised, everything that went on at the estate soon became common knowledge in the village. Mrs Browne had actually been at the party and had seen some of the photographs in the window of the newspaper's offices. That prompted me to tell her the reason for my visit and I asked if the church kept any historical records, as I was eager to learn more about the original workers on the estate. She assured me they had a comprehensive library of information dating back hundreds of years, including the registers of births and deaths in the village.

Like many other long-term residents her family had worked on the estate and she remembered her mother telling her stories. When the priest returned, she introduced us and explained why I was there.

'I'll be delighted to show you the old records. You might also find a look round the cemetery interesting.' As he led me into his study I noticed one wall held a bookcase full of ancient manuscripts. 'Do take a seat, Gina. Was there a particular period you were interested in?'

I explained about the photograph of my great grandmother and assumed it would have been some time after the turn of the century. I knew my grandmother's married name had been Mulholland, and we traced her in the marriage registers. She had wed a local man from the village and, tracing backwards, I discovered great grandmother Georgina's name had been Allston. What did surprise me was her rank was given as *Lady*. I wasn't sure whether it was due to her marriage or if she was actually from aristocratic stock. Tracking further through the records, I made the amazing discovery that she had married the lord of the manor, and my grandmother had been born the year before the fire. That meant I was actually related to the original owners of the estate which was now my home. If the stories were true, the blood of the despot who had tortured and murdered the young girls found in the cellar ran through my own veins. It was a frightening thought. The vicar mentioned I looked rather pale and suggested we take some fresh air.

The memorials nearest the church were quite modern, but he led me to the furthest reaches of the

307

cemetery which was almost derelict and very
overgrown. Here the graves were obviously much older
and it was difficult to read the faded inscriptions.
Eventually our steps took us to the mausoleum, the
burial place for the original nobles and their
descendants. I started shaking, and rather than show
myself up, wandered off from the vicar to try to regain
my composure. I remembered the original lord and his
son had been well respected and liked by the villagers
and the people who worked on the estate. It was only
the grandson who had been hated, and shown bad
blood, although it seemed he was the man my great-
grandmother had married.

Lost in thought, I glanced at the nearest grave
and could just make out a few letters carved into the
marble. Bending down, I pulled away some of the
weeds covering the other letters, and scrubbing at the
accumulated grime managed to read the inscription,
*Here lies Georgina Mary Allston beloved wife of Lord
Henry Allston. Born 1890, died in childbirth 1919. At
Rest.*

It seemed my great-grandmother had died
giving birth to my grandmother. I knew from the
records I had seen that she had been married in 1910,
and from the knowledge I already had it appeared her
husband was twenty-five years older than her. The
records confirmed she was from a good family so
perhaps he had married her to try to show propriety. It
might also be the reason they had been married for nine
years before she gave birth to their first and only child,
my grandmother.

I felt I had learnt enough for one day so, calling
Woof, thanked the vicar and his housekeeper for the
information and their hospitality and set off home. I

needed to talk to Steve about all I had discovered but wouldn't see him until the following evening. That night the dreams returned but this time there was a difference. It was still set in the cellar of the estate but I was the one sneering at the prisoners chained to the wall. There were no young females cowering in horror; these were all males, ranging in age from a lad of fourteen or fifteen to a strapping fully-grown man in his thirties.

Chapter 42 Reality

The next day was a working day, and the normal struggle to commute, handle bosses and customers, and fit twenty hours work into eight helped bring me back to reality. Lunch was forgone in the hope of leaving at a reasonable time for my meeting, and Penny had left me remnants of the party food so there was something available for my guests. When I arrived home I fed Woof, then let him out for a run while the food was keeping warm in the oven, ready to serve later. Descending to the cellar to select a bottle of wine, I remembered my dream of the previous night and expected to feel some trepidation. Surprisingly, I felt totally powerful and in control; maybe I had more of the despot's blood in me than I realised.

After a shower I changed into palazzo pants and a silk top, and set out the dining room table in preparation for our meeting. Everything was ready when I heard the first ring of the bell and opened it to greet Arthur, closely followed by Bernie and finally Steve. Over a glass of wine Arthur updated us with his suggestions for possible employees. He gave a brief summary of each person he had interviewed, and his recommendations for who we should accept and how they would fit into the team. He also had a list of others who would be suitable once the groundwork had been completed and we needed more expertise.

After some discussion we all concurred with Arthur's suggestions and agreed a salary pay scale. There were a few boys Arthur had rejected, and out of interest I asked his reasons for not selecting them. He seemed reticent at first but then explained that although they were well qualified, he didn't think they had the 'ancient understanding' necessary to commit to the project. Although I was slightly mystified I accepted his explanation, especially when Steve and Bernie seemed to understand exactly what he meant. Our discussion turned to financial matters and what payment we should offer Arthur. Always the perfect gentleman he suggested he looked round the cellar and grounds to give us privacy while he orientated himself with the layout.

While he was gone, we settled not only what we should offer Arthur but also the main details of the partnership agreement between Steve, Bernie and myself. Bernie had taken notes and told us he should have the engrossed agreement ready for our signature by the weekend. When Arthur returned he was very satisfied with the figure we suggested, and eager to start the preparations for the vineyard straight away. He offered to contact the labourers with a view to starting work the following Monday, and somewhat overwhelmed with how quickly things were moving, I agreed. Before I knew it, my pipe dreams had become a reality.

By the time I held the wine sale at the end of June the ground was prepared and actually looked like a vineyard. The sale was even more successful than I could have imagined, and I was amazed at the profit when I reckoned up the final total. Even after paying for all the expenses of the open day there was enough to cover the cost of the machinery and the wages for the best part of a year. I had only used up about one tenth of the stock, and with another sale before Christmas and a further one next summer there was every likelihood of paying off the mortgage within the year.

Chapter 43. Full circle.

Before I knew it, autumn had arrived. The grapes were already growing on the vine and I couldn't believe it when Arthur said we would shortly be having our first harvest. My research had indicated it usually took at least a year to settle, but somehow everyone else involved had been confident we would be sampling the wine by Christmas. When I queried the unbelievable progress, sly glances were exchanged between Arthur, Steve and the other people involved. They all came up with explanations at the same time which made me even more suspicious.

'The ground was ready from when it was a vineyard before.'

'It's been a good summer.'

'We have the expertise.'

'It's the secret ingredient.'

For some reason it was the last comment which convinced me there was something I wasn't being told. Although there wasn't enough to be commercially viable, it was a good testing ground to iron out the possible problems for full scale production. As Christmas approached I had a sense of déjà vu. It seemed unbelievable that only a year ago I had been engaged to Paul and expecting to spend the rest of my life with him in our new home. We had already arranged that Steve would come over on Christmas Eve and spend the holiday with me. The lease on his flat was due to expire at the end of January and rather than look elsewhere he would move in with me.

We celebrated Christmas with our first bottles of "Chateau Alderslay." Christmas morning Steve woke me with breakfast in bed before we went down to open our presents. His gift to me was a beautiful diamond necklace.

'It's gorgeous, Steve. Thank you so much.'

'There's something else to go with it.'

Seeing the small box, I assumed it was matching earrings, so I was overcome when he bent down on one knee and presented me with an engagement ring as he asked me to marry him. For a moment I gazed at in in disbelief, then half laughing, half crying, of course I said yes. He slipped it onto my finger and I wore his ring as we attended the church service, followed by a social gathering in the village hall where we wished all our friends and neighbours a Merry Christmas. No one seemed at all surprised at our engagement, although I became emotional at all the congratulations we received.

Although Paul had been tentatively accepted when we first moved here, I felt the villagers preferred it that Steve would become the new lord of the manor. So much had happened in one short year my fate felt predestined. Finding the house, splitting up with Paul, meeting Steve, discovering my heritage and resurrecting the vineyard all seemed as if they were meant to be. My dreams of the cellar were a recurring event, but instead of a nightmare, became part of our lives. Steve and I married in late October the following year. We decided on that date so we could have a honeymoon after the main harvest season. It was a wonderful day and all the villagers attended our celebrations.

A year later I gave birth to the twins, Tia and Remy. Once they started to crawl they were a handful, wanting to explore everywhere, and the darlings of the local villagers who were delighted we were continuing the family line. We didn't allow them down into the cellar. They would learn more about the family business once they were old enough. For now they were happy to spend their time with Bambi, who was fully grown. Woof had also started his own family. On one of our walks, we had come across a half-starved wild female who looked part wolf and part Alsatian. Initially I had tried to shoo her off but Woof persuaded me to take her home with us. At first she wouldn't come into the house so I put down water and food for her in the grounds. I was worried she might harm Bambi but she settled into the estate as if she had always belonged there, and she and the fawn became friends. Gradually she accepted me, and under Woof's protection became house trained. Their three gorgeous pups were born on the same day as my own offspring.

History had come full circle, and although modernised, the estate reflected the way it had been in my great-grandmother's time. The vineyard thrived, and as the years passed I learnt the secret of its success. We now had a permanent staff, all from the village, and our reputation was spreading. *Chateau Alderslay* won several prizes in major wine competitions, but the villagers closed ranks when outsiders tried to delve too deeply into the ingredients involved in production. I had researched more of my heritage and discovered fascinating facts about my ancestors. At every turn I came across familiar names and realised that many of the inhabitants of the village were interrelated. It seemed unbelievable that within forty minutes commuting distance of the capital, my home could be so insular. Initially I had regrets at giving up my day job, but with the passage of time become so much a part of the local community it seemed a life-time away. Gradually I lost contact with my old colleagues and immersed myself in village life.

Chapter 44. Blood is thicker than water.

Several years have passed since I first discovered the estate as a young, naïve girl looking to find a first home to share with her fiancé. That Gina would send back a steak in a restaurant if there was even the slightest hint of blood. As I became engrossed in the business, little by little I was shown what it entailed, and I don't mean tax returns or employee regulations. Everyone from the local village newspaper to the police sergeant seemed to be involved, and available to resurrect the conspiracy of secrets which had ensured the success of the original vineyard.

Despite our best efforts, suspicions leaked out and I found reporters from the national newspapers on my doorstep demanding to know more about the *Chamber of Horrors* discovered in my basement. In my role as Lady of the Manor, I directed them to the local police who came up with the story of renovations uncovering an ancient graveyard. Their efforts to entice gossip from the villagers came to nothing and we were left in peace.

Occasionally an outside police force interfered when a homeless vagrant was reported missing after last being seen in the vicinity of our village. The sergeant, who had first discovered the bodies in my cellar, filed his reports and we all supported his view that we had last seen the tramp moving on his way to pastures new. A few local girls were reported missing by their families, but there were no mysterious circumstances. They were all discovered living in London with their boyfriends, having escaped to the bright lights from the monotony of staid village life. We had learnt from the mistakes of the past, and there was no other hint of scandal.

The cellar and lower cellar were now given over to the needs of the winery, but Terry created a separate section to house the secret of the vineyard's success. We had our good years and our not so good years with the wine production, as was normal in the trade. Unlike other producers, our superb vintages were not so much dependent on the weather. It was more to do with what - or rather who - was available at the time to provide the final ingredient.

I should have been more shocked when I discovered the other secrets of the house, but like my great grandmother I learnt to accept my destiny. The blood of the ancient squire flowed through my veins, but at heart I was a decent woman looking to repay the debt I owed to the villagers who had become my family.

Fate had drawn me to this remote place, and the phantoms of the past had guided me in restoring things as they had been in the days of my ancestors. At the beginning I was an innocent, unaware of my ancient heritage and the calling of the primeval spirits guiding my every move, but blood is thicker than water and my destiny had been pre-ordained.

Why else would I have split from Paul, and found a new partner who understood and was part of the ancient traditions? Why else would I have decided, against all the odds, to resurrect the vineyard and truly become part of the closed village community? Like my great-grandmother I had found my animal companions, the descendants of hers, and through me her spirit lived on. I had even begun to understand why she had married the despot lord of the manor despite all the horrors that must have been her lot in daily life.

Our white wines were sold to supermarkets and restaurants as house table-wines, but it was the rich, blood reds which won awards with their distinctive taste. For the sake of the vineyard, I learnt to ignore the screams of the lonely wanderers who unwittingly stumbled into our production process. Without their plasma we would have been only an average producer of fine wines, and after all, we have a reputation to keep up. As long as solitary travellers stumble across the village and contribute their life blood to our ancient, secret recipe the vineyard will prosper.

Cheers.

If you've enjoyed this book please consider leaving a review on Amazon, Goodreads or your favourite book purchasing site.

Spreading the word on social media is also invaluable in helping authors gain a wider readership.

The more you shout, the more we can write.

Thank you.

If you would like to keep in touch, receive special offers and be the first to hear news of forthcoming publications, please consider joining my email list. You won't be bombarded – I hate spam as much as you do.

Sign up here:
www.voinks.wordpress.com/sign-up